I0761958

Emily Kazmierski

Also by Emily Kazmierski

Don't Look Series

Don't Look Too Close (a prequel novella)

Embassy Academy Trilogy

Deadly First Day

Lethal Queen Bee

Killer Final Exams

Ivory Tower Spies Series

For Your Ears Only

The Walk-in Agent (a Julep Short Story)

The Eyes of Spies

Spy Your Heart Out

Spy Got Your Tongue

Over My Dead Body

Other Novels

Malignant

All-American Liars

Life Among the Ashes

California, United States
Cover Design: Parker Book Design

Printed in the United States of America

First Printing, 2021

www.EmilyKazmierski.com

For Adam.
There's no one I'd rather
watch Seinfeld with.

Chapter 1

Day 91, Monday

I left every single one of my plants behind when I moved in with Aunt Karen.

After.

Most people find orchids to be finicky plants. They bloom only if precise conditions are met, or not at all. I was always drawn to their particularity and resilience.

Not anymore. Not now that I'm the one clinging to life as a shriveled, nearly dead stub of brown in an airless, smothering situation.

The newly purchased blouse I pull over my head still has the tags hanging from the back collar. Its sharp edges are making the tender skin between my shoulder blades itch. I bend awkwardly, trying to reach it, and only manage to pull out a few strands of my overlong, hickory brown hair. What I wouldn't give for a broken-in tee and jean cutoffs.

Helplessness threatens to overwhelm me, making me collapse on to the edge of the too-small twin bed, pawing at the bright red comforter with black polka dots. I'd have deemed it too childish to use if Aunt Karen hadn't told me she'd purchased it because it reminded her of my favorite anime show about a teenage girl whose superhero alter ego is a ladybug. I didn't have the heart to tell her I'm not interested in it anymore. Or any of my other former hobbies.

None of it makes me light up like it did Before.

The old house creaks as someone moves down the hallway.

I look up, my pulse skittering.

"Does everything fit all right?" Aunt Karen stands in the doorway, her perceptive brown eyes skimming over me. Her dyed red hair is starting to grow out, leaving a stripe of gray at her scalp.

I bite my lip, nodding. "This outfit okay?"

"The blouse looks nice on you. Feminine."

Not like my old clothes.

The older woman moves into the room, dressed for her new job at the grocery store in a slouchy green polo and khaki slacks. Her eyes glance over my face and away. "Where's your bracelet?"

"Oh. I—"

"Your parents would have wanted you to wear it," she encourages, picking up the sterling bangle from the top of the dresser and watching with keen eyes as I snap it on to my wrist.

The clothes tag rustles when I move, sparking Aunt Karen's continued scrutiny. "What is that?"

"Tag. Would you mind...?" Presenting her with my back, I pull my hair forward over my shoulder. My skin prickles at the exposure, but I hold myself still.

Aunt Karen excuses herself to get some scissors from the kitchen, returning with a bright red set that ironically also still has the tag on. The older woman gives half a smile as she yanks it off and tosses it in the wastebasket under the small desk in the corner. "It's amazing the things you have to buy when you move. Being back in this house feels like going back in time."

Her eyes take in the room around me before she moves closer.

I'm grateful she doesn't see me flinch as she draws closer with the gleaming shears.

Carefully, as if she's afraid I'll collapse if she touches me, my new guardian cuts the tag out of my blouse and tosses it.

"How are you feeling about your new school? You know how you're going to introduce yourself yet?"

I shrug. I've been dreading this, so instead of making a mental plan like I normally would, I've kept putting it off. I guess I'll figure it out if anyone asks. Probably no one will.

"Practice makes permanent. You should run over what you want to say in the car on the way over. Want me to role play it with you?" The woman crosses her arms, studying me.

"No, thanks. I'll manage." Shouldering my backpack, I follow her out on to the landing. The door to the master bedroom has been shut tight. In the short time I have resided in this place, I have never trespassed there.

The temperature drops as we descend the stairs. Under her breath I hear Aunt Karen grumbling about how inefficient the old house is with its minimal insulation and seventy-year-old windows. While the upstairs is near too warm, the downstairs feels like a freezer. I consider going back upstairs for a sweater but don't. The second I step outside, I'm slammed by a wall of air so hot it steals my breath. It's not even 8 AM and already almost 90 degrees. The jean skirt I'm wearing chafes, the blouse tacky against my skin. It's got to be twenty degrees warmer here than at home.

Home.

My eyes threaten to well over, but I force the tide back. I can't arrive for my first day of school with puffy eyes and splotchy skin. I get into the passenger side of Aunt Karen's sedan once she unlocks it and click my seatbelt into place.

Despite the ocean of sadness that washes over me, I'm relieved to be out of the old house that has been in the family since it was built in the 1940s. The white paint peeling off the clapboard siding and the weathered front porch testify to the truth of it. Against the side of the aged structure, the AC unit shudders as it tries to keep pace with the climbing heat.

I look up at the house, all of its windows and blinds shut against the outside.

As Aunt Karen backs out of the driveway, something in my chest loosens. I'm nervous about going to a new school where I won't know anyone, but it's got to be better than that house, where every move I make is catalogued and deconstructed. The idiom *walking on eggshells* has never been so concrete in my mind as now.

The car moves down the street past orchard after orchard of almond trees. Apparently, it's the town's major crop, along with milk. This side of town is all farm land; the other side flooded by the sea of black and white cows at the dairy. You can smell the stench from the freeway.

In town, we pass the grocery store, a big box store, barber shop, furniture store, boutique dress shop, a beauty parlor with faded photos in the windows, and a coffee shop/diner. That's it—that's the entire town.

I make quick work of my breakfast, wadding up the foil wrapper and tucking it into my pocket. Aunt Karen wouldn't like me leaving it in the car's spotless interior.

The school looks pretty much how it did during orientation a couple days ago. A long, single storey white building with a gymnasium at one end. A knight on a horse is painted on the side of the gym over a banner saying, "Go Lancers!" Behind that is the football stadium, which looks well-kept even though the metal bleachers are ancient.

The parking lot is separated into two sections: the teachers' cars mostly sedans and minivans, while the student lot is full of trucks with extended cabs. Many are downright filthy, hinting at the popular pastimes of rodeos and off-roading. I wrinkle my nose as Aunt Karen pulls to a stop right in front of the main building.

Every student standing on the sidewalk turns to gape as I unbuckle my belt and move to open the door.

Aunt Karen stops me with a firm hand on my arm. "Do you have your recorder?"

"Oh. Yeah." Unzipping the front pouch of my new backpack, I unbury the small silver device and turn it on, careful to keep it low enough that no one outside the car can see it.

"Don't forget to check it between classes to make sure it's still going." Her tone is admonishing.

"Don't worry, okay? I won't forget." *I know how important it is.*

She watches me for a beat. "I'll be here to pick you up after school. Wait right out front."

I promise to comply before climbing out of the car. She doesn't pull away as I move toward the clump of students on the front steps. Their conversations hush as I draw closer. All eyes are on me—the new girl.

I try to muster a small smile, but one by one their expressions register my face and flick away, as if they're afraid to stare. My hand comes up to cover the white scar that cuts a line from my left nostril all the way to my hairline. Dropping my chin, I let my hair fall in front of my face like a curtain.

The metallic blue front door flies open, almost knocking me in the head. I gasp, jumping back.

"Crap. Sorry. I'm sorry! Megan?"

My reddened face whips up to lock on the boy who just tried to murder me with a door. The gangly boy with an anime tee and thick black plastic glasses frames gives me a sheepish smile. Adjusting the backpack strap he's got slung over one shoulder, he holds out a hand. "I'm Noah Lopez, your student liaison. Welcome to Valley High." He steps back, motioning for me to go through the door he holds open.

We step into the administration building. The aisle passes the high counter manned by a secretary and out the other side to the open-air courtyard.

My heart is staging a revolt in my chest cavity. I can do this. I can.

The secretary gives me a warm smile. "Good morning! I gave Noah here your schedule. He'll show you around, okay, hon? And don't be afraid to ask if you need anything."

"Thanks." The middle-aged woman's warmth is a sharp contrast to the chilly reception I got outside, making me wonder if someone started a school-wide game of Hot and Cold I don't know about.

"How'd you know my name?" I ask Noah as we pass through the courtyard. Low hills of dead grass roll between the concrete walkways, each mound crested by a sapling supported by wooden stakes, like miniature kingdoms guarded by groups of students. Nearest us, a jock catches sight of me and turns to whisper in his buddy's ear. A ripple goes through the open space, and my ears flame.

Hopeful for some semblance of normalcy, I ignore the clamminess in my palms. Resist the urge to cover my face in my hands.

Noah chuckles. "You're the first new kid we've had since Joey Donner moved here in third grade. Small towns, you know?"

"Right. Is this the part where you ask me all about where I'm from and stuff?"

"I figure you'll tell me all about that whenever you're ready to. Being new must be tough." The smile the boy throws my way makes me relax a fraction.

The morning light glows behind the apple green leaves of the nearest tree, unearthing an urge I haven't felt in three months. Taking out my new phone, I peel the protective film off so I can take a couple quick photos. Squatting gets the composition I want. When I'm satisfied, I straighten to find my would-be assassin watching intently.

"You a photographer?" he asks. "Can I see?"

I hesitate, but hold out my phone.

"It's pretty. You're good. You should talk to Mr. Baugh, the art teacher, about getting into his advanced art class. I'm in there, too."

Embarrassed by his easy compliment, I tuck the phone away, murmuring a quiet thanks.

Noah's focus moves to my face. I wait for him to zero in on the ugly line marring my skin, but he doesn't. Good, because despite what I told Aunt Karen, I have no idea what to say about it. Something like relief flutters in my stomach.

"Here's your schedule," Noah says, leading me along one of the walkways. "Mr. Tobin, fifth period. He keeps his room freezing cold, so you might want to bring a blanket to keep in your locker. A ton of people do. Last year there was even a competition to see who could find the ugliest one. And don't ever be late to Ms. Parker's class or she'll make you wear a sombrero for the rest of the period." He laughs, running a hand over his black wavy hair. "Hat hair is no joke, is all I'm saying."

His smile pulls a ghost of one out of me in return. The expression feels foreign on my face. I can't remember the last time I smiled.

Posters line the windows of the classrooms we pass advertising football, a club for future farmers, and cheerleading. I stifle a wince, hoping my tour guide didn't notice.

He doesn't miss much, unfortunately. "You have something against the great sport of cheerleading?"

"Not really," I say with a noncommittal headshake.

"Okay… So, here's your first period class. If you want, I can come back after and walk you to your next one. Make sure you don't get lost?"

"Sure. Thanks," I add as an afterthought.

"See you then, Megan." He ducks his head before moving off.

When I step inside the portable classroom, no one is here yet.

A janitor is standing behind the teacher's desk with a wastebasket in hand. "Morning," he grunts, setting down the empty receptacle and leaving quickly, glancing back once. Probably to get a better look at my scar.

Settling in a desk in the back row, I take out my phone and look at the photo of the leaves. It *is* pretty good. Chewing on the inside of my cheek, I debate for a second before opening my social media app and posting it. It's the first one I've shared since Before.

Almost immediately a couple of people I used to chat with leave comments. Maybe I haven't been completely forgotten.

It would be nice to start posting photos again. As long as Aunt Karen doesn't find out.

Before class starts, I unzip the front of my backpack under the desk to check the small device she gave me. It's still recording.

Chapter 2

Day 95, Thursday

Noah is waiting for me when I leave my English class, and I fall into step beside him. He's been super nice since my first day of school, helping me find all of my classes, tipping me off so I could avoid the worst foods in the cafeteria, and telling me which bathroom to avoid since it's the school's unofficial smoking room. I'm pretty sure he was only supposed to show me the ropes my first day, but he's still around. We're accidentally becoming friends.

"Four days down." Noah meets my eyes, turning to walk backward without breaking contact. His hair hangs down over his forehead, but he pushes it back with one of his spindly brown hands.

"One hundred seventy six to go."

He barks a surprised laugh. "That bad, huh?"

"I miss home. That's all."

Noah hesitates. Licks his lips. I can sense it coming. The question he's avoided asking for the past three days. "What do you miss most?"

My body relaxes. This I can answer truthfully. "The beach."

"We have beaches. They're probably not the same, but…"

I give a noncommittal head bob. He doesn't press. I like that about him.

The gates in front of the school are open wide as everyone hurries off campus. Done with one more day of high school. A bottle-neck forms in the open gaps between the tall, blue metal boundaries. It reminds me of a documentary I saw about toll booths in India and the constant beeping of their horns. Here the constant is the grumblings of impatient jerks.

When an idea hits, I halt in my tracks and am rewarded by an elbow to the back.

"Watch it," some guy growls as he pushes past me toward freedom.

Noah, when he glances over his shoulder and sees that I'm no longer following, pushes gainfully upstream toward me. "Forget something?"

Making up my mind, I meet his watchful eyes. "Can you show me where the drama club meets?" I'd try to find it myself, but I'm still getting my bearings and I don't want to be late for the first meeting of the semester.

"So you're a thespian, huh?" Noah perks up. His brown eyes shine as if I've given him insight into my very soul.

"Something like that." Very like that, actually. I'd just started going on auditions. Had actually landed a small part on a popular police procedural. But then…

A custodian exits the bathroom abruptly, making me skirt around him as I backpedal through the crowd.

The drama club meets in the school's theater behind the gym. It's a large, black box with platforms centered around a lowered stage. The group does all of their plays in the round. I've never experienced that before. Anticipation filters through me. It'll provide a unique challenge.

Noah says his goodbye and goes, leaving me standing in

the theater doorway alone. The interior of the dark, cavernous space is cool, a reprieve from the punishing heat outside. Metal frameworks run along the ceiling, holding the colored lights that are trained on the center of the room.

Squaring my shoulders, I make my way down the aisle toward where the club's members are sprawled out on the platforms talking and laughing. A guy tosses a cheese puff into the air and catches it to the squeals of a couple of younger girls. When I get close enough, they turn to stare.

My instinct to puff up and make myself as large as possible to intimidate them prickles under my skin, but I ignore it. It took a lot of compelling arguments to convince Aunt Karen to let me participate in drama club, and the last thing I need is to ruin it by creating a scene my very first time in the building.

"You're Megan, right? I'm Fiona. Welcome to drama club." A tall Black girl with long, multi-colored braids stands and greets me, brushing her hands on the front of her jean shorts.

"Thanks. I heard you guys were doing *The Mousetrap* this semester. It's a great play."

"Yeah, it should be fun. Why don't you come sit with us?" She leads me to one of the platforms and introduces me to her friends. "Marisa, our Mollie Ralston. Viv, Costuming. I usually work lighting. What about you?"

I glance at Marisa, wishing desperately I could tell her I played that role when we'd done the play back home. But I can't. It was part of my deal with Aunt Karen. No front-of-the-curtain parts. "Stage crew all the way."

"So you've done this play before?" Marisa asks, holding up a cracked-spine paperback. She shoves her raven hair back when it falls in her eyes.

I nod, enthusiastic, and tell them about how, at my old

school, we staged the murder mystery play in a train car as a nod to Agatha Christie's most famous book, *Murder on the Orient Express.*

"The police officer was a woman? Nice touch," Marisa says, tapping the cover of her book thoughtfully. "I suggested to Esau that we do this one with an all-female cast, but he said no."

"He glared, is what he did," Viv puts in.

"Directors." Marisa huffs a strand of hair out of her face.

"Seriously," I put in. My nerves are jangling. I've never met this Esau person, but he sounds like a terrible director. Hopefully he's learned there is no "I" in team. T. E. A. M. Team. Clap clap.

"Excellent. Want some popcorn?" Fiona pulls a clear ziplock out of her bag and holds it out to me.

"She's always trying new flavors," Marisa puts in, smoothing her hair into a high ponytail.

I run my fingers through my own mousy brown locks, hesitating when my eyes land on the bag of green-tinted kernels. I don't want to alienate these girls. How bad can green popcorn be? I take some. Chew slowly.

"So… can I ask you a question?" Viv asks, her green eyes bright with curiosity.

Here it comes. I brace myself.

"How'd you get that scar?" She points to her own cheek while looking at mine.

Thick, hot blood running down my neck.

Pulling as the doctor yanked my face back together.

Taking off the white gauzy bandage to see the angry red line that cut through my cheek.

Stark black stitches against tanned skin.

"Shut it, Viv. It's rude to ask," Fiona scolds her before

turning to me. "Sorry, sorry. You don't have to answer that."

My head shakes. I exhale. "It's fine. Running with scissors. Stupid, I know."

The girls recoil in chorus.

"That must have hurt," Viv says, gritting her teeth.

"You have no idea."

"All right, let's get started." The commanding voice rings through the room, hushing all other conversation.

Everyone turns toward it.

A male figure is silhouetted by the afternoon sun. The door thuds as he advances toward us. I blink him into focus and my eyes widen.

"Who's that?" I whisper to Fiona.

"Our director—Esau Chavez. He's a senior and the leader of the club. It's his first semester directing. Miss Crabtree, she's our advisor, has an office through there," she points down a hallway, "but she pretty much lets us do our thing. She'll pop in from time to time to make sure we're actually working, though."

I can't help but notice that many of the other students' attention is riveted to the director as he walks between the platforms and stands with his arms crossed in the center of the stage. And no wonder. He's north of six feet, with sun-bronzed skin and black eyebrows like slashes above his eyes. Black hair in two French braids that hang down his chest. Large gauges in his ears. Whoa, is all I can think when I look at him.

Esau's jaw works as he surveys us. "Nice to be back with everyone. I'm looking forward to working on *The Mousetrap* with you guys. If we bust our butts, this play will be great. Maybe the best the town has seen in years." His eyes pause on me. "Who are you?" There's a note of accusation in his voice that makes my hackles rise.

"Megan Pritchard," I say, standing with chin raised. "I just moved here, and I'm interested in working with the stage crew. I've done this play before, so if you're interested, I've got some ideas on how to—"

"I'm directing, so no thanks. I've already got a strong vision for how I want this thing to look. I'm sure Fiona can find something for you to do backstage, though." Esau turns away to talk to a guy on the opposite platform. Dismissing me. Blocking my view of the other half of the group.

Embarrassed, I take a step closer. "I really think you'll be able to learn from my experience."

Esau tenses, glancing at me over his shoulder. "If you're not interested in listening to your director, there's the door." One long arm points toward the exit.

My skin glows red hot as he stalks off toward what I assume is the advisor's office.

"Holy smokes." Marisa fans herself with her script. "That was a scorcher." There's no missing the piqued interest in her expression. "He's pretty hot, huh?"

I catch myself before I can make a snarky comment about grumpy alpha assholes.

Fiona rolls her eyes. "Ignore him. He's got a stick up his butt about the show, but he's not a bad director."

Not wanting to argue, I keep my mouth shut. A good director would want to hear from everyone on his team. Would want any ideas that would ensure the success of the show. Esau Chavez is clearly on an ego-induced power trip.

Pulling a baggie of baby carrots out of my backpack, I crunch down on one.

Esau, who is standing in the mouth of the hallway, glares at me. "No eating in the theater."

Surprised, I stare at him, carrot gripped in my fingers.

"No food. Period."

I put my snack away, eyebrows rising when he doesn't make everyone else stow their crap. It's been less than five minutes and I'm already starting to hate Esau Chavez.

Fiona puts her popcorn away in solidarity. Marisa shakes her head.

Aunt Karen is focused on the radio when I climb into her car, but she doesn't forget to hold out her palm for the recorder. I hand it over, not bothering to hide my annoyance at her brusqueness.

The radio talk show host is going on about security footage at some gas station in the southern part of the state. After a quick look at me, Aunt Karen turns it off.

"You don't have to do that," I say, even though I don't want to listen.

"It's fine." The way her hands tighten around the steering wheel indicates otherwise. She maneuvers toward the street. Viv waves enthusiastically from where she's standing next to Fiona, Marisa, and several other drama kids near the tailgate of a filthy pickup truck. I wave back before we're too far away.

The silence in the car is oppressive. I wish my guardian would turn the radio back on. I may not want to hear the latest grizzly news coming out of southern California, but it might be better than the dead air in the already stifling car. Ugh, I wish she'd get the AC fixed in this thing.

I suck in a breath. Aunt Karen must hear the desperation in it, because she turns up the fan. Hot air blasts against my face, making me gasp, and she turns it down again.

"What were they talking about?" I gesture toward the radio. My stomach churns, afraid of the answer yet compelled to ask. Fear and anger twine in my belly, because even before my guardian speaks, I know she's not going to say the words I have dreaded and craved hearing for months. An indication that the hell I'm in is finally coming to an end.

The woman levels a heavy look at me, considering. "There was a possible sighting of the Mayday Killer outside a gas station, but the police don't know where he went. Or even if it was truly him."

A shudder runs through my core.

Chapter 3

Day 96, Friday

I try to drown out the noise as I crouch and line up a shot of the herd of feet stampeding through the courtyard as the last bell of the day finishes reverberating between the buildings.

"Megan?"

A tap on my shoulder makes me whirl around, falling flat on my butt.

Noah's peering down at me, his curly hair haloed by the blazing afternoon sun. "I was calling you, but I guess you didn't hear me. Want help up?" He holds out a hand, which I consider taking but don't.

I stand slowly, brushing the bits of yellowed grass off my bare legs.

"Inspiration struck, huh?"

"Something like that."

He lopes beside me as I head for the theater. It's my second club meeting. Hopefully I can get on Esau's good side somehow. Otherwise, drama club is going to be pretty much torture.

Shouts and scuffing shoes emanate from the gym as we pass by, and a janitor's cart is standing abandoned in the propped open doorway. I walk a hair faster.

"Wow, you walk fast," Noah says, matching my pace. "Hey, I was thinking about going to the Santa Cruz boardwalk tomorrow and was wondering if you'd like to go?" He ducks his head a little, almost like he's nervous.

I looked up the boardwalk the other day, and it does look really fun. There are tons of rides and booths with fried cookies and candy bars. Plus, it's literally built right on the sand. I can almost feel the warm grit between my toes.

"That could be fun. Who all is going?"

Noah stops in his tracks, mere feet from the door to the theater. Adjusts his glasses. "Oh, um, a bunch of my friends. They'll like you. Promise."

I shear off the hint of a smile that threatens to blossom, choking it with the flicker of envy that lights in the pit of my stomach. "I'll have to check with Aunt Karen. Can I text you?"

"Sure. Sounds great." With a wave, he jogs away.

In the theater I sit with Fiona, Viv, and Marisa. They've sort of welcomed me into their group. It's nice to have people to sit with at lunch instead of finding a grassy hill to conquer by myself.

Looking around to make sure Esau isn't here yet, I take out the cheesy puffs in my backpack and crunch into them. What he doesn't know won't hurt him. But leaving orange fingerprints all over the theater might. I lick my fingers clean as I absorb the conversation of the girls around me.

Marisa takes a sip of her drink, ending the story about her mom, who used to be a dancer on Broadway.

"So, are you guys going to the boardwalk tomorrow?" I ask. "Noah said a bunch of people were going."

Fiona leans closer, snagging a cheesy puff. "I haven't heard of anyone planning to go out there. You sure he said tomorrow?"

I nod, relaying the conversation I had with Noah.

Fiona exchanges glances with Marisa before looking at me. "You know what it sounds like? Like he was asking you on a date."

"Agree," Marisa puts in. "Plus, he's still walking you to all your classes, right?"

"Yes," I whisper, not comfortable with where this conversation is going.

"Don't you think that's overkill for a student liaison? One or two days, sure. But five?"

"He's just being nice," I say, hearing how flimsy an excuse it is.

Fiona's head tilts to the side, lips quirked upward. "The question is, are you interested?"

My tongue gets tied in my mouth as I struggle to find something to say. I've known Noah for less than a week. He's nice and all, but I'm definitely not ready to go on a date with him. That is, if Aunt Karen would agree to it, which she won't. I shake my head. "I don't know."

"Looks like we're going to the boardwalk tomorrow then. Who's in?" Fiona smiles as Marisa and Viv cheer their enthusiasm at the idea.

The theater door flies open and Esau steps inside, eyes scanning over the group of us assembled on the platforms.

Ducking my head, I try to stow the cheese puffs without crinkling the bag.

The grumpy director strides closer. "Pritchard, go see if the art teacher has any extra paintbrushes we can use to touch up these platforms. And once again I'll remind you that there are no snacks allowed in the theater."

"I don't have any snacks." I stand up, tucking my backpack under the platform.

One of Esau's thick eyebrows arches. He looks pointedly at my fingertips, which are tinged orange. Oops.

"Sorry," I mutter. "Can you tell me where the art room is?"

"I'll take her," Viv volunteers. "It's right next to my ceramics class."

"I need you here to inventory our costumes. She's a big girl. You can find it on your own, can't you?"

Esau's condescending tone makes me frown as I march out.

What an ass.

Rounding the corner, I slam into a solid body. The air gets sucked out of my lungs as I fall backward. A vice-like hand grips my elbow, keeping me from falling. Strong fingers dig into my arm, unearthing memories that I don't want to relive ever again.

I yank my arm until it comes loose. My pulse pounds in my temples. My eyes round when I see it's only a janitor looming over me.

"You all right?" he asks in a scratchy voice.

I stare, blinking him into focus.

"Watch where you're going next time, okay?" Then he's gone.

Gasping for air, I lean against the side of the building. Telling myself over and over that I'm safe. There's nothing to be scared of.

Of course that's not true.

Esau spends the rest of the afternoon ordering me on stupid errands all over campus, leaving me no time to work with Fiona on the lighting and stage setup for the play. Each time I return to the theater with whatever random items he sent me to fetch, his nostrils flare. Then he sends me out again.

There's no time to share any ideas about how to make our production the best it can be. At least now I know where everything is on campus.

When Aunt Karen picks me up from school, the look she gives me is not reassuring. I know without asking that the police haven't caught him yet. Maybe they never will.

Chapter 4

Day 97, Saturday

This interrogation has got to be over soon.

"What route are you taking to the beach?" Aunt Karen asks.

Ready, Fiona holds out her phone, navigation app open.

"That looks like a windy road."

"I've been driving for two years and never had an accident." Fiona tucks the phone into her large rattan beach bag. Her braids are up in a high twist on top of her head like a crown.

"And your car is in good shape?"

"My dad checked it over last week. He's a mechanic at the dealership." Fiona winks at me. She's holding up under my guardian's pop-quiz really well and rocking her two-piece Hawaiian print bikini and sarong too.

"Fiona's really responsible," Marisa adds with a firm nod. "She's in charge of the entire stage crew for drama club, and we've never had any on-set accidents." She's wearing a full coverage rash guard over her terra cotta skin.

Viv giggles into her hand, averting her eyes when Aunt Karen zeroes in on her before looking at me.

"You'll be careful? Not go on any dangerous rides? Or

swim out too far into the ocean?"

One hand lands on my hip. "I'm not a baby. I know how to stay alive."

A tense beat passes, and Aunt Karen scowls as if the statement is dubious at best. The stairs of the old house creak, but I don't look toward the noise. There's nothing there to see.

"I swear Megan will come home in one piece," Fiona says, holding up a hand in what looks more like a Vulcan salute than scout's honor.

"You'll go straight to the boardwalk and straight back. No extraneous stops. And make sure to wear enough sunscreen."

"Yes, ma'am." Swiping my bag of snacks and a water bottle out of the fridge, I hurry my new friends out of the house before Aunt Karen can change her mind. Mercifully we didn't mention there would be boys, or there's no way she would have let me go. She's got the overprotective jailor vibe down pat. It's mortifying.

I can't blame her.

"Take the front," Viv says as we near the car, "so you can enjoy the drive. It's really pretty."

Thanking her, I do. I'm relieved, because the last time I was in a car on a mountain road I may have thrown up into my favorite sun hat. RIP.

"Wow, your aunt is something else," Fiona says once we're all safely in her white four door.

"I thought my parents were bad," Marisa says, sticking her head between the two front seats to plug her phone into the radio.

"Says the girl in a rash guard down to her ankles," says Fiona.

Marisa swats at her. "Not funny. You know how my mom is about skin care. Besides, she's kind of right. I do not want to end up leathery and brown like all the surfers who don't wear sunscreen. I'd never get any more acting gigs."

Bubble gum pop filters through the radio, making a thrill shoot through me.

I'm actually going to the beach! With friends!

Not even a quick glance at the depressing sight that is my new old house can tamp down my excitement.

We tumble out of the car into a parking lot teeming with people. Everyone looks like a pack animal, arms full of umbrellas, beach chairs and towels, coolers, and sand toys galore. Looking out at the golden beach and blue water, a knot of homesickness makes my stomach flip. I cover the misery that washes over my face by pretending to dig into the plastic bag of supplies I brought. Only look up when I've got my more unruly emotions under control.

"You coming?" Fiona asks.

I catch up to her and the other girls.

"The guys have a fire pit. Noah got here at the butt-crack of dawn to reserve one."

"That was nice of him," I mutter.

Viv bursts out laughing. "Noah is always like that. An over achiever. He has a good look, though. Those thick frames work for him. And wait until you see him in the knitted sweaters he wears through the winter."

"You like him?" I ask as we scramble over the concrete barrier that separates the parking lot from the wide stretch of sand. Bright white life-guard booths with red numbers on the sides stand at regular intervals in both directions, and between each one is a large concrete fire pit. Each one is already surrounded by clusters of people even though it's before noon.

"Noah? No way. We've all known each other way too long

to date. That's why pretty much everyone around here is so curious about you." Viv wiggles her eyebrows in my direction.

"Me?"

"You're a mystery."

"Fresh blood," adds Marisa.

"Don't scare her," Fiona says, tossing an arm around my shoulders. "Don't worry. We won't let anyone eat you."

I laugh at the absurdity of this conversation. "I think I can handle it. Just keep Esau away from me."

"If you say so. We're here!" Fiona whistles.

A bunch of male heads whirl in our direction. Noah comes jogging over. "Can I help with anything?" He takes the heavy shopping bag from my hand, smiling shyly down at me. My eyes skitter over his white tank and out to the aquamarine waves.

"Here. Thanks." Marisa shoves her monstrous cooler into the boy's other hand.

Viv flings herself at a tall, wiry redheaded girl.

I survey everyone as we draw closer to the fire pit where we'll be all day and into the evening. "You've met pretty much everyone," Fiona says. "Noah, Dariel. The ginger is Erin."

I chant names, hoping it'll help me remember. Dariel, whose mischievous smile and high box fade I remember, is in drama club with us. I'm pretty sure he and Fiona have something going on. Erin is new.

"Erin's my boo. She goes to the Catholic school," Viv says, still draped around the wiry carrot-top. The girl tugs Viv closer, looking for all the world like Viv's the only sun in her orbit. Viv giggles when the taller girl tickles her side.

"And you know Esau," Fiona finishes, gesturing with one hand toward the guy who's brooding at the edge of the group. His black hair is up in a man bun and holy cheese he doesn't have a shirt on. Boy is C. U. T. CUT.

He's also glaring at me.

My ears burn as I help Noah fan out the Mexican blanket I brought. I ordered it off the internet the minute I had my new address. I had one just like it once, draped over the foot of my bed. A memento of a fishing trip to Mexico with Dad when I was ten. My throat closes as my gaze rakes over the tight cotton weave, dyed orange and pink. Dashing my hand across my eyes, I turn away.

Down the beach, there's a long wooden platform built over the sand, with stairs leading up to it. The entire length of it is jam-packed with booths and shops. I can smell the greasy cooking oil from here. Towering above the colorful buildings are the rides. A classic wooden roller coaster. An old-fashioned log ride. A zero gravity spinner. An air-gondola ride that spans the length of the boardwalk.

"Welcome to paradise. Swimming first, or rides?" Fiona throws her arms out wide.

"Swimming," I say. I'm aching to feel the salty ocean current on my skin.

"Okay. Let's take a quick dip, and then we're getting fried twinkies!" Viv cheers.

I blink. "Fried what?"

"Twinkies. You haven't lived until you've tried one," Viv says, rubbing her hands together like a supervillain in a cartoon.

We run toward the water, laughing and hooting. Dodge sand castles and practically naked sunbathers. It's fantastic. It's a gorgeous day. It's…

Freezing cold!

My entire body grows goose bumps on my goosebumps as I gasp, the water up to my chest.

"It's hecka cold, right?" Noah calls from a few feet away.

"I bet the new girl doesn't last five minutes," Esau taunts, wading past with a splash. His thick arms pump through the water with ease.

It rankles, especially since I know he knows my name. And betting on my endurance in cold water? Ha.

I push deeper, farther, swimming with strong strokes of my arms and swift kicks of my legs. The ocean and I are one. Twisting, I float on my back, letting the current slowly push me in toward the shore.

I'm the last one out, not giving in until I'm shivering, my fingers and toes like dried prunes.

Esau looks down his nose at me as I catwalk past him to where the girls are crowded around my blanket, chowing down on watermelon slices Marisa brought in her massive cooler.

I dig into my bag for my dry clothes and pull them on.

Down the beach, there's an especially loud outcry from a group of people playing an aggressive game of volleyball. Near the net, a man lies sprawled in the sand, his teammates cheering around him. It looks like fun.

When I reach into my pocket for the tube of lip balm I keep there, my fingers come away with a scrap of paper instead. Confused, I unfold it.

Pencil scrawl cuts across the paper, the strokes so heavy they've punctured the paper. *I've missed seeing you*, it reads. Gasping, I shove it back into my pocket.

I don't know how, but my worst nightmare is coming to fruition. He's found me. I don't know how. I've been so careful. Trying not to let my hands shake, I smooth my hair up into a wet ponytail as best I can, scanning the stretch of beach. It's crawling with people. I don't see any sign of *him*, but in this crowd spotting a single person is nearly impossible.

A ways away, a law enforcement SUV is parked on the

sand, and the officers are leaning against the front bumper. It's reassuring.

My heart thunders in my chest as I will myself to focus on the chattering conversations of my friends all around me. I'm okay. I'm surrounded by people. He can't be here. He *can't.* The last possible sighting was hundreds of miles away.

But that doesn't really mean anything, does it? He's been on the run for months.

My hands won't stop trembling as I focus my attention toward the group I'm encircled in, no longer willing to risk a look behind me.

Chapter 5

"You ready for this?" Fiona asks, taking a swig from one of the fruit punch pouches Noah brought for everyone. A huge, rickety-looking wooden rollercoaster sprawls along the boardwalk. Its boards are peeling in places where the whitewash has nearly worn away. A string of cars thunders past us, occupants screaming. Whether in thrill or terror, it's hard to say.

My mind returns to the note hidden in my pocket. Half of me wants to ask Fiona to take me home, but the other half knows what will happen if I do. Once she sees it, Aunt Karen will never let me come back to this place. This beautiful place. Up until I found that note, it was the most at home I'd felt in months. I'm fighting a mental battle to get back to that place.

Steading myself, I meet Fiona's eyes. Safety in numbers is definitely a thing. So instead of giving in to my fear, I nod. "I'm ready."

Marisa and Viv whoop, standing up and brushing the sand off their damp swimsuits. Viv's solid black monokini makes her olive skin look fantastic.

"Let's do it," Noah says, trying to brush off his white tank, which clings to his lithe frame.

Sprawled out on his towel like a Greek god, Esau snorts. Then pushes himself up to his full height. He practically blocks out the sun when he hovers behind me like that. Why did he even come, if he's going to be such a butthead the whole time?

"Come on. Fried Twinkies first!" Viv says.

"Did you forget what happened last time?" Fiona eyes the girl warily.

Viv's cheeks rouge. "Okay, fried Twinkies after!"

"What happened last time?" I whisper to Marisa, who imitates spewing everywhere with gesticulating hands. Our resident actress, everyone.

We surge through the crowd, dodging patrons chowing on cotton candy. Bells ding as little kids spend money on most-likely rigged carnival games. A guy walks past carrying the largest stuffed panda bear I've ever seen. My eyes practically bug out.

"You got a thing for panda bears?" Esau huffs.

"No." I cross my arms. No need to mention the life-sized panda I used to sleep with.

"No fighting, kids, or I'm turning this car around," Fiona says.

My foot catches on an uneven plank, and I go flying, my heart lurching into my throat.

A strong arm snakes around my waist, righting me. "So clumsy," Esau grumbles near my ear.

My face heats as I shove him away.

"Are you okay?" Noah asks, his soft brown eyes on mine.

"I'm fine. Thanks," I say pointedly, refusing to thank Esau. With heart still hammering, I scurry to catch up with the girls in the line for the roller coaster, sandwiching myself between Fiona and Marisa. The boys are right at our heels.

Screams reverberate as the train cars rumble up to the highest point of the track. Then go plummeting down toward the boardwalk. A plaque to one side of the entrance states that the ride has been in operation since 1924. There must be something like trepidation in my face, because Noah leans nearer.

"It's not that scary," he says. "It's my favorite ride, actually."

I'd like to tell him about a similar roller coaster back home. My favorite ride ever. Instead, I bite my tongue.

We shuffle through the line, Marisa polling us to see which coaster to hit next.

"We don't need an itinerary," Viv says, "aside from the Twinkies."

"It never hurts to be prepared," Marisa says, swiveling to point at Erin. "Speaking of, babe, you look a little pink. Did you put sunscreen on?"

"Knew I forgot something," Erin deadpans.

"Oh you," Marisa says, clucking her tongue.

"I vote for the gondolas," Esau says, surprising me into turning to where he's standing at the back of our group. "It's quieter."

"Our director has spoken," Marisa decrees. "Gondolas it is."

"We're not in the theater," I say. "We don't have to do what Esau says."

"Oooh," Fiona crows. "Them's fighting words."

Esau crosses his arms, glaring at me.

I'm so dead at our next drama club meeting on Tuesday. Esau's going to make me climb the ladder to adjust the lights a hundred times. Or send me on so many gopher trips I miss the entire thing.

Once we're at the front of the line, Marisa and Fiona pair off. Viv links arms with Erin. I turn around and come face to face with Esau.

"It's you and me, new girl." Esau's dark eyes are piercing.

"Where's Noah?" Annoyance flares in my voice.

"He asked to switch."

Standing on tiptoes to see past Esau, I catch a glimpse of Noah chatting with another girl from school. Looks like she's into him. Oh.

Sucks to be me. Stuck with Mr. Grumpus over here.

Fiona catches my eye, looking at Esau. "Sorry," she mouths.

I shrug like it's no big deal.

When it's our turn to board, we slide into the ride's cars. They look like old-fashioned mine carts with a bench seat and a lap bar. Esau plants his feet, his legs taking up most of the space. Leaving me a tiny bit of footroom.

"Stay on your own side," I hiss, but he doesn't move.

Slamming my thigh into his, I try to shove him away. His thick legs don't budge.

"You're the worst," I mutter.

He ignores me.

The roller coaster clickety-clacks as it climbs to its highest peak. Anticipation coils in my belly as we pause at the top. I can see for miles. The deep blue of the ocean. The swaths of golden sand. The large houses along the shore.

A scream rips out of my lungs as the ride dives toward the wooden planks below.

Esau laughs at my surprise, the sound emanating from deep in his chest.

We skid around the first sharp turn and my body slams into his. I scramble to get away, but the g forces push me against him, not letting up. By the time the ride ends a minute later, I feel battered and bruised from fighting to stay in my own space.

"I didn't know you were so desperate to be close to me," Esau taunts, glancing at me with ebony eyes.

"You wish," I splutter, looking away.

Noah catches up with us as we're dumped out on to the wooden planks of the boardwalk. "How was it?"

"Super fun. Esau and I are bosom buddies now."

"Sure," he drawls, looking between Director Grumpy Pants and me. Esau's displeasure is obvious.

"Twinkies next," Viv says, grabbing my arm and drawing me away. "You like fried food, right? You're going to love them."

"I'm a vegetarian," I say, "but I'll see what they have."

"Perfect!"

Oh my goodness, deep fried Oreos are delicious. And possibly heart-attack inducing. Three of them dusted in powdered sugar and drizzled with fudge sauce were enough for one day.

"Run lines with me? I don't have mine memorized yet." Marisa asks as we're standing in line for the gondolas.

"Sure," I say, glancing over my shoulder at the burbling crowd. No familiar figures. *I'm safe,* I chant in my head. With a mental effort, I look to where Esau's standing, seemingly absorbed in watching the volleyball games out on the sand. For once his face is relaxed enough that he doesn't look like he's about to murder someone. I wonder what's up his butt? You know what? Never mind. I do not want to go there.

"I don't have another copy of the script," Marisa says with a tap on my shoulder, "so we'll have to share."

"That's okay. I don't need one."

Marisa's eyes widen as Fiona and Viv gape at me.

"I've done the show, remember? I practically have it memorized." I'm flustered, as if they could tell I was thinking about a certain broody director a minute ago. Clearing my throat, I school my features into an easy smile.

"Let's see what you've got," Fiona says.

Marisa gives me an act and scene.

I close my eyes, letting the words come flowing back. How it felt to stand on the stage in my costume, the lights in my eyes. Lines flowing from my lips like honey. The applause, afterward. Beaming faces in the audience that I'll never again behold.

Marisa begins, and I stay right with her. Line for line. Word for word.

By the time we're done, everyone in our group is staring at us.

"Wow, that was… really good," Noah says.

"No kidding. You're going to try out next semester, right?" Fiona asks. "You'll be cast for sure."

I shake my head. "Acting isn't for me. I'm much more comfortable behind the curtain." Lies on top of lies.

"Nonsense. Esau would have cast you, right Director?"

Esau's eyes zero in on mine. "Like she said, she's better off backstage."

I open my mouth to retort, my ego stung. But we've reached the front of the line. "Girls only," Marisa says, grabbing my arm and tugging me into the bright pink gondola with her, Fiona, Viv, and Erin.

"Later, Fifi," Dariel calls to Fiona.

Noah frowns slightly as us girls arrange ourselves in the suspended pink car, but Esau merely rolls his eyes.

I settle in as we rise into the air, glad to get a break from his scornful gaze.

The back of my neck prickles as if I'm being watched.

Peering over the side of the gondola, I look down at Noah

and Esau where they're climbing into the next one. They sit as far apart as possible. Neither of them is paying us any attention.

Down on the boardwalk, people criss-cross the wooden planks. Eating. Yelling. Laughing. My eyes dart back and forth, looking. For a moment I see a cruel mouth under a down-turned cap, but when I blink the man is gone. I swallow the nerves.

"Now that we're alone, want to hear something really freaky?" Fiona leans forward.

"Ghost stories, yes!" Viv grins.

"This isn't a ghost story. It's absolutely true," Fiona says. "On the drive out this morning, I thought we were being followed. This blue car with dice in the mirror was behind us for almost an hour."

"What?" I whisper, gripping the plastic seat with white fingers. So it's true. He followed me here. Waited until we were all swimming to leave me that note. My throat constricts. No, no, no, no, no. Every law enforcement agency in the state is looking for him. And there were police on the beach. There's no way he could have gotten past them without being spotted.

But it happened anyway.

"Don't freak out!" Fiona cries, waving her hands. "It was a false alarm. They turned off a different street."

I shudder, focusing on the central white pole that anchors our floating tram. Try not to picture a certain heavy gait. Brutal hands. The figure I thought I saw in the crowd below.

It wasn't him.

Couldn't have been.

I've missed seeing you.

Now I'm even lying to myself.

Chapter 6

Day 101, Wednesday

Aunt Karen said that someone moved in right across the street the day after we moved into the old house. But I've never seen him. He must be a gamer or something and never comes outside. It kind of weirds me out that there's someone living there I've never laid eyes on. What if it's him?

I've missed seeing you.

Ducking down in my seat, I munch on my toaster pastry.

"Why are you slouching like that?" Aunt Karen asks. "Sit up so we can go."

She's going to think I'm ridiculous if I tell her. Or maybe she won't. It's worth a shot.

"What if our new neighbor is, you know?"

She stares at me for a moment, surprised. "Don't be ridiculous. You think I wouldn't know if our new neighbor was a wanted fugitive? Give me some credit."

I'm not ready to let it go. "Have you seen this person? Actually met them?"

"Yes, I've met them. His name's Justin. He's quiet is all. I've known him forever. We went to school together, back in the day."

"You did?"

"It's a small town, Megan."

"If you say so," I mutter, chewing on the inside of my cheek. My instincts are whispering that there's more to this Justin person than my guardian is saying, and I've learned not to ignore them. It's too much of a coincidence that he moved in right after us. Or maybe I'm jumping at shadows.

Maybe if I know a little more about the guy, he won't creep me out so much. "Where did he work before the school?"

"The dairy." It's an automatic response. She pulls up outside the school. "Got everything?"

I pull open the front flap of my backpack to reveal the recorder and push its start button.

"Good girl. See you after school."

It's a half hour before school starts, so there isn't anybody here yet. Aunt Karen had to go into the grocery store early, for what she didn't say. I figured I'd rather be at school early than have to walk from the house. The concrete steps are warm in the morning sun as I pull up a seat and take out my phone.

I've posted a few more images since the leaves, and I've gotten some good feedback. I scroll back through my feed, pausing on a photo I took of my orchids blooming where they hung in my window back home. Large yellow flowers. Small crimson blooms. Pale pink petals so tiny they don't even look real.

A dingy white car pulls into the lot and Noah climbs out, pink box in hand. He waves when he spots me and jogs over. "Want a donut? I thought you might be in the mood for some breakfast since your aunt doesn't cook."

I'm a little embarrassed that I told him that. It's true, though. I have never eaten so much takeout in my life. "I wouldn't say no to a chocolate bar."

"I got one of those. Actually, I wasn't sure what you liked, so I got half a dozen. Here." He opens the pink box, holding it out.

I thank him, taking one. This was so nice of him. Besides, the toaster pastries I've been eating don't last very long in my stomach.

"Okay… So for our art project, here's what I was thinking." Noah goes on, detailing an idea about combining my photos with his love of anime to create a collage of one of his favorite characters. I nod along, not really listening.

I'm glad he took me to meet the art teacher, Mr. Baugh, because the advanced class is way better than being stuck in art 101 with a bunch of freshmen. Mr. Baugh took one look at my social feed and told me to request a transfer. It's not a photography class, specifically, but Mr. Baugh hopes to get filmography and photography sections going in the next couple of years. It's nice to have classes with Noah, since I somehow don't have any classes with Fiona, Marisa, or Viv.

"Want to get together tomorrow night to work on it? At your place?"

"I can't. Drama club."

Noah takes a sip from his coffee cup. "We'll figure it out."

I'm glad he's not pushing, because I already know what Aunt Karen would say if I asked about having friends over.

"Are those donuts?" Fiona calls as she, Viv, and Marisa walk over from their cars.

"Yep. Want one?"

"Don't mind if I do," Fiona says, plucking an old fashioned out of the box. Marisa takes the one covered in sprinkles.

The janitor walks right past us and around the corner.

I jump, realizing that he walked right up to us without

making a sound. I have to be more alert. Relax, I tell myself. You're being paranoid. The man didn't pay us any attention.

"So… the school janitor. He's weird, right?" I try to act casual as I turn back to my friends. Probably fail.

"Who?" Fiona asks, peering over my shoulder.

Marisa follows suit. "Oh, you mean the new guy, Justin?"

"He's new?" I squeak.

"Yep. And super cute."

Fiona grimaces.

Viv leans in conspiratorially. "I heard a rumor he got fired from his last job because he was caught with a student. You know what I mean."

"Really?" Marisa's bright eyes are glued to Viv.

I'm fighting to keep my eyes from glazing over. This Justin is new at the school. He's *new.* Which means he could be the physical manifestation of the phantom who destroyed my life. Fiona's voice cuts through my terror haze.

"They wouldn't let him work at the school if any of that was true," Fiona says, shaking her head.

"They do background checks before they hire any new staff," Noah says.

That may be true, but what about criminals the police can't identify? What if they don't have a record? A background check on someone like that wouldn't turn up a single, bloody thing.

Chapter 7

Day 102, Thursday

Esau is in a *mood* today, barking orders at the stage crew and making his actors run the same scene over and over until it's beat perfect. His exacting, demanding nature is both eye-roll inducing, and something else I don't care to think about right now.

"Again," our director commands, throwing his black braids behind his back. The gauges in his ears are flat black under the lights. Marisa and the other actors reset the scene, adjusting their bodies into the forms Esau has told them to use. Fiona and one of the stage crew guys are on a ladder tinkering with the filters over the stage lights. White becomes blue becomes orange.

"I hate the orange," Esau says, glancing up the ladder. "Go back to blue."

"Got it." Fiona switches out the filters with a deft hand, passing the unwanted ones down to me.

The actors take the scene from the top.

Esau produces an old digital camera from under his chair and starts filming, pivoting around the stage in a slow arc. His dark eyes are laser focused on the scene before him as he easily steps over a pile of cables.

My eyes widen and I duck behind the ladder to avoid being filmed. Whatever he's doing, I can't be on camera.

"Feeling shy?" Fiona asks, hopping down from her perch with a dull thunk. She nods toward Esau with her chin.

The director's back is to us now, his camera zeroed in on Marisa's face. It's her turn to speak, but her expression has gone blank. Her eyes casting around for the words that should be on the tip of her tongue.

The others are staring at her now, waiting for her to pick up their practiced rhythm.

Silence.

Esau's shoulders tense. The camera catches all of it.

Marisa's eyes meet mine, frustration in her golden eyes.

I mutter the line just loud enough for her to hear.

She picks it up, and the characters are off again.

Esau eyes me over his camera. Which is trained right on me.

With an eep I sidestep behind Fiona, feeling a lot like a little kid hiding behind her mother. I wait until the brooding director moves on.

"I need some help with the sound system up here. Fiona?" Dariel calls from the booth at the back of the room, where I can barely see his high, box faded hair over the rail.

"You coming?" Fiona says over her shoulder, gesturing for me to follow.

"Will there be kissing this time?"

"No promises," Fiona laughs as we climb the stairs. We work with Dariel upstairs for a few minutes, trying various lighting cues and sound effects, noting where they'll work best in the show.

"What's with the camera?" I ask Fiona as I adjust the soundboard per Esau's direction.

"Esau's got a channel on a streaming site, and he's trying to get some traction as an influencer. Last I checked, he only had a couple hundred followers." With a shrug, she turns to Dariel. "Let's try that last cue again, yeah?"

Dariel winks at her.

I like Fiona. She's a capable stage manager. She knows how to do pretty much everything backstage and puts people where they're the best fit. She busts her butt when it counts, but she also knows how to have fun with it. Unlike someone else I know.

From up in the booth, it's easy to track Esau's movements with his camera. He spends the next several minutes filming the actors before getting some footage of the stage crew painting a backdrop.

Marisa forgets another line and I call it down to her.

"What's Esau's handle?" Nudging Fiona with my elbow, I wait with my fingers poised over my phone. I'm curious about Mr. Grumpy's social. She helps me find it, and immediately I can see some areas where Esau could improve. I'm not internet famous, but I have a few favorite creators I follow, and it's easy to see the differences in their most popular content and what Esau's doing.

"You gonna tell me your deal about being filmed?" Fiona asks.

Dariel climbs out from under the sound board with a cable snaked around his arm. "BRB, boss lady." He bounds down the stairs, placing the cable with careful hands.

I lean over the edge to make sure Esau isn't anywhere nearby before I answer. "Would you believe me if I told you I just don't like having my picture taken?"

Fiona's braids wave back and forth as her head shakes. "You've got nothing to worry about."

I raise an eyebrow, daring her to mention my scar.

She doesn't.

My attention returns to the soundboard. "Aunt Karen has a thing about the internet. She says it destroys privacy. You should hear her ranting about how it's her job to protect me from creeps, especially on the computer. I shudder to think what she'd do if she found out I was on Esau's feed."

"So she's one of those."

I nod in the affirmative. Hope that's enough of an explanation. There's no way I'm telling Fiona about the tiny crack in my guardian's expression I glimpsed when I told Aunt Karen about the note. She tried to hide it, but it was there.

"Anything else we need to do up here?" Dariel asks, eyeing Fiona with a flirty grin as he climbs the stairs.

"Shut up." Fiona grins.

"Pritchard! Get down here."

"Ohhhh, somebody's in trouble."

"Shut up, Dariel," Fiona says through a chuckle.

Great… What does the great grumpus want now? I take my time on the stairs, knowing that each second it takes me to get down there needles Esau. I can't help it. Getting under his skin gives me more satisfaction than a lot of things these days.

When I finally reach the stage, he's glaring, corded arms crossed over his chest. "Didn't know you were an old lady," he says. "Should we install a ramp to help you get around faster?"

"What do you want, Esau?"

"Your new job is feeding the actors their lines if they need 'em."

"No more gophering?"

One of his thick black eyebrows lashes upward. With a grunt, he walks away. It's not exactly a promotion, but I'll take it nonetheless. Anything is better than pinballing all over campus on the stupid errands he's tasked me with every other time the drama club has met. Maybe I won't need to shower as soon as I get home tonight, slick with sweat from running.

The rest of practice goes smoothly, with most of the actors not needing much prompting. They've pretty much got their lines down with a few hiccups here and there.

Marisa, though, isn't doing well. Whenever Esau is listening, she gets even worse. By the end of the meeting, her face is red with frustration. Strands of her black hair stick to her neck.

"You need to have everything memorized by Friday. Your performance today was unacceptable."

Marisa cows before Esau, eyes on the floor. She nods, chewing on her lip.

"Friday, all right?"

I can't stand by while Esau presses someone into submission. I won't. "She heard you." Stepping forward, I put an arm around Marisa's shoulders.

"Excuse me?" Esau's dark eyes blaze.

"She knows what she needs to do, okay? You can drop it."

"No, I can't *drop it*. As the director, it's my job to make sure the show runs smoothly. You want Marisa to embarrass herself in front of everyone? Because I don't."

I'm seething with rage as my new friend's eyes start to glisten. "Where do you get off? In case you hadn't noticed, your stomping and growling has everyone on edge. Marisa was doing fine until you started barking at her. If anyone should be embarrassed, it's you. Your actors are too stressed out by you, Mr. Grumpy, to remember their lines."

Esau's eyes are narrowed to slits. He looks between Marisa and me. Grunts. "That's enough for today. See you all on Thursday." He goes backstage, helping the crew clean up so everyone can leave.

Dariel calls down to me from the booth, asking for help with some cables.

"Just a sec," I call back. Drawing closer to Marisa, I whisper, "You okay?"

"Yeah. I'm fine. These lines… ugh."

As one of the show's leads, Marisa does have a lot to memorize. It took me a long time to get my lines down when we did this play at my old school, and I'm a pro at memorizing. There's so much I wish I could say to Marisa, tell her about my experiences. Instead, I give her a tap on the shoulder. "I'm around if you want to practice sometime."

"Really? Thanks." She stoops to gather her stuff and I high-step it up the stairs to where Dariel's waiting. There's a small window behind the sound booth, covered in black cloth to block out the light. I push it aside and peer out to the mostly empty parking lot.

But in the far corner there's a dusty sedan. Blue. And if I squint, I can just make out fluffy dice hanging from the rearview mirror.

In my head, I know it's an overreaction, but my heart plunges into my shoes.

"Hey Dariel, whose car is that? The blue one?"

Dariel takes a look over my shoulder. "Dunno."

"Be right back." I run down the stairs and out the door, ignoring Esau's indignance when I brush past him. The car's engine starts as I hit the asphalt of the parking lot and sprint toward it. Tires screech and the acrid smell of burning rubber hits my nose as it lurches toward the exit.

My heart beats in time with my feet slamming over the hard ground. I'm almost there.

Too late.

The car speeds away before I can see more than a glance of a hand on the steering wheel. It was a man, I'm sure, but beyond that…

"Everything okay?" Fiona asks from behind me, making me whirl around.

Catching my breath, I nod. "Fine."

Fiona looks formidable with one hand on her hip. "If you say so. Let's go back inside."

Everything is *not* fine, but what's one more lie?

Chapter 8

Day 106, Monday

Closing my locker, I startle.

Esau is leaning against the wall, looking at me with an inscrutable look on his face.

"Hey." I roll my eyes, not looking forward to the lecture I'm about to get for speaking out of turn in drama.

Lockers slam around us as people exchange books and binders, or dig through the detritus in their assigned spaces for an errant bag of chips or red vines.

Marisa, Fiona, and Viv approach, but Fiona takes one look at Esau standing next to me and keeps the girls moving down the hall. I stare after them, wishing they'd stopped to rescue me from Mr. Grumpy Pants's forthcoming tongue-lashing.

Esau draws my attention back to him with a hand on my arm.

My mouth opens in surprise as I look down at his brown fingers on my pale skin. I don't know what to make of the gentle touch.

He withdraws, dropping his hands behind his back. "How are your classes going?"

I stare, my brain stalling, still trying to figure out why he's talking to me. The way I look around down the hallway for a sightline on any of my friends must be comical, because when I turn back to Esau, he's smirking.

"Your classes?" he prompts.

"No one makes me move heavy scenery around or peel gum off the floor, so I can't complain."

He strokes his jaw and I can't help wondering if he's suppressing a chuckle. Esau's ebony eyes meet mine. "Look, I have a favor to ask."

My chin hits the floor. "You're asking me a favor? Seriously?"

Esau's teeth clench. "Forget it." He turns away, but I catch the sleeve of his white t-shirt. The look he gives me over his shoulder makes me drop my hand as if it's been burned.

"Wait. What was it you were going to ask? I'll help, if I can."

Exhaling out his nose, Esau opens his phone and holds it out to me. "Fiona said you're good at this stuff."

Taking the device, I peer down at Esau's social media account. I scroll through, and immediately I can spot several mistakes he's making. My teeth nibble on the inside of my cheek. Esau does not take suggestions well, so I hesitate even though I could school him on what he's doing wrong.

"Spit it out," he all but commands.

"When you put it that way." I rattle off several suggestions and my reasonings.

Esau nods, his eyes flicking over my face. "See you around." And then he lumbers away.

I stand in the middle of the hallway, shocked that he actually sought me out to ask my advice on something. Plus, it was weird that he asked about school before getting to the point. It's not like he cares about my day. Why bother?

The warning bell clangs through the corridor, making me

and everyone else lingering before their next class scurry toward their next period.

I slide into my seat in art class as the tardy bell is ringing. Mr. Baugh catches my eye from the front of the room and gives me a look.

"Sorry," I mouth. I feel bad for being late because I like this class, and I like Mr. Baugh. He seems genuinely kind and interested in his students, unlike some of the other teachers. Besides, art class gives me an excuse to take more photos. In the past two weeks I've taken hundreds of new ones, so much that they're clogging up the storage space on my phone.

At the front of the room, Mr. Baugh reminds us to keep up with our reading before telling us to split up into pairs to work on our semester projects.

Noah grins at me. "We still need to get together to work on our project."

"How about Sunday? We could meet at the diner in town."

He shakes his head. "I'm babysitting my younger sister and brother that day."

A flare of frustration goes through me. Why is it so hard to find a time to get together to work on our project? And if I'm being honest, I'd like to get to know Noah better, too.

"That's okay," I say. "I used to babysit all the time. Little kids like me."

Noah's wide brown eyes study me. "You sure? They're kind of a handful. I can't promise you won't end up dressed like a firefighting princess. Or holding a lizard."

"I like lizards."

He laughs at the hesitance in my voice. "Okay, Sunday it is. I'll text you my address."

I'm relieved, not only because Aunt Karen has made her

displeasure at having random people in her space clear, but also because the idea of inviting friends over to the old house feels wrong somehow. How can I expect Noah to be at ease there when I never am? Worrying my lip, I wonder if the place will ever feel like a home, or if it will always feel like simply a place to hide.

Aunt Karen is gone on one of her mysterious long walks. She goes practically every evening after dinner, but she won't say where. I feel kind of bad. Suddenly becoming a guardian when you were childless before has to take some adjusting. She needs some space; I get that.

Still can't say I like it when she's gone, though. The creaks and groans the old house makes creep me out. The drone of the AC sounds more like cultic chanting the more I focus on it. And the grove of eucalyptus trees out back? I shudder to think what could be hiding in there.

Which is why when the girls from drama club showed up, I was so on edge I slammed the door in their faces to a chorus of *Hey* and *Aren't you going to invite us in?* I took a second to breathe before I opened it again.

Once I recover from my shock at being visited at Aunt Karen's house, I slip out the front door. "What are you guys doing here?" I ask, crossing my arms, deciding that looks too aggressive, and uncrossing them again.

Fiona's mouth pulls down. "Sorry, should we have texted first or?"

"My house is chaos—Mom's having the kitchen remodeled," Viv says.

"My mom doesn't know how to butt out," Marisa adds. "She thinks my friends are her friends, so it's better if we don't spend time there."

"Last time we were at Marisa's place her mom tried to watch Clueless with us, but she kept ranting about how awful their acting was," Viv starts to grin and Marisa swats at her with a Shh. Viv is not put off. She mimics Marisa's mom, clutching the fake black pearls she's wearing and using a nasal voice. "Like, *Oh my God, you know not to scrunch up your entire face when you fake cry, right?*"

I turn to Fiona, waiting for her excuse. She gives a playful shrug. "I came to see your aunt Karen. She's cool."

Inside, a door slams.

"Is she home, by the way?" Fiona looks past me, her brown skin already glistening in the stale air. "Can we come in? It's kind of stifling out here." She takes a step toward the door, but I block her.

"No! Sorry. Aunt Karen doesn't like having people over. I think it's because she needs to detox after dealing with customers all day at the grocery store. Sorry, again."

The girl shakes her head. "It's fine. We should have texted. We'll go."

"No! Please don't. Do you want some lemonade?"

"Absolutely we do," Viv says, quoting a character from *The Office.*

"Nice one, Jim," Fiona says, thumbing at Viv.

"I think it would have been really fun to play Angela. She's so catty all the time. I could really get into that," Marisa says.

I don't know how this happened, me standing on the front porch discussing an old sitcom with friends from my new school, but here I am. The word reverberates through my brain. I have friends. At my new school. A small smile flits over my lips.

"So, lemonade?" Viv prompts.

I start, promising to bring it right out. In the kitchen, I

remember that Aunt Karen doesn't cook, so there aren't any lemons. Or sugar, aside from the sugar replacement stuff she uses in her morning coffee. She must not sleep well, because she doesn't speak until she's had at least two cups of the stuff.

Ha! I'm in luck.

There's a can of lemonade concentrate in the freezer. It's crusted over with freezer burn, but it should be fine.

By the time I step out on to the porch with a pitcher and four glasses, all three of my friends look like they've been in a sauna—they're panting with the heat and dripping sweat. They pretty much have, it's so ungodly hot out here.

"You know, let's go in the house, okay?"

"Oh thank god," Marisa says, fanning herself with her hand.

"You sure your aunt won't mind?" Fiona asks, taking a glass from me and slamming back the lemonade before pouring another.

"It's fine. Let's sit in the living room." It comes out too loud. Embarrassment makes my ears heat. But the relief of being in the air conditioned room overpowers it. We plop down on the old leather couches, scratched here and there, and drink our lemonade.

"BRB," Viv says. "The restroom is?"

"Down the hall, first door on the right." Once again, too loud. I slurp down lemonade, hoping it'll make my pits stop sweating.

"Can I get some more ice?" Fiona asks, peering into her glass where the last shards of it are rapidly dissipating.

I shoot out of my seat. "I'll get you some."

"I'll help." Marisa is at my heels all the way into the kitchen.

Opening the freezer, I use a plastic cup to scoop the ice.

The fridge is so old it doesn't have a dispenser in the door.

Marisa tries to whisper into my ear, making me jump sky high.

"Sorry," I stammer. "What was that?"

"I need help," Marisa says, barely above a whisper. "With the play. I have to get my lines memorized. If I don't…"

"I, um. What do you normally do to memorize your lines?"

Marisa shakes her head. "This is my first big role. Last year I played a tree."

My mouth drops open. "Your…" I swallow. Try again past the cotton in my throat. "Your largest role before now was as a tree?" It all makes sense. The nervous fidgeting when members of the crew watch the actors practice. The flubbing of lines. The frantic help-me stare she kept throwing my way at our last meeting. She was anxious because this is all new for her.

The girl nods, eyes on mine. "Now you're getting it."

"But I thought you…"

"Look, I just, I have to get it right, okay?"

"I know there are techniques you can use to…"

The front door opens and shuts.

"Oh, hello. Fiona was it?" Aunt Karen's voice sounds friendly on the surface, but I know better.

Bolting from the kitchen, I rush into the front of the house. "We were just hanging out here in the living room. See? Lemonade."

Aunt Karen looks from Marisa, who clearly was just in the kitchen with me, to Viv, who picks this moment to come back from the bathroom. The simmering annoyance behind the woman's eyes makes me gulp down more cloyingly sweet lemonade.

She shakes it off, her hand moving from the small of her back. There's a lump under her shirt like she stuffed something down the back of her waistband. Some of that expensive chocolate she eats when she thinks I'm not looking, perhaps? Not wanting to think about sweaty chocolate any more than never, I shove the thought away.

Aunt Karen makes small talk for a few minutes before ushering the girls to the door. They leave, full of lemonade and probably wondering why my guardian is so overprotective. Aunt Karen twists the lock on the door and turns, hitting me between the eyes with a look so cold I wish I had a sweater.

"Megan," she asks, "what did I say about visitors?"

"I know. I'm sorry."

Aunt Karen's expression softens. She takes a couple steps closer. "I asked the sheriff about that blue car you've been seeing."

"You did? What did he say?"

Her frown tells me everything I need to know before she even speaks. "It was a dead end. The owner died a year ago, and nobody has registered as its new owner."

"So what you're saying is it's a stolen car, and anyone could be driving it."

She puts a gentle hand on my shoulder. "Just, follow my rules, okay? And you'll be fine. I'll keep you safe."

I don't have a choice but to believe her.

Chapter 9

Day 108, Wednesday

Noah's house is a small blue bungalow set back from the road in a stand of gnarled oak trees. The dairy and its sea of monochrome bovines is right next door. The smell is intense, even inside Aunt Karen's car with the windows rolled up.

"Let me know when you need me to come get you," she says, her eyes drooping to my backpack before settling on my face. "You have everything?"

I assure her that I do before sliding out of the car. "I'll text you."

The gravel spreads over the ground as Aunt Karen pulls away, leaving me alone on the long drive. With a deep breath, I start toward the house, the rough stones jagged under the soles of my sandals.

An unearthly squawk makes me jump and whirl around.

There's a black-and-white striped chicken standing a few feet away, its dark beady eyes locked on me. Luminescent green feathers plume out behind the bird.

I don't think I've ever actually seen a chicken in person, and this one is kind of pretty. I hunch over to get a better look.

It lunges toward me with a bird-like war cry.

With a screech, I take off for the house, hoping that I'm

faster than the foul fowl hot on my tail.

"Ouch!" I yell when the demon bird's sharp beak makes contact with my heel. "Noah! Help." My eyes slide between the bungalow's white front door and a large oak tree with a horizontal branch just low enough for me to grab.

The demon bird squawks, making another jab at my heel.

Cutting off the gravel path and dropping my backpack into the dirt, I leap onto the lowest branch of a sprawling oak tree and pray chickens can't fly. They can't, right?

The spawn of bird satan ruffles its feathers in the sunlight as it stalks around the trunk of the tree. Cocking its head like a velociraptor, it looks up at me. The bird clicks its beak together and pecks at the ground. I don't know where chickens are on the animal intelligence scale, but I'd swear this thing is pretending to forage so I'll climb down from the long, rugged branch where I'm perched.

Fat chance, bird.

The chicken flaps its wings and leaves the ground, swooping just underneath my dangling feet.

Eep! Thankful I'm wearing long shorts instead of a dress, I move to a crouch.

The bird makes another attempt and goes back to fake foraging. Evil, wily creature.

Taking a peek at my heel, I hiss under my breath. It's bleeding from a small hole where the freaking aggressive bird bit me. I look to the house twenty feet away. Back down at the bird. Should I make a break for it?

The front door opens and Noah steps out. He's got a bright purple feather boa around his neck, and his wavy black hair is tousled over his forehead. It's almost enough to make me chuckle despite my current situation.

Noah's mouth drops open when he catches sight of me

huddled in a tree like a trapped raccoon. "Megan? Crap. Napoleon! You stupid rooster." Jogging over to the base of the trunk, Noah shoos the bird who I swear glares at me before trotting around the side of the house. If I didn't believe birds were somehow related to dinosaurs, I do now.

"Here, let me help you down." Noah's hands land lightly on my waist, and I jump down from the branch. "I'm so sorry about that. I was going to come out and warn you about our guard rooster, but my sister got me invested in building a blanket fort and… You're bleeding! God, Megan, I'm so sorry. What a disaster."

"It's okay. Thanks for the hand down."

When I meet his eyes, I'm surprised to see a tinge of pink in his cheeks. Is Noah blushing? He seems to realize that his hands are still on my waist, because he pulls away and scratches the back of his neck. "Let's get you inside before Napoleon remembers he likes the taste of human flesh, okay?"

I force a laugh, but I'm wary of the demon bird until we're safely inside.

Noah was not exaggerating about the blanket fort he and his siblings have made. The entire front room of the house is a canopy of blankets upheld by dining chairs, a floor lamp, and lots and lots of wooden clothespins. One snaps and flies through the air as a little girl crawls out the nearest flap in the fort and looks up at me with open curiosity.

"Anza, this is my friend Megan. Megan, my sister Esperanza. Anza for short."

The little girl grins, showcasing a gap where her two front teeth should be. "Are you here to see our fort?"

A little boy crawls out of the flap, takes a peek at me, and scuttles back under the blankets.

"That's Matteo," Noah explains. "He's shy around new

people."

"Come on. Let me show you our fort. It's the biggest one we've ever made. Noah helped, but Mattie and I did most of it."

"You did? That's impressive."

The little girl nods, still grinning, but Noah begs off, telling her we have homework to do. He leads me around the giant patchwork of blankets to the dining table, which is missing all but one chair and a long bench. Noah gestures for me to take the chair before folding himself on to the bench. It's so tall, the boy's long legs barely fit under the table. When I try to get him to switch, he waves me off. "I'm used to it," he says with a small smile.

We've just pulled our class notes out when Esperanza approaches us, towing her younger brother behind her. "We're hungry," she says. "Can you make us quesadillas? With just cheese. No tomatoes."

Matteo whispers in Esperanza's ear loud enough that I can hear he doesn't want beans in his either.

I stifle a laugh.

Noah sighs, pulling his gaze toward mine. "You don't mind, do you? Want one?"

"Go ahead. Kids have to eat, right?" Esperanza returns the warm look I send her way. Matteo is hiding behind her, and she's just tall enough that it works.

Noah excuses himself to work on quesadillas while Esperanza climbs onto the bench and grabs one of the coloring books Noah pushed to the far end of the table when we set up shop. Pulling a bin of markers toward her, she goes to work on a rainbow unicorn, showing me her progress after each color.

I look around for Matteo, but he must have disappeared into the blanket fort again.

"Did you know that my brother and I are raising a pig?" Esperanza says with a giddy grin.

"You what?"

"Her name is Piglet, and once she's big and fat we're going to sell her and buy a car just for us."

A whine comes from somewhere under the blankets. Noah catches my eye from where he's standing at the stove, a knowing smile playing over his features.

Esperanza leans closer to me. "Mattie wants to buy new video games, but I think a car would be better."

"A car would be pretty awesome. I don't even have a car."

The little girl's eyes widen and she dives under the blanket fort, loudly informing her brother of my lack of vehicle. Esperanza is sweet, and I'm betting Matteo is too.

I scroll through the images on my phone, trying to decide which one to post. I've been posting most days, and it feels great to put my work out there again. The likes and comments don't hurt either. I've reconnected with a couple of girls I used to do photo challenges with, too.

"How'd you get that big white scar on your face?"

Noah's jaw drops in horror at Anza's bald-faced question.

"Were you born with it? I was born with a strawberry mark on my arm. See?"

I look down at the little girl's arm where she's pointing to a mark that really does look like a strawberry.

"Anza! You don't ask people rude questions like that," Noah scolds. "Sorry about that. Six-year-olds, you know?" It would be easier to shrug off if Noah wasn't scanning my face with intent eyes, the question clearly visible there. How *did* you get that scar?

I don't want to talk about this. "I have to go to the bathroom," I blurt.

Noah tells me where it is, and I hurry away from Anza. Don't follow me, don't follow me, don't follow me.

The quesadillas are almost ready. The delicious scent of melted cheese wafts as I go down the hallway. An elaborate collage of photo frames runs the length of the wall, broken only by the closed doors. There are photos of a young couple who must be Noah's parents. I recognize his nose on the woman's face, but his smile is definitely from his dad. Baby Noah grins at me, his hair slicked up in a mohawk of soapy bath water. Beyond this are photos of his siblings as babies, swaddled in pink and blue blankets and wearing hospital beanies. His mother smiles at the camera with tired eyes. Interspersed between the faces I recognize are images of a boy I can't place.

"Hey Noah, do you have another brother?" I call.

When he doesn't answer, I peek into the kitchen.

Noah's jaw is tight, his eyes fastened to the griddle where the quesadillas are browning.

I'm starting to get to know Noah, and the look on his face makes it clear that I've stumbled on to a sensitive topic. Biting my lip, I retreat into the hallway.

Did he say the bathroom was the first door on the right, or the second?

Taking a guess, I open the first. Definitely not a bathroom. Instead, my eyes fall on a twin bed, unmade with a rumpled blue comforter kicked down to its foot. There's a small, well-loved wooden desk and chair in the corner. I turn to take in the rest of his room, hoping he's okay with me being in here.

Above the bed there's a large poster of an anime character with wolf ears and red clothes standing next to a girl in a green and white school uniform. I'm guessing this is a safer topic. "You're an Inuyasha fan?" I toss out, hoping he can hear me over the crackle of melting cheese and browning tortillas.

No answer.

Still, I'm pleased that he has a poster of one of my favorite anime shows. A spark of something like enthusiasm ignites in my chest, but it's quickly snuffed out by what I see next.

Taped to the back of Noah's door are articles and maps. A collage of face sketches done by a forensic artist have been printed from a printer low on ink. Headlines cut from newspapers shout at me in thick black letters. *Serial killer. Gruesome murders. Artist rendering. Mayday murders. If you have any information on the identity of this person, please call...*

My stomach lurches at the soulless look of the man in the sketches. They're not great, but my mind fills in the rest. The room starts to spin and my pulse goes thready. Someone is breathing hard, and it takes a second to realize that the ragged inhales are coming from me. Something deep in my belly recoils. Recognizes the base undercurrent in that gaze. Recalls the one and only time I beheld someone with that animalistic sneer on their face.

Panic gurgles in my throat, making me lurch backward when the door swings open.

"There you are. The quesadillas are…" Noah's words drop off at my ghostly expression. "What's wrong?"

I swallow, throat dry. My eyes bob between the boy and the murder board he's got hidden behind his bedroom door. Tears threaten, but I bite my tongue, fighting them back.

Understanding dawns on Noah's face and he opens his mouth to speak.

I'm shaking my head. My entire body is quaking as I back away from him toward the hallway. I can't talk about this. I can't. Before he can get even a word out, I bolt.

Scrambling down the pebbled drive, I dig my phone out of

my backpack and panic-dial Aunt Karen.

"Megan? Are you okay? What's wrong?"

"Please," I choke out. "Come get me. I can't stay here."

"Don't panic. I'm coming!"

"Too late," I mumble after the phone line goes dead. My fingers glide over a folded piece of paper as I return my phone to the front pouch of my bag. Dread fills me as I stare at it. I've seen those ripped edges before. Plucking it out, I warily unfurl the lined sheet.

Don't try to find me. I'll come for you when the time is right.

The tide of panic in my chest rises as I swivel around, looking for the boogie man hiding in the trees. *When the time is right.* What does that even mean?

Noah is standing on the porch, watching me with a worried frown. He acts as lookout until Aunt Karen pulls up in her car and I scramble inside, slamming the door to ward off the demons chasing me.

Day 87

The room is immaculate. A row of cabinets lines the wall, each labeled with something more ominous than the last: utensils, gauze and skin grafts, prosthetics.

My fingers curl around the edges of the chair I'm sitting on until they hurt, but I don't let go.

Don't dare look to the mirror in the corner, afraid of what I'll see reflected there.

I have to do this. There is no other choice.

"Are you ready?" Aunt Karen asks, her eyes steady on mine.

I nod, once.

"Hold still," the woman wearing latex gloves scoots her stool closer and studies my face. My cheek. The cleaning cloth stings as she rubs it over my skin.

She examines the reference image on the computer screen at her elbow before sliding her concentration to land on the planes of my face. Pulling her tray of tools close to her knee, she selects one and holds it up.

I feel nothing as the woman pulls the skin taut and gets to work.

I refuse to close my eyes, forcing myself to watch as the branding scar
blooms
on my
cheek.

Chapter 10

Day 109, Thursday

I've been thinking about the second note, but no matter how much I wrack my brain, I can't figure out how it got into my backpack, unless it happened at school. The only times I don't have it are during PE and drama club. Someone must have snuck into the locker room while we were outside running a mile despite the heat and put it in my bag.

Which means the killer has help from someone on campus, or he's here.

The new janitor comes to mind. It could be him, despite what Aunt Karen says.

Noah smiles uneasily as I walk into art class and slip into my usual desk next to his. He tries to catch my eye, but I busy myself with the time-honored tradition of digging around in my backpack, pretending to look for something.

"Megan?" he asks, putting a gentle hand on my arm. "Can we talk?"

I sigh. "I don't really want to talk about it," I say. "I just want to—"

"Good afternoon, everyone!" Mr. Baugh grins at us from the front of the classroom. "I hope everyone is ready to spend this period working on their projects?"

A flurry of answers—some eager, some half-hearted—come from my classmates.

I'm equally unenthusiastic. I hoped Mr. Baugh would give us something we could work on individually today so I could keep avoiding having that conversation with Noah. It's only been two days since the discovery of his murder board and the second note and I Do. Not. Want. To. Talk. About. It. But instead of working on my own interpretation of Starry Night, or making a cast of my own face with papier mâché and breathing straws, I've just been sentenced to an hour of stilted conversation and nerves strung tight.

The pairs around us are already getting to work, and I'm still staring down into my backpack at nothing.

"Megan, please," Noah breathes. "Let me explain."

"I don't want to hear an explanation about how you're a serial killer groupie or something. Not today." Okay, so maybe my tone is a tad harsher than I intended, but seriously? The guy has a map of everywhere the Mayday Killer has been spotted on the back of his bedroom door. What else am I supposed to assume than that he has an unhealthy interest in what happened?

For all I know, Noah could be helping the devil.

Noah scratches his ear under his glasses. "You think I—wow." He mouths the last word, his own face turns down toward his desk, and he doesn't say anything else.

A twinge of guilt curls behind my breastbone at the crestfallen look on his face, but I let it stand. At least now I won't have to hear anything else about the killer who's already taken twelve lives and has managed to elude the police for nearly six months now. Hell, despite all of their technology and man-power, they don't even know *who he is.*

For the rest of class, Noah works on the outline for our

collage while I sort the photos on my phone by color to see how many more will be needed. He doesn't say anything else, which is fine. It's not uncomfortable at all.

"Looks like someone doesn't hate you, after all," Fiona says when I walk into drama club.

"What are you talking about?" After the painfully awkward period I spent with Noah, I had been hoping that drama club would be a positive change of pace. Having a friend group again feels fantastic. We have so much fun that it's almost easy to overlook what a bossy ass Esau is to me ninety percent of the time.

"You told him that he should be using natural light and portrait mode for his social account, right? Take a look." She holds her phone out to me and I take it, scrolling through Esau's feed and noting that he's done both. Instead of dark, grainy photos, the newer ones are well lit and crisp. He's also cleaned up his profile. Another suggestion I made.

"That doesn't mean anything. He still hates me."

"Right," Fiona says, arching a brow. "He hates you. I gotta say, I do not look at guys I hate the way that boy looks at you."

I roll my eyes. "Then you clearly aren't looking carefully enough."

"What are we looking at?" Viv asks, popping her round face over Fiona's shoulder. She's got a bunch of sewing pins in a watermelon-shaped cushion at her wrist. She's been hard at work in the hallway, sewing and altering the costumes for the play, and she's pretty talented. The color palettes she's putting together for the characters make my mind come alive with so many ideas.

Too bad our director has his head stuck up his—

"We're talking about how Esau looks at Megan."

"Oh, I like this conversation. How does he look at her?"

"Like he hates me," I say at the same time that Fiona says, "Like he wants to eat her face."

All three of us bust up laughing at the absurdity of the idea. Viv mimics chomping with one hand, making us laugh even louder.

"Plus," Fiona says, once we've all calmed down. "Dariel had something very interesting to say about that day we all went to the boardwalk."

"What about it?" I hate how curious I sound.

Viv's cheeks go round as she grins. "I heard about this!"

Fiona puts an arm around each of us and pulls us in mischievously. "He told me that when we lined up for the mine carts, Esau asked Noah to switch places with him so he could ride with you."

"No way!" I say much louder than necessary.

Viv cups her face. "Isn't that the cutest thing you've ever heard?"

"That is absolutely not true. There is no possibility on earth that Esau wants to do anything other than order me around until I'm so sick of it I quit drama club." Too bad for him. I'm not a quitter. On a dare, I once climbed to the top of a human pyramid with a sprained ankle. The look on my mother's face when I limped off the field afterward? Let's just say she wasn't thrilled.

My eyes start to burn, and I blink rapidly to clear them.

"Are you okay?"

The deep timber of Esau's voice makes me freeze. Is he talking to me? I swivel my head slowly toward where he's standing a handful of feet away, his arms crossed over his stupidly attractive chest. There's a thick, blue rubber band around one of his wrists. His eyes lock on mine. He's waiting for something.

Oh.

"Yeah, I'm fine. Thanks." My mind is struggling to keep up. Grumpy Pants Esau just asked me how I am? Do I look sick or something? Because there's no way he could have noticed that my eyes were threatening tears, could he?

"The stage crew could use your help painting the sets today." Esau's nostrils flare as he inhales. His eyes flick over my face before he turns away. Snapping the rubber band, he stalks off.

And there it is. He was simply wondering why I wasn't already working on something. That makes a whole lot more sense than the ludicrous idea that he was actually checking on my emotional wellbeing. Because come on.

Fiona moves closer. "You're sure you're okay? I thought you were going to lose it for a second there."

"I'm fine, really." Shaking my head to clear it, I point toward where some of the members of the stage crew are painting a fake window on to one of the backdrops. "I'd better get to work before I get yelled at."

Viv makes chomper hands again.

Fiona chuckles. "Or eaten."

I'm in the back of the theater, wearing a trash bag to protect my clothes from paint, when I hear a loud shutter click. Spinning around, I see Esau standing in the center of the stage talking to a middle-aged woman in a bright red skirt suit. Beside her is a twenty-something guy holding a professional camera with a lens that's so long it's obscene.

"Who is that?" I hiss at the girl nearest me, Josie.

"No idea," Josie says. Unphased, she goes back to painting the hydrangea bush she's been working on for the past hour.

Esau and the woman talk back and forth for a few minutes before I notice she's holding a recorder in one hand. The camera man is tramping around the theater, taking photos of anything and everything. He takes a photo of Fiona coiling a cable and asks her if she'll sign a release in case they use the image.

"Definitely! I've never been in the newspaper," she replies, signing the page on the clipboard he holds out to her.

Newspaper? Wait, that woman is a reporter?

My stomach churns and I'm pretty sure I'm turning green. Lurching up from where I sit on an overturned milk crate, I tear the plastic bag off my body and wad it up into a ball. "I have to go to the bathroom," I tell no one in particular. Then I bolt toward the rear stage door, away from the reporter lady and her co-hort's giant camera.

I cannot be in the newspaper. I don't know anything about the madman who's after me, but drawing attention to myself cannot be a good idea.

When the time is right...

Fiona yells, "Wait!" as I pull the door closed behind me.

Leaning back against the prickly stucco wall of the structure, I take a couple of deep breaths. Everything is under control. The reporter didn't talk to me at all. She doesn't have my name. And the camera man would have had to get a release if he wanted to use any photos of me. Which he didn't do. So I'm fine. There aren't going to be any mentions or photos of me in the local newspaper.

No extra incentive for anybody to come after me.

Still, that was way too close.

Chapter 11

Day 113, Monday

Four days since the fiasco at Noah's house. Now that I've had a lot of time to agonize over how I reacted, I feel terrible about it. Seeing those articles and photos, the map of places where there have been possible sightings of the Mayday Killer over the past four months, I panicked. I made some assumptions about Noah that probably weren't fair.

There's no way someone as gentle and sweet as Noah is helping a killer.

I should have let him explain why he'd gathered all of that stuff behind his bedroom door instead of running out of there like a small dog running from a pack of coyotes. Which is why, when I sit down next to him in art class, I don't look away when he glances at me.

When I don't immediately turn away, he perks up.

"Does this mean you're talking to me again?"

A quick survey of the classroom confirms that there's no one sitting in the desks immediately surrounding ours. There are a couple of guys in the far corner washing paint brushes in the sink. A girl in the front row is doing pencil sketches in a notebook.

"Yeah. Look, Noah, about Sunday—"

"I'm sorry you had to see that," he jumps in with an earnestness that makes my chest loosen.

"It's okay. You're allowed to have hobbies. It's just that I, all of the Mayday Killer stuff, freaked me out."

Noah lowers his head. "It sort of freaks me out too."

We look shyly at each other, our gazes skimming before pulling away. I've missed talking to him the past few days, and his candid admission brings home how much. There's something so easy and open about Noah, like what I see is what I get. There's no pretense with him.

"So you're not a serial killer fanboy?" I ask, still needing to hear his answer.

Noah's eyes widen behind the black frames of his glasses. The incredulous laugh that bursts from his mouth is sort of cute. "So that's what you thought. Huh."

I shrug. It sounds ridiculous now that he's said it out loud. Noah is far too kind and gentle to be a secret murder fanboy. Or worse.

"It's nothing like that. The thing is, I'm interested in true crime stuff. And since the Mayday Killer is still at large…"

Mr. Baugh comes in carrying a stack of old newspaper clippings that he plunks down on his desk.

The girl in the desk on Noah's other side shifts closer to him. Is she listening in on this conversation? She takes out a book and starts to read.

I pull my shoulders down from around my ears. I'm getting more than a little paranoid.

Noah glances over at the teacher before leaning closer to me, voice lowered. "Since he's still at large, a lot of people in the true crime community are trying to find him."

"The sooner the better," I breathe.

"Exactly."

“That makes a lot of sense.”

Noah visibly relaxes. “Right? Hey, you wouldn’t want to help me gather info on him, would you? Because there’s a lot out there, and it would be awesome if we found something that could help.”

The bell rings, and Mr. Baugh starts walking up and down the now-full rows of desks. “All right everyone. Today we’re going to exercise your ability to improvise creatively. Each of you will be given a newspaper article, and it’s your job to come up with a collage piece that conveys the emotion of the article.” He goes on to detail the list of supplies we’re allowed to use and reminds us that it’s a timed exercise that ends when the bell rings signaling the end of class.

Noah scans his quickly before pushing out of his chair and loping to the back for supplies.

I’m glued to my chair. My heart is pounding loudly in my ears. Licking my lips, I glance up at Mr. Baugh. He’s talking to another student near his desk, gesturing to the sheet in her hand. His gaze skims over me without lingering.

I look back down at the paper sitting on my desk. Did he hear my conversation with Noah? Is that why he gave me this article?

Flat on my desk is a story on the Mayday Killer.

Emotions flash in my chest like fireworks as I scan it. Anger. Sadness. Guilt. Fear. But which of those can I possibly convey in an art project that I have to finish in the next forty minutes? Better yet, which one can I dwell on without poking at the riptide of tears that’s always hovering behind my eyelids? I breathe in through my nose and out my mouth, willing my fracturing nerves to steady. This is no big deal; I lie to myself.

Choosing the sensation I gauge to be the least risky, I get to work.

When Noah sits down beside me with supplies of his own, I whisper, "I'll help you with your research. Maybe we'll find something."

And if it helps the authorities find him sooner, it still won't be soon enough.

Aunt Karen got delayed at the store, so she sent a deputy to drive me home. But then the deputy got a call on her radio about some emergency across town, so she left me half a mile from Aunt Karen's.

Luckily for me, it's a scorching hot day.

Gasping in the heat, I slog toward the old house.

The asphalt is rippling with it as I trudge along. No one else is out, and whenever someone parks on the street, they hurry inside their destination as quickly as possible, slamming the door closed behind them.

I am dying to duck inside one of the businesses to get a break, but I really just want to get to safety. Besides, I'm not much for being stared at. It's the downside of such a small town. Everyone knows everyone else, except me. I stick out like a sore thumb.

The downtown melts away and I make a right toward the neighborhood where the old house sits. The road is flanked on both sides by almond orchards. From what Aunt Karen has said, the farmers here used to grow all kinds of different crops, from cherries to citrus, but there's more money in almonds.

Ahead, the road undulates like the ocean's waves. I blink, aware that what I'm seeing is a trick of the eye from staring so long. Then I stop. Look behind me. There's no one there, but I could swear I heard footsteps.

I keep walking, focused on listening to see if the footsteps pick up again. My heart skitters, and I take a deep breath. I was hearing things. Probably from being out in this heat for too long. Because of course the first time Aunt Karen would be unable to pick me up it has to be the hottest day of the year.

Despite the exhaustion in my limbs, I pick up my pace. Sweat drips down my back.

There's a flicker of movement in my peripheral vision, and my head snaps toward it. Just a tree branch caught in the breeze.

I freeze. There isn't any breeze. The air is dead and still in this heat.

But that means…

I stare at that branch, but it's not moving now. I must have imagined that, too.

Repeating it over and over in my head doesn't keep me from breaking into a jog.

And then I hear it. Footsteps matching my pace. Someone is definitely nearby and trying to hide their footfalls in mine. I don't want to think about what that means.

I whirl around to look. If I can identify them, they'll stop. They'll have to. Right?

There's no one there. I must be imagining it. It's all in my head.

But it wasn't last time.

When the time is right.

I dash away, my backpack slamming into my butt with every step. Textbooks weigh it down, causing the straps to dig into my shoulders. My shoes slam the pavement with each stride forward.

I can still hear the footsteps. Matching each of mine. This time I don't dare turn around. I'm too afraid of whose face I'd see.

I run all the way to Aunt Karen's neighborhood, rounding

the corner toward her house without glancing behind me. The devil himself could be giving chase and I wouldn't know. Sometimes it's better not to know.

My body slams into something hard, and I fall backward, winded.

Firm hands grasp my wrists and arrest my motion. "Whoa, are you all right? A t-rex chasing you or something?" Justin the janitor shoots an appraising glance at me before looking over my shoulder. When his expression remains easy, I chance a peek.

The street is empty save for a few parked cars. Whoever it was could be hiding behind one. Watching.

"You're awfully red. Maybe you should go inside. Hot out here."

I take in a great gulp of air and force myself to meet Justin's eyes. "Thanks," I stammer. "I'm just going to…" Motioning toward the old house, I skitter up the walk before he can say anything else.

I don't take another full breath until I'm inside with the deadbolt thrown home. Peer out the peephole.

The street is empty.

Chapter 12

Day 117, Friday

My focus in drama club today has been sloppy, my brain in a fog. I'm pretty sure I'm coming down with a cold or something, after spending all week tiptoeing around school waiting for the other shoe to fall.

Now, I plod around the theater trying to keep my head clear while wishing I was at home, curled up in my bed, watching anime and eating my mom's homemade chicken noodle soup.

Which is why when Esau chews me out for nearly knocking Marisa out with one of the set pieces, I take it, necessarily chastened.

Marisa sits on an overturned milk crate with a wet paper towel pressed to her forehead.

"I'm so sorry!" I croak, but she waves me off.

"It was an accident, right? You weren't trying to take me out so you could take the lead, right?" She winks at me.

I give a choked laugh, not sure how to respond.

Esau hits me with a glare that sends a shudder down my spine. "You have to be more careful, Megan. How would you feel if we'd had to stop practice to take Marisa to the hospital to make sure she doesn't have a concussion? You're not paying attention today, and we don't have time for these kinds of mistakes. The play opens in six weeks. You're not terrible at this, so don't act like it."

Even with his gruff voice and cold expression, it's the first compliment Esau has ever given me.

I open my mouth to explain my brain fog, but I'm cut off by a string of sneezes. I manage to aim into my elbow. I always sneeze in fours. Weird, I know.

"God bless you," Esau mumbles.

"Thanks?" I give a watery laugh.

He rolls his eyes. "If you're sick, you should go home."

"I'm fine," I say. "We've only got a half hour left. Thanks for the concern, though."

"It's not you I'm worried about. It's my actors. You're a walking health hazard today."

Am I hallucinating, or is there a glint of amusement in his eyes?

"Just try not to make any more mistakes in the next thirty minutes, okay?"

And there's the Esau I've come to know and loathe.

"Yeah."

He stalks off to yell at someone else.

I'd absolutely hate him if I didn't understand a little about what he's going through. It's his first time directing, so he's responsible for every single person in this theater, from the actors to the lighting and stage crew, to Viv, who spends most of our meetings behind her sewing machine, whipping up costumes, making alterations to old pieces, and sewing whatever else Esau asks her to with a smiling mouth full of sharp pins. Our advisor is basically non-existent. As far as I can tell, she spends all of our meetings in her office reading on her Kindle. Fiona told me she took a peek once when the woman was out and discovered tons and tons of vampire novels.

Fiona rolls her eyes at me playfully as our grumpy director tromps up into the sound booth to confer with Dariel about the lighting. I thought Esau would relax as rehearsals progressed, but it seems like he's only getting more and more tightly wound.

Esau's exacting mood makes our practice run long, so I'm late meeting Noah at the library. When I rush inside the old brick building, I spot him using one of the computers at a round table in the far corner. He waves when he spots me.

"I wasn't sure you were gonna show," he says when I slide into the chair next to him.

"Sorry. Esau kept all of us late."

He laughs. "I do not envy you. Esau can be pretty intense sometimes."

"Tell me about it."

The librarian behind the information desk shushes us, making me clamp a hand over my mouth to stifle a giggle.

"Should we get started on our research?" I whisper.

Noah gestures to his computer screen. "Yeah. Here, let me show you."

"What are you working on?"

Noah hesitates before continuing at my nod. "I'm looking through the articles on the Mayday Killer's victims to try to find some commonality. Usually with serial killers, there's a reason they pick their targets. It's not all random. But so far I haven't come up with anything."

"What have you looked at so far?" I ask, hoping I sound casual. He can't know how much I've got riding on this.

Noah lets his head fall against the chair's back and looks up at the ceiling. "Their jobs, income levels, religious beliefs…"

My mind speeds as I try to think of some other aspect Noah could research. What can I give him? The back of my neck tickles like I'm being watched. My pulse beats a staccato rhythm in my throat. Did the phantom who chased me home from school the other day follow me here too? I dig deep for courage and whirl around to look.

Justin's here, talking intently to the librarian and gesturing toward the non-fiction section. He could have followed me here, easily.

"Small towns…" I murmur, but I don't believe that's all it is.

"What was that?"

"Nothing. It's just, I see the same people everywhere."

"Small towns." Noah huffs a laugh.

We focus on the articles he's got open on the computer, scrolling through the research he's put together to look for some kind of link between all of the victims. I keep surreptitiously looking over my shoulder to keep track of Justin as he meanders through the stacks.

"They all have kids," Noah says, nudging me with his elbow.

The contact sends a frisson of surprise along my skin. My mouth is dry, so I take a drink from my water bottle. "Doesn't everybody?"

"You're right. A vast majority of people do." He keeps scrolling. "I feel like I'm missing something, but what?"

I glance around the library again to double check Justin isn't anywhere within earshot. When I can't spot him, a cold sweat breaks out over my skin.

"Megan?"

I give myself a mental shake. "What about location? Maybe they're all close to the same freeway?"

"No, that's not it. I've got a map at home that shows all of the spots where he's struck, and they appear to be random. I don't think it has anything to do with geographical location."

We talk for over an hour, tossing possibilities back and forth. Noah makes some notes in a spreadsheet on his phone, even though we don't come up with anything new. I'm a potent cocktail of relief at being back on speaking terms with Noah, and anxious energy surrounding our subject matter. I'm surprised when my stomach growls.

"You hungry?"

"I'm starving. I didn't realize how late it is."

Noah licks his lips nervously. "We could go to the diner and grab some dinner. I can pay if you want."

My eyes fly to his warm brown ones, surprise lining my face. Is he asking me out on a date? Something that feels surprisingly like anticipation rises in my chest at the thought of a date with Noah. I try to talk myself out of it. I've only known him for three weeks, and beyond the fact that he's a true crime fan, likes anime, and babysits his siblings, there's so much I don't know about him.

There's so much he doesn't know about me. So much I can never tell him.

The elation turns to dread as I realize what I have to do.

Noah's smile curves downward as if he already knows.

"I can't. I'm sorry."

This boy who's becoming one of my friends shakes his head, looking away. "It's no big deal. I should probably get home and help my mom with dinner anyway. Thanks for your help today. You gave me some new ideas to look into."

"Glad I could help."

We gather our stuff into our backpacks in awkward silence and walk to the front door.

"You need a ride?" he asks.

"No thanks. Aunt Karen's coming to get me."

"Sure." After saying goodbye, Noah crosses the parking lot to his car with his shoulders hunched.

I stand just inside the library, wondering if I've just torpedoed our friendship.

When Aunt Karen pulls up, I climb into her car and strap on my seatbelt. "I think the janitor, Justin, was following me the other day. And he showed up at the library a little while ago."

My guardian's hands tighten on the steering wheel. "Why do you think he was following you?"

"I could hear footsteps, so I ran. Then there he was in front of me. There wasn't anyone else around. And today, he was pretty much the only other person in the library the whole time we were working in there."

She's quiet for a minute, thinking. I can't read the expression on her face. Don't know what she'll do with this information.

At the next stoplight, she shifts to look at me. "I know you're scared. Believe me when I say that I'm doing everything I can to keep you safe. The authorities are throwing everything they've got into finding the Mayday Killer. He's not going to lay a hand on you. Wait, I'm not finished. Justin is not the Mayday Killer. He is not after you. You have to trust me."

Frustration hits me. She's not taking my suspicions seriously. Not at all. Just like my parents, and they were made to regret it.

"Aunt Karen, please just have them look into him, okay?"

"He's not going to hurt you," she says, emphatic. End of conversation.

If she won't believe me, I have to do something. I have to

find proof.

Chapter 13

Day 118, Saturday

This is the first time I've been to Noah's house since the discovery of the murder board, and it feels a little awkward. Even though I'm pretty sure Noah was being honest about being a true crime fan, it feels strange knowing there's a detailed map of the Mayday Killer's movements tacked to the back of the boy's door. The grizzly images and meticulously clipped newspaper articles don't mesh with Noah's wholesome appearance somehow. I can't make the two ideas fit together in any real way.

I can't shake the feeling that there's something Noah isn't telling me about his interest in the serial killer. Who's still at large, by the way. I clench my fists, willing the anger that threatens to spark into flame in my chest to cool.

Esperanza and Matteo zoom past, the little boy knocking into me as they skid giggling over the worn wooden floor of the dining room. Noah offered to set them up with a movie in the living room so we could work on our project in his room with minimal interruptions, but I told him it would be easier to spread out on the dining table. Thankfully, he bought it.

"You got any other homework you want to get out of the way before we dive in?" Noah plunks his backpack down on the long wooden table and starts pulling out books. "I've got some I need to finish up."

"Same." I sit across from him and unzip my own backpack, only I don't see my history book. I flip through the textbooks shoved into the small bag once, twice. It's not there. Crap. We've got a quiz in class tomorrow that I really need to study for, and I can't do that without my textbook.

I shoot a glance at Noah, who's already deep into his own work. I could walk to the school and back, but it's a couple miles each way. Plus, it's super hot out there right now. I'd be a flushed, sweaty mess by the time I got back. Noah can't drive me because we're supposed to be babysitting the kiddos.

Slipping my phone out of my bag, I text my aunt asking her to stop by the school and get my book. She should be done with her shift at the grocery store by now. It takes a few minutes for her to respond, and when she does, she says she's still at work. There was some glitch in the system and they're having to tally sales by hand.

Noah and I both look up when we hear footsteps moving away from the front door. It unnerves me that I missed the signs of someone approaching.

Esperanza and Matteo come skidding down the hallway and into the living room. "There's someone here to visit!" Anza cries, climbing on the couch to look out the front window.

Glancing over his shoulder at me, Matteo whispers in his sister's ear.

"No, it's not Tia Maria, silly. That's a man."

Noah catches my eye and smiles.

I can't help returning it. The little girl's speech is so matter-of-fact that it's hard not to laugh.

"Wow," Noah says, staring at me.

"What?" I put my hand up to brush at my face.

He blinks. "It's just, I've never seen your full smile before. It's, wow."

I bite my lip as warmth fills my cheeks. Pushing away from the table, I cross toward the front door. Esperanza beats me to it, unlocking it and swinging it wide just as Justin swings into a muddy brown pickup and drives away. The smile drops off my face.

Noah's on his feet in a second. "Anza! Shut that door. You know the rule."

Looking stricken, the little girl obeys.

I turn to look at Noah, trying to mask the hot slush of emotions roiling through me. "Rule?"

"She's not allowed to open the door unless there's an adult with her. I'm sure some of the parents of the kids you babysat had the same rule, right?"

"Oh. Yeah. I forgot about that."

Anza gives me a warm smile, her ebony eyes sparkling. Her waist-length black hair falls in a shining river down her back. When she wraps a tiny hand around my fingers, my insides heat. I haven't felt such naked trust in a long time.

On the top step sits a book. My history book. Somehow Justin knew I'd lost my history book. He knew because he must have been watching me close enough to notice. I scoop up the book and scurry inside.

Justin may not have gone far, and if he's been watching me… I recoil when I imagine him pawing through everything in my locker in search of my history book. He would have had to use the keys he has access to for his job. They can't just go into our lockers, can they?

A huge red flag of unease unfurls in my mind, making me hold the book tighter against my chest. It might be the proof I need to convince Aunt Karen that the guy she's known since she was in school is watching me.

Esperanza and Matteo are so riled up that Noah caves and puts on some kiddie show for them in the living room. He bribes them with gummy bears to keep them quiet.

I sit there staring at my history book and trying to focus, but all of the noise from Noah and his siblings is distracting. I keep having to read the same sentences over and over. I'd get so much more done if I was at Aunt Karen's, shut behind my bedroom door with my headphones in my ears. I'm going to have to stay up so late tonight to get through everything.

"Can I ask you a question?" Noah's words are gentle and inquisitive, bringing my attention up to his eyes. They slide over my face in a way I've seen a hundred times since school started.

And here I was thinking he simply wouldn't ask. Not like all of the people at school who can't help themselves at the sight of such an ugly, permanent reminder of trauma scrawled across my face.

"I got it in a car accident," I say, "and no, I don't want to talk about it." It comes out with more bite than I intended, and I almost wish I could take it back. Try again. It's not his fault he was curious about the vivid white seam that bisects my cheek.

Noah nods, returning his attention to his books. There's something in the line of his shoulders that makes me pause. If I knew him better, I might know if that meant he was embarrassed or hurt or annoyed, but I don't.

"I had an older brother."

My head jerks up at this. Noah has murmured it like one would a confession, soft and quick, as if trying to avoid being overheard. It doesn't escape me that he says he *had* an older brother. Past tense. "You did?" I lick my lips, then push it further. "Where is he?"

"He died. He was killed." The bleak look in his eyes

behind the thick black frames of his glasses guts me. It's obvious he's exposed a festering wound by uttering those first two words, so I don't press for more. He's not ready for it. Neither am I.

But I recognize it for what it is: an offering. He sees my trauma and offers up his own in trade. So that we're even. So that I don't feel so alone. For a hundred reasons that I can't begin to understand.

Something unfolds in my gut, beckoning me to acknowledge it. Acknowledge the newly uncovered truth that Noah too has known loss. The heavy black curtain of death being lowered down too soon. The stumbling in the dark after the lights have been snuffed out.

"I'm sorry," I whisper. It's not enough. Those paltry words will never be enough. Not knowing what else to say, I change the subject.

"He used to work at the dairy, right?" I ask, giving up on my homework.

"Who?" Noah's black brows furrow in confusion.

"That janitor guy, Justin." I toss my thumb over my shoulder.

"Not that I know of."

I go still. "Are you sure? Aunt Karen told me he worked there before he got the job at school."

"I don't think so," Noah says, shaking his head.

"And you're sure." I frown. I know I sound more combative than is necessary.

"I mean, the dairy is pretty big, so it's possible I just never saw him, but…" Noah tousels his hair and shuffles through his papers.

"But?" I'm leaning forward over the table, the hesitance in Noah's tone drawing me in like the gymnastics finals at the summer Olympics.

He sighs. "I don't want to say your aunt was wrong, but I don't think that guy's ever worked at the dairy. I can ask my dad though. He's worked there for twenty years, so he'd know for sure." Pulling his phone out of his pocket, he starts tapping on the screen.

"Wait. No. Don't do that. I must have misunderstood her. Maybe she meant he'd applied at the dairy." I shrug it off even though my blood is pounding in my ears. There's no way I misinterpreted what Aunt Karen told me. *Where did he work before he started at the school? The dairy.* Either she was wrong, which doesn't jive with the careful competence my guardian exudes in pretty much every area aside from actual parenting. Or she lied.

Chapter 14

Day 119, Sunday

The newspaper article on Esau came out today. I've been scoping out Aunt Karen's newspaper each day so I wouldn't miss it. I'm curious about what he said to that reporter.

Every morning, Aunt Karen leaves that day's rolled-up paper in the middle of the kitchen table while she's making her coffee. She uses one of those French presses and lots of flavored creamer. Then she sits there in her dark shirt and pressed pants and reads in silence. "It's useful to keep up to date on current local events," she said the first time I saw her reading an actual newspaper and couldn't stop my eyebrows from rising into my hair. I didn't know anyone still read a physical newspaper, since everything is available online. I didn't even know they still printed them.

This morning the newspaper is twice as large as during the week, and Esau's brooding face is right on the front, above the fold. Aunt Karen's attempting to make breakfast, so I snatch it off the table and fall into a seat to read it. I barely speak to Esau during drama club, so who knows why I'm interested in an article about him, but I am. It starts by talking about his humble upbringing—those are the literal words the journalist used. I smother a huff into my palm. Aunt Karen looks at me over her bottle of creamer, then turns to the giant stack of plain, buttered, almost-burned toast she's made.

Quietly, I keep reading, but stop again to take a bite of the peanut butter and banana wrap I threw together.

Reading all of this background info about Esau is making me feel kind of voyeuristic. Like, if I wanted to know about his childhood I should ask him in person, not read about it in a newspaper. Then I shake the feeling away. If Esau didn't want everyone in town reading about it, he wouldn't have told the reporter. Fair is fair.

"Is that you in the newspaper?" Aunt Karen bellows, tearing the pages out of my hands and bringing them closer to her face.

Dropping my breakfast on the table top, I scramble out of my chair. "No. I'm not in any photos. They didn't ask permission, and they have to have…" My voice dies when I look where Aunt Karen is pointing. Sure enough, there it is, my profile behind Esau in the photo. In color. In the county newspaper.

"I thought I told you to stay away from cameras! Do you realize how many people will see this?"

"Most people don't even read these anymore," I say, trying to placate her. Aunt Karen is just trying to keep me safe.

"That isn't funny." Each word is clipped, as is the sharp look she sends my way.

I cross my arms. Go completely still. She's right. It's not funny.

"If you can't stay away from the press, I'm going to pull you out of school."

"No, please don't. I promise to hide the next time someone shows up with a camera. It probably won't happen again," I add hastily.

"I'm calling that good-for-nothing editor right now," Aunt Karen decrees, scrolling through her phone. "I have his number here somewhere…" She puts the phone to her ear and paces across the kitchen.

"What can they do? It's already been printed," I say halfheartedly. "Besides, he already knows where I am." She's clearly not heeding me, her back turned as she taps her foot on the dingy linoleum floor.

"They can take it off their website!"

Apparently she was listening.

"Can you believe he hasn't been home to see his family in five years?" Marisa says contemplatively as she takes a long swig of her mint grasshopper milkshake.

Despite the fiasco this morning, Aunt Karen agreed to let me meet my friends at the only diner in town for milkshakes this afternoon. After a lot of groveling and promises that I'll never let anyone take my photo ever again.

It's a blistering day and Main Street is like a ghost town. Except the diner, which boasts a whopping thirty milkshake flavors. Pretty much everyone from school is here. Noah is sitting across the diner on a counter stool, flanked by Esperanza and Matteo.

Despite all the buzz about the article, Esau is absent. Frankly, I wouldn't want to be out with everyone talking about me either.

"I can't imagine not seeing my mom for that," Viv says from behind her vivid pink cherry milkshake.

"Same," Erin says, her arm slung behind Viv on the back of our corner booth.

Next to me, Fiona nods, looking down at her phone screen. "I had no idea he wanted to be a film director. It explains why he's so uptight about everything being perfect at practice all the time."

Next to her, Dariel nods.

"Seriously," Marisa says.

"I wonder why none of the teachers have tried to start a film class," Fiona muses.

"Mr. Baugh says there aren't funds for it," I say, thankful to have something safe to add to the conversation.

"And that quote about Megan!" Fiona crows, reading in a fake man-voice. "There's a girl in my drama club who is constantly questioning how I direct, the choices I'm making, and it's been challenging. But you know what? I secretly enjoy it, because every one of her questions makes me re-evaluate what we're doing and why."

I caught the line when I read it this morning. Even more surprising than the fact that Esau mentioned me of all people in his interview is that I don't hate it.

"You vex him, and he likes it," Viv teases, winking at me.

"Ugh, Megan, you're so vexing," Fiona says through her laughter.

I focus on my chocolate peanut butter milkshake. The best flavor, obviously.

"I wish it said what kind of tractor he drives," Marisa says, dreamy eyed. "I wonder if it's an International or a John Deere."

"John Deere," she and Viv say simultaneously, like it's obvious.

The rest of us burst into laughter.

"I bet you'd like to see his tractor," Viv says through her giggles, prodding at Marisa with the hand that isn't on Erin's thigh.

"Shut up," Marisa says, an indignant flush to her cheeks.

"He's hot, but no. Besides, I think he'd rather show Megan his tractor."

My neck heats. "Gross. Like I want to ride a tractor with a sweaty, bossy grump."

The table falls silent.

Crap, I may have gone a little too far.

That's when I notice everyone looking past me with guilty expressions.

"He's right behind me, isn't he?"

Fiona nods. "Yep."

I turn, my eyes climbing past the sweaty white t-shirt and messy bun of black hair to settle on a pair of annoyed eyes. "Esau, I…"

His gaze locks on mine. "Grumpy, huh?" He pulls his t-shirt up to wipe the sweat off his forehead, and everyone suddenly is very interested in their food. My eyes jump back up to his face, but from the wicked tilt to his mouth, he definitely thinks I was peeking at his abs.

"See you around," he says, walking past us to the counter to order.

I watch him walk away, his words from the article on a loop in my head.

"Film is supposed to be evocative. It pushes the boundary of human experience in a way that is intensely relatable and inspiring. At least, that's the kind of film I hope to make someday." I can hear Esau speaking the words in my head.

That longing to provoke emotion in other people is a feeling I can relate to. Whenever someone comments that they love one of my photos, it cements in my mind my love for photography. The ability to capture a feeling in an image in a way that other people understand is breathtaking. Empowering. The shared experience makes the hours of shooting and editing worth it.

I study Esau while he orders his milkshake and stands to one side to wait. Somewhere behind that grumpy, bossy exterior is a guy who wants to relate to other people through film. Through emotion.

I can't hate him for that.

"Hey, isn't that your aunt?" Fiona asks, nudging me.

I turn to look out the window. "Yeah." She must have decided she wanted a milkshake.

"Maybe she's come to yell at you about that photo some more," Fiona says. "She is so strict. If I was ever in the newspaper, my mom would buy copies to send to all of our relatives."

Aunt Karen steps out of a shop across the street and walks toward the diner. Even in the oppressive heat, she's wearing dark slacks and a short-sleeved button-down.

I wave at her through the window, but she must not see me, because she keeps going. Passes the front door and goes around the side of the building. That's weird.

"I'll be right back."

Fiona slides into the aisle so I can climb out of the booth. I go outside and have to gasp at how hot it is compared to the interior of the diner. It's like walking around in molten lava. The hair hanging down from my ponytail sticks to my neck. Maybe Esau had the right idea about the bun.

I round the corner but don't see Aunt Karen. She must have gone around back, but why?

I walk to the back of the building and freeze. Aunt Karen is there, but so is Justin. He's got my guardian pinned to the wall.

I open my mouth to scream at him or yell for help. He's attacking her! Where's her gun? I thought she always had it on her. My mind reels as I stand hot glued to the concrete, the heat seeping in through my sandals and searing the soles of my feet.

Oh.

Justin leans into Aunt Karen and kisses her. Her hands fly up to his hair, and they're one beast with hands and lips and teeth.

Gross.

I back away as quietly as I can, stunned. Aunt Karen is secretly dating Justin. It explains so much—why he's always around, the warmth in her tone when she mentions him, the casual way his name rolls off her lips.

Then it hits me. The reason she lied to me about him working at the dairy. She's covering for him. The only question is, what are they covering up? There's no question his past is shady, but is it murderous?

Chapter 15

Day 122, Wednesday

Noah's map of sightings of the Mayday Killer has another pin. Another couple is dead, stabbed ruthlessly over and over on their couch. Their children found the bodies when they got home from playing soccer in the park with friends. I wish I could send them something, anything to let them know they're not alone, but the press are withholding their identities since they're minors.

It's the right call. The sickos and freaks who come out of the woodwork when there's a serial killer involved make my stomach turn.

And I didn't see Justin at the school today. Which is why I've spent the afternoon looking for him on social media and searching his name on the internet to see what I can find out. There's not a trace of him anywhere. Any mentions of him on the web have been scrubbed eerily clean.

Visions of viscous, crimson blood on bright green latex gloves swim across my vision, tainting the hung map red. It creeps across the wall, inching closer and closer to where I'm sitting at Noah's desk with my refurbished laptop. I'm supposed to be going through my backlog of photos to find ones that are the right colors for our project, but all I can see is red.

My throat tightens. "I need to go."

Noah jumps up from where he's sprawled on the carpet, head propped on his hand. "What's wrong? Are you okay?"

"I'm fine."

Ever so gently, his fingers brush my elbow. "You sure? You look a little pale."

"I'm wiped. Long day."

He huffs in agreement. "It's almost dinnertime. We could order pizza or something."

It's a sweet gesture, and I try to plaster a smile on to my face, not sure if I succeed. "Thanks, but not tonight. I really should get home."

He nods, adjusting his glasses up his wide nose. "Maybe next time."

I pack up my stuff quickly, avoiding looking at the back of the door. Avoiding Noah's eyes. I'm afraid if I meet his gaze, he'll be able to see the panic behind my own. The fear and revulsion that war inside me.

On the way home, I ask Aunt Karen if she can pick up a couple things for me when she's at work tomorrow.

The old house creaks and groans when we unlock the door and step inside. Despite the sun's high position outside, all of the blinds are closed to shutter out the radiant heat. Dropping my backpack onto the floor with a thud, I head to the kitchen for snacks and the cardboard box I know is on the back porch. I hesitate before unlocking the back door, an uneasy feeling in the pit of my stomach.

If Justin's working with the Mayday Killer, he could be waiting back there to help finish what the murderer started.

I spend a long minute peeking through the back window to make sure there's no one hidden out there before I unlock the door, snatch the box, and slam it shut in a blink. Slide the bolt into place with heart stammering behind my ribs.

A while later, Aunt Karen comes back downstairs wearing an oversized tee and yoga pants. "What's going on in here?" she asks as she comes into the kitchen. Her hair is down around her shoulders with the ponytail crease still visible. It's the most casual I've ever seen her.

"I made spaghetti," I say, gesturing to where two pots are sitting on the stove with flickering blue flames underneath. It gave me something to focus on other than the grizzly news from earlier. Not even the orchids she brought home from the grocery store for me could hold my attention.

"Thank you. I'm starving." My guardian dishes herself some food, exclaiming over how delicious it looks. I'm flattered even though it came out of a jar ready-made. It's probably not that good.

We eat in quiet, the old house settling around us as the temperature slowly falls with the sun.

Aunt Karen thinks she's being covert by sneaking glances at me whenever she takes a drink from her water glass, but I see her. And ignore her. I don't have anything to say. Noah's map surges to the front of my mind, zeroed in on the newest pin.

Actually, maybe I do want to talk.

"The Mayday Killer struck again."

"I know." My guardian's tone is measured, as if she's afraid to give her voice free rein.

"Hanfield is less than an hour away from here."

Aunt Karen's fork stills over her plate. She sighs. "The police are doing everything they can to apprehend him. They're building blockades and checkpoints. All public transit is being checked. That… man can't hide forever. He'll be caught. Soon."

"It's been six months since his first." *And he's been able to evade capture the whole time.*

Aunt Karen starts to reach across the table to where my free hand is lying, but straightens the napkin in her lap instead. "I promise you I won't let anything happen to you while you're living under my roof. I probably shouldn't do this, but I could teach you how to handle my firearm. I'll show you where the safe is, if that would make you feel safer. What do you think?"

I bite my lip, curious. "No, I don't think I'd like that."

"If you ever change your mind."

We go back to eating in the silence. Aunt Karen's gun is never far from my thoughts. Before any of this, I had never fired a gun. My parents were staunchly anti-firearms and hadn't kept any in the house. But now? I'm afraid of what I would do. What might happen if I had access to a life-ending weapon.

"You know, if you ever need anything and I'm not here, you can ask our neighbor across the street, Justin."

She says it so lightly, like there's nothing behind it. Sometimes her cool manner of speaking scares me just a little. Even if I was freaking out and Aunt Karen wasn't here, I don't think I'd have the guts to go across the street and ask Justin for help.

"He gives me the creeps. And I think he's been following me. What if he's dangerous?"

"Who? Justin?" Her incredulous tone slides right under my skin.

My voice rises. "He brought me my history book after I left it at school. At Noah's. How did he know where I was? And how did he know I needed my book?"

Aunt Karen finishes chewing her bite. "He's not

dangerous. I asked him to grab the book for you."

My eyes swim as the spaghetti on my plate morphs into blood and grit smeared across the floor. I push my plate away, squeezing my eyes shut. She asked him. That actually makes some sense. Maybe I'm making more of Justin than is really there. My tense muscles relax just a bit.

Aunt Karen eats a couple more tiny bites. I don't blame her for her reticence. The noodles are still a little crunchy.

"There's something I have to ask you," she says finally, putting her silverware down and pushing her plate back. "Did you know an Anderson family? Maybe from that summer camp you used to go to?"

I go completely still. Suddenly Aunt Karen's hesitance to eat and her somber manner make sense. She was trying to figure out how to deliver the death blow to my day. Because the Andersons? They were friends of mine from camp. We spent long hours swimming in the lake, paddling around in plastic kayaks, and hiking through the woods. They were *friends* of mine.

My throat clenches. The only reason she'd be asking me about them right now, this moment, is if something catastrophic happened to them. When I look up at Aunt Karen, the sympathetic curve of her eyes tells me everything.

I know which family was ripped apart this morning. The Anderson kids' lives are damaged beyond repair, just like mine. Water wells in my eyes, making my guardian's sad smile blurry.

"I got a call a couple of hours ago. They thought you should know, but you can't tell anyone. Do you understand?"

I nod, struck silent by the heavy weight on my sternum. Nate and Kate, I'm so, *so* incredibly sorry.

"You okay?"

It's a stupid question, so I don't answer.

"I'll clean up here. Why don't you take your new flowers up to your room?"

"I don't want them anymore."

"You texted me asking me to buy them not two hours ago."

"That was two hours ago."

Why should I even bother trying to move on with my life, having any hobbies or passions when they could all be torn away from me at a moment's notice? And flowers, of all things? They're beautiful, but so fleeting. So mortal.

"I'll leave them in the window behind the sink, in case you change your mind."

Once, I left one of my orchids in the back window of my mom's car by accident, and by the time I remembered it, it was completely singed. The leaves had bubbled up in shades of yellow and black. The whole thing crumbled the next day, no matter how much water I gave it to drink. It had already been marked for death.

I stare down at the orchids' petals, wondering if the healthy parts of me have been burned too, until they're so destroyed by the searing pain that they're not salvageable. Maybe I'll live the rest of my life like a leafless orchid. Unable to thrive and grow and flower, even under ideal conditions. My eyes fall to Aunt Karen's hand, still outstretched over the table. If I was even in the ideal conditions.

"I think there are some grow lights in the garage if you'd rather."

"No thanks. Why would there be grow lights in the garage?" I ask over my shoulder.

"I'm pretty sure one of my cousins was growing weed in there at some point." Aunt Karen winks. "It's worth a look."

"Maybe later." I scoop up a few of the plants and carry

them gingerly to the living room where I've left the rough-cut lightbox I made this afternoon. I may be a burned-out shell of what I used to be, but I can still fulfill my part of the project I'm doing with Noah. All I need is a few more photos in specific colors.

As I position the plants and take photo after photo with my phone, I can't keep my mind from wandering back to the Mayday Killer. What motivates him to keep killing? Take more lives? Why not find a cabin in the woods and hide out where he'll never be found? He could read a thousand books, grow a garden, live out his days in peace. It would be an act of compassion, one I'm not sure he's capable of.

Instead, he continues to hunt and kill. This time striking a family I knew. It's unfathomable. My chest tightens painfully as I imagine what it was like for Nate and Kate to walk into the house sweaty from a soccer game in the park, laughing and talking trash. I imagine them halting in the hallway as a strong, salty scent hits their noses. The questioning glances they give each other as they move deeper into the house. The way grief engulfs them like flies in a Venus fly trap when they discover the killer's handiwork.

Sucking in a few quick breaths to expel the evil images, I try to focus on my project. It's innocuous enough to keep my thoughts shallow, where it's safer. Sitting back on my heels, I scroll through my photos. I've got some good ones that I think Mr. Baugh will like. And there are a couple that will look great on my social feed.

Chapter 16

Day 123, Thursday

Gingerly, I pull the poster board out of the back of Aunt Karen's car, frowning at the bend in one corner. It was perfectly straight when I loaded it. The imperfection will have to do. An audible sigh escapes me as I slide my backpack onto my shoulders. Aunt Karen eyes the pink and orange dress I'm wearing—it's a louder print than most of the clothes she bought for me—but doesn't say anything. The tightness around her mouth is enough of an indication of her displeasure at my clothing choices.

I don't know if she expected me to change once I picked up on her displeasure, but I wasn't about to do that. I'm tired of all the drab, neutral colors that make up most of my new wardrobe. A little splash of color was warranted. Welcome to parenting teenage girls, Aunt Karen. Maybe someday we'll even get into a fight about my post high-school goals, just like my mom and I used to do.

Because apparently taking a gap year to pursue my dream is not a valuable use of my time. *So few people make it in the industry*, she'd said. As if I didn't already know.

I sniff, remembering the way Mom's eyes would crease as she tried to convince me that taking a gap year would put me behind. The conviction in her voice when she insisted I at least consider going straight to a four-year school. Sharp pain cuts through my chest and I shove the memories away.

Time to put my game face on.

Reaching up, I pretend to swipe paint along my cheekbones. Face paint was a normal part of my school attire once. School spirit, yay! But now? I barely even wear makeup except for concealer. The scar shows right through it, so why bother?

Hoisting the poster board so I can maneuver without ramming into anything, I march up the steps.

Noah is at the top, kicked back on one of the concrete walls and reading a graphic novel I'm familiar with. "Hey," he says when he sees me, hopping up and pocketing the book. "Whatcha got there?"

I turn it around so he can see the aesthetic I spent a ton of time on last night in an attempt to keep my mind off everything else. Pops of neon color contrast with dark, shadowy images of gritty urban streets and rain-soaked pavement. It's a physical representation of the lighting idea I've worked up for *The Mousetrap*, printed out in cerebral color. Hopefully Esau will go for it. Sure, the first five times I tried to show him on my phone he blew me off, but it'll be much harder to ignore the poster board in my hands. At some point he's got to see that my ideas are good ones. He has to.

The corridor is buzzing with activity as people arrive for school. Lockers slam and backpack zippers open and close, but the thing that gets my attention is the whispering. Down the hallway, a group of boys are watching a video on their phone. Justin is mopping what looks like a pool of jello salad but which I know from the smell is vomit. I still think he's a little weird, but maybe that's because I see the devil everywhere these days.

As Noah and I draw closer to the group of boys, I hear snatches of a reporter's voice. She's talking about the homicidal maniac who's rampaging through our state without a care in the world. He's slipped through the police perimeter again.

My chest constricts.

"Everyone's pretty freaked about the Mayday Killer." Noah says just above a whisper.

"They should be," I murmur.

"Pardon?"

"I said, it looks that way."

"Right." Noah's dark hair bobs as he nods, his eyes narrowed just slightly. "You gonna carry that all day?"

I shake my head. "I'm gonna run it to the drama room before first period."

One of the guys in the huddle spots us and gestures to his friends. "Hey Noah," he calls. "I bet you're pretty upset by all this, yeah?"

Noah stops, his entire body going stiff. He doesn't look back at the guys, all of whom are now focused on us. On him. One of them flicks a glance at my scar before returning his attention to the boy beside me.

Noah clears his throat, but his words still come out unsteady. "I don't know what you mean."

"You know, how your brother was murdered, and they never caught the guy? What if it's the same guy?"

This dude's words ring in my brain. The man who killed Noah's brother couldn't be the Mayday Killer. That was ten years ago. The MO was different. It couldn't be. Could it?

"Aren't *you* scared?" I ask, as much to shut up my brain as to shut up these jerks.

The group of dudes look at me in surprise, a huddle of

poser shirts and slack jaws. Finally, after what seems like forever, the guy who started it says, "Sure, I'm scared. Big, bad killer man is on a rampage, and the police haven't managed to catch him yet." His liberal use of air quotes tempts me to glare, but I manage to contain it.

"The police are doing everything they can to apprehend him, and they will." Great, I'm parroting Aunt Karen now.

"Some job they're doing. He's killed what, fourteen people by now?"

"Fifteen," Noah says. He seems to come back to himself, his body unclenching. The pulse in his neck is going at break-neck speed, though. Something about this conversation has him rattled, but what? "Did you know that criminals sometimes stay on the FBI most wanted list for years? It's harder to catch fugitives than it looks on TV. There's a lot of work and research that goes into it."

"Don't they have witnesses, though?" another guy asks.

"Witnesses are unreliable," Noah explains. "You could have ten people recount the same event, and they'd each tell you they heard a different number of gunshots. It's not an exact science. Memory can be faulty, or it can be manipulated."

A beat too late, I add, "That's true."

The warning bell clangs, making me jump. Whatever spell was cast to create the cohesion of students listening to Noah's conversation with the bro dudes is broken as people scatter, hurrying to reach their classrooms before the tardy bell rings.

With a quick glance at Noah, whose breathing is slowing to normal, I hurry to first period and slide into the desk beside Dariel. At the front of the classroom, the teacher is fiddling with his laptop to get it connected to the projector. So we've probably got ten minutes before class will actually start. Everyone else seems to feel the same way, because chatter breaks out all over the classroom. A box of Twizzlers gets passed around, and I take one. I love these.

"Dude, what is that? You got a presentation today or something?" Dariel picks up my poster board and looks over it, head bobbing in approval. "Looks like someone's getting an A in art class."

I can't help but laugh. "Thanks, D, but this isn't for Art. It's for Esau."

His red brows pull together. "You made this for Esau? Wait, is this a confession of love or something?" He flips it over and looks at the back, which is blank. "You forgot to sign it, Meggie."

"Don't be ridiculous," I say, suppressing a smile at the nickname. No one's ever called me that, but I could get used to it. Taking a corner of the board, I give a light pull. I don't want to damage it before I can even show it to Esau, but suddenly I don't want Dariel scrutinizing it anymore either. "I'm hoping if he sees a visual of the lighting scheme I've been trying to sell him on, he'll let me try it."

Up front, the projector makes a loud beeping noise, drawing my attention. The teacher is hovering around the projector, pressing buttons in a way that does not look good. A few rows over, the class techie gets up and trudges up there, tapping the teacher on the shoulder so he'll stop his assault on the projector long enough to look at her. Poor techie girl.

Dariel leans closer. "We're talking about the same Esau, right? Esau Chavez? Control freak? Man bun? Always barking orders?"

I roll my eyes and frown. "He's going to hate it."

"I mean, probably. Yeah." His fingers tap a rhythm on the desktop.

My frown deepens. "My ideas for this show are good. I

just have to make him see that somehow."

"Good luck with that." Dariel chuffs incredulously.

"Thanks," I mutter. "I'm going to need it." I spend the rest of the day going through what I'm going to say to Esau to get him to try my lighting so that by the time the last bell rings I have it memorized. It's a welcome break from the conversations all around me. Death, fear, and confusion are the rule of the day. Not for me. Not anymore, if I can help it.

My opportunity to show Esau my vision for the show comes sooner than I expected it would and goes a lot smoother too. Esau isn't in the drama room when I get there after class. Marisa and one of the other actors are running lines in the middle of the stage area. She's still using her script, I notice. Fiona and Dariel are upstairs in the booth, and it does not sound like they're working. In the far corner near the hallway, the whir of Viv's sewing machine draws me closer.

My eyes land on the fabric and my feet halt abruptly. Blood is pooling around the machine, inching outward toward my sandals. A pair of hands lie cut and bleeding in the middle of the widening puddle. A dinged wedding band glints on a twitching ring finger.

A cry escapes from my throat. If I don't back away, it's going to seep into my shoes. But I can't move. The haze of terror in my brain is blocking all communication with my limbs. I squeeze my eyes shut.

It's not real. It's not. I'm not in that place anymore.

I force my eyes to open and refocus.

A puddle of scarlet cloth is lain out in a swath around Viv's machine, but the whirring has stopped. Viv is staring up at me with wide, attentive eyes. "Megan? You in there?" she asks.

Almost too late, I manage to nod. "Sorry. I zoned out for a second there."

Viv studies me, her expression not quite believing. Then gestures past me. "Fiona's calling you."

"Right."

Fiona is standing on the stairs leading to the booth, and when she spots me she grins. "Esau's not coming today."

"What?"

"There was some problem at the farm, so he had to rush home after last period. You know what this means?"

"Everyone's leaving?" I'm surprised at how disappointed I am to hear that. Despite constantly butting heads with Esau about aspects of the show, the afternoons I'm able to spend here rather than cooped up in the restless quiet of Aunt Karen's house have become my safe space. The only time I can truly be myself without fear of being scrutinized by my overprotective guardian.

"Haven't you ever heard the phrase, 'the show must go on?'" Fiona plants a hand on her hip.

"I'm not following."

Holding up my collage of inspiration photos, Fiona raises her eyebrows.

My eyes run over the flashes of neon color in the images. Then to everyone around us, who for some reason are looking at Fiona and me as if we're in charge around here.

"You think?" I ask.

"Let's try it. We can reset the lights afterward." Fiona grins. I do too.

Excitement hums in my veins. This is my shot to set up the lighting scheme how I want. Run through the show the way I imagine it should look. Take some photos. It's going to be so fantastic even Esau won't be able to argue. It'll show him my vision is just as valid as his. I'm making this happen, thanks to Fiona.

"Thanks, girl," I say. "All right everyone. Esau's not here today, so we're going to try something a little different. Dariel?"

"Your wish is my command, Meggie."

A thrill runs through me as my fellow club members listen and comply with my requests. Bodies scramble around the drama room, setting up for a run through of the first act. Fiona's on a ladder changing the colored films over the lights. Up in the booth, Dariel gives me a thumbs up. A sense that I'm right where I'm supposed to be makes my chest puff up.

My phone chimes in my pocket. A text from Noah. I start to ignore it, but a word in the preview snags my attention. I scan the message quickly. It shoots an arrow that pops a gaping hole in my ballooning heart and sends it careening toward my feet as it loses all of its air. He's gotten in contact with someone who's willing to share some of the police's case files with him. Crime scene images, too. It's the break in the case he needs, Noah insists. Will I meet up with him Monday after school to look through it for leads?

It's the break we both need, really. If I'm going to figure out who's behind the killings and protect myself, a look at the police files would be useful. If I can stomach them.

"We're ready," Fiona calls as she climbs down the ladder. "You look a little green. You okay?"

Shoving my phone back into my pocket, I meet her eyes. "I've never been more ready." It's definitely a lie.

Chapter 17

Day 127, Monday

Noah meets me outside my seventh period class. "I thought we could go straight over to the library from here, if that's okay?"

"Sure," I say, steeling myself. I know what I have to do. It's a matter of self-preservation. Aunt Karen won't let me go gallivanting around in search of a killer, but I can still do some digging. Plus, I have to keep tabs on Noah's research to make sure he doesn't find out. And he would never understand. He's too honest, too good to understand. He'd never look at me the way he does, with his warm brown eyes shining behind his black plastic frames.

We cross campus, walking through the football field and out the back gate in a clump of students. Most leave through the parking lot, but those who don't have cars often leave this way to avoid the crush of traffic at the front gate. Even from this distance the honking and shouting coming from the lot are clear.

I'm relieved to be with Noah this afternoon. Friday afternoon Aunt Karen couldn't pick me up, she was held up at the grocery store, so Justin drove me home. It was all kinds of awkward. But somehow not bad. It was way better than walking home alone. There was no feeling like someone was following me, even though I know someone is. The notes alone are proof that the Mayday Killer is either here, biding his time, or has a lackey he's using to scare me. There's someone in this town tracking my movements. I'm not just another small town teenager heading home from a day of mind-numbing classes.

Today, Noah and I walk through downtown. "You interested in a milkshake before we hit the books?"

I chew on my lip, worried he'll take it the wrong way if I agree. I've felt a little bad for turning him down ever since he asked me out a couple weeks ago, but Noah hasn't brought it up again. He also hasn't done anything that makes me think he's bummed about it either. It must not have been a big deal to him. Maybe he just wanted something to do on a Friday night. Besides, it's stupid hot out here, and a milkshake sounds divine.

"Sure, I could go for one."

"Excellent." He holds the door open and gestures for me to lead the way inside.

My stomach gives a tiny flutter at the attention, but I ignore it. It doesn't mean anything when Noah offers to pay for my milkshake, and I decline.

Twenty minutes later we step outside onto the sidewalk, me sipping on a chocolate peanut butter shake and him drinking a root beer flavored one. We chat about anime all the way to the library, arguing good-naturedly about which ones are the absolute best. We laugh as we stumble into the brick building, sighing at the relief of the cool air.

"Man, I love this place," Noah says as we make our way to the back to the table where we usually sit. "It's so quiet, unlike at home."

"Who's home with Anza and Mattie this afternoon?"

"Mom's off today. I think she needed a mental health day,

you know?"

I can only imagine how difficult Mrs. Lopez's job as a nurse in a local elderly facility is every day. I'm familiar with the concept of taking a mental/emotional rest. I could use one myself, but as Noah pulls a stack of papers out of his backpack after scanning the area to make sure we're alone, I know today is not that day.

The top page is a crime scene photo on a plain paper with a printer low on colored ink. The image is in black and white, but it doesn't lessen the impact of seeing a pair of bodies slouched forward on a couch, their throats slit.

My stomach revolts and I squeeze my eyes shut.

"Crap, sorry. I forgot to warn you." There's a shuffle of papers. "It's okay to look now."

When I open my eyes, the crime scene photos are gone. An apologetic smile from Noah doesn't make me feel any better.

"Sorry about that. I haven't had a chance to look at any of this yet. I kind of wanted to wait until you were with me. I hope that's not weird."

"Not weird." My stomach disagrees with a gurgle.

Noah takes another sip of his shake, his eyes still on my face. Then he slides some papers across the slick tabletop toward me. "Why don't you start with this list of survivors? Do some googling and see if you can find any connections between them that the police might have missed."

"I doubt they missed anything," I say, but take the sheets. My perusal of the alphabetized list is both agonizingly slow and as fast as I can force it. I can't get past a deep sadness for each name on the list. The person behind it whose life is irreversibly changed. Kate and Nate Anderson are not yet on the list.

"Find anything interesting?"

I shake my head.

"It's just, you've been staring at that one page for five minutes."

I push my gaze up to his. "It's a little overwhelming."

"I get that. Want to look at something else for a bit? I can trade you."

"No," I say too quickly. My fingers tighten on the papers in my hand. "This is interesting."

After a beat, Noah goes back to scanning the rest of the file.

I wait until I'm sure he's not paying any attention before I look down at the papers in my lap. At the top of the final page is one single name printed by itself. Clenching my teeth and breathing deeply through my nose to calm the quaking in my stomach, I silently fold the paper in half and tuck it under my butt. Then I throw myself into the rest of the list with as much gusto as I can muster.

I'm deep in concentration when a hand lands on the tabletop next to the paper I'm reading. Noah and I have been working in silence for over an hour, and the movement makes me startle, gasping in surprise.

"What was that for?" I ask, managing to glare up at the guy standing beside my chair.

Esau is looking at me with an inscrutable expression. "That's what I was about to ask you. What were you thinking on Friday? I'm gone for one practice and you change everything about the production."

My gaze flits to Noah, who is watching us carefully. Something in my look must convey the idea that I want privacy for this conversation, because Noah clears his throat and adjusts his glasses. "I'll be right back," he mumbles as he goes.

"You were gone for two practices, okay? And I changed

one thing. One! I thought if you saw how it would look with the neon lighting, you'd like it. Besides, I put it all back when we were finished."

Esau sighs, pulling over a chair from another table, turning it backward, and sitting in it. His arms cross casually across its back and his dark eyes pierce my own.

This is the part where he chews me out for messing with his precious production. I kind of understand why he's so uptight about every aspect of our play, from the actors' delivery to the costumes to the lighting. Esau is the director, so we're supposed to be working toward his vision. He was planning for this far before I came along, and probably didn't anticipate butting heads with the new girl at school. There's no way he saw me coming; I never saw any of this coming either. My throat dries and I swallow, forcing it open.

I steel myself for a whispered scolding just as Noah reclaims his seat across the table. He must have asked someone at the information desk for access to the library's newspaper archive, because he's got a stack of them in his hands.

Esau glances at Noah, then leans closer to me. "Your lighting. It wasn't… terrible."

A surprised laugh escapes from my mouth.

"Don't get carried away," he says, but there's a hint of a smile at the corners of his mouth. "Let's get together later. We can talk it over. See if we can come to some kind of—"

"Compromise?"

"Yeah." He swallows. It's clearly killing him to admit that someone else's idea isn't the worst thing he's ever heard. But I can't help it. Half a smile tips my mouth up. I've worked my butt off in drama club, and it's nice to finally get a little credit for it.

"I'm not sure if I can. My aunt…"

"She's pretty strict. Yeah, I've heard," he adds when my eyes widen.

"I'll ask her, but I can't promise anything."

"We'll figure it out." Esau unfolds himself from the chair and replaces it under the next table. "See you around, Noah."

"Yeah," Noah says with a casual chin lift.

Esau walks right past Mr. Baugh, who is talking to the librarian at the information desk. When he turns, he sees us and gives a small wave which Noah and I return. Small towns, I think.

As Noah and I dig back into the case file, I can't help but notice the ease between the two of us is gone. There is no easy banter about anime characters or the superior milkshake flavor. And worst of all was the look on his face when I told Esau I'd ask about meeting up with him later. Noah didn't look sad, exactly. He looked disappointed.

Maybe he hasn't forgotten about asking me out, after all.

Maybe it meant more to him than I realized.

I steal a glance at him across the table. His black wavy hair has fallen forward over his brow as he reads. Absently, a finger itches the side of his nose behind his glasses. He's not as broad as Esau, but there's a quiet confidence about him that I have to admit I like. I almost wish I could… No, it's for the better this way. Who knows how long I'll be living with Aunt Karen anyway. It might be for the next eighteen months until I finish high school and go off to college. Or it might be another week.

Noah's arms are propped on the tabletop as if he's trying to shield the crime scene photos he's studying. I shudder, picturing that single name alone on a sheet of crisp white paper. Not for the first time, I wonder what will become of her.

Chapter 18

Hours Later

It took me forever to finish my work tonight, so it wasn't a lie when I told my guardian that I had a headache and was going to bed early. A glass of water and a Tylenol fixed that. Now I lay still in bed, breathing in and out evenly so if Aunt Karen decides to check on me, she'll think I'm asleep. She turned the hall light off and retired to her room two hours ago. So that's looking unlikely. I'm pretty sure I've heard her moving around downstairs in the early hours of the morning a few times, but it's almost midnight now, not 4 AM. Slowly, the noises from next door went quiet, signalling that the house is asleep.

Bright blue light from the full moon shines in through the gauzy curtains over the large window, turning the striped rug shades of blue and purple. Outside, an owl hoots from its perch in one of the eucalyptus trees that stretch out in a grove behind the house.

Under my pillow, my phone vibrates.

I slide it out and read the message.

I've been waiting for this text for the past hour since Esau messaged me that he was bored and I should meet him tonight to talk about the play's lighting. If I didn't know any better, I'd think he enjoyed arguing with me. But if I can convince him of my vision for the play, it'll be worth the risk I'm taking leaving the house.

Peeling back the thin coverlet, I sit up, fully dressed. With careful hands, I pick up the stuff on the desk under the window and set it on the floor. The old house creaks, making my pulse leap. I go still. Waiting. Nothing stirs.

My eyes fall on the silver bracelet sitting on the corner of the desk, and I slide it on so she's with me.

Climbing onto the wood veneered desk, I crouch to open the window. Hopefully it cooperates. I haven't actually tried it since I claimed this room. It's been so hot outside we've had the AC running constantly. It didn't even occur to me that it might not open until right this second, but it's a distinct possibility judging by the layers and layers of paint on the sill. After some maneuvering, and time spent pushing and pulling at it, I'm able to dislodge the sliding lock. Moment of truth time.

The window screeches as it rises, causing my heart to sledgehammer my ribcage. Frozen, I strain for any trace of movement that indicates Aunt Karen heard. She could barrel into the room any second. If she catches me fully dressed and attempting to sneak out, she'll probably put me on full house arrest. GPS anklet and everything.

Mercifully, nothing happens.

That's right, I think. I make magic happen. This is happening.

Climbing out, I stand upright on the patio cover that runs along the front of the house. Inching forward, I sit with my legs over the edge. Good thing I know how to fall without seriously hurting myself. Leaning forward, I aim for the patchy grass, keeping my legs loose.

My sandaled feet hit the grass and slide out from under my body, landing me on my butt.

A huffed laugh pulls my attention to the side of the house where a tall figure materializes out of the shadows.

I go tense with fear until I realize it's Esau moving closer to me, his black hair streaming around his shoulders over his white tee.

"You were supposed to wait in your truck," I hiss, standing up to brush myself off. "If Aunt Karen hears us, she'll kill us both."

"You're late. I came to make sure she hadn't busted you," he whispers back.

"Does it look like I got caught?"

Esau shakes his head, amusement playing about his eyebrows as he looks at me. Snaps that intriguing rubber band. "Come on." I can't help but notice the way the moonlight caresses his hair as Esau leads the way down the driveway to the street. The scuffed and muddy pickup truck he drives is parked in the shadow between the streetlights a couple houses down.

The truck's doors shut after us, and I turn to look back at the old house. The way its shadow looms long over the dry grass. The way it's set back from the road and surrounded by trees makes it look sort of like a creepy farmhouse in a horror movie. No lights have come on. There's no movement. Looks like I'm going to get away with sneaking out. Take that, Warden Karen.

The interior of the truck is much cleaner than the outside, except for a rip in the upholstery in the middle of the bench seat. A satisfied smile rises as I face forward.

"You ready?" Esau asks, glancing over at me, arms slung over the worn steering wheel. At my nod, he starts the truck, expertly using the stick shift to chug down the street. I never saw anyone driving stick before, but the way Esau does it so easily is kind of attractive.

Thankful that it's dark enough to hide the pink climbing into my cheeks, I look out the window. The downtown is silent as we coast through. We're the only car stopped at the red light. Down a side street, headlights flash as we pass. I guess someone else is awake in this sleepy town after all. I try not to think about who it could be. So far, whoever's passing me angry notes has only done it during the day. Hopefully, the dark of night will hide me from prying eyes.

Forcing that idea away, I turn to Esau.

His left hand hangs casually out his window, which is rolled down all the way. We're driving slow enough that the breeze picks up strands of his hair, making them float around him in a dark crown.

Using the hand crank, I roll down my own window and breathe in the fresh country air. There's something so serene about being almost the only people awake. The quiet and the dark are like balms in my soul, shoring up some of the tiny cracks that have splintered in my core. I didn't know it, but I desperately needed this. The freedom of being out of that house, out from under Aunt Karen's thumb, even for just an hour.

Esau slows the truck as we approach the farm where I suppose he works, but I'm not ready for this to end.

"Keep going," I say, shooting a glance at the boy beside me to gauge his reaction.

Esau actually smiles, and he speeds past the wrought-iron gate topped with metal roosters.

We drive around in the tranquil stillness of midnight for over an hour, reveling in the cool, damp air. After about twenty minutes, I'm shocked to discover that I'm comfortable here with Esau. He's not barking orders or glaring at me or sending me on stupid errands. Hell, we're not really talking at all, but it feels… right somehow. Like this is where I'm supposed to be tonight.

After a while, Esau turns on to a dirt road beside a wide almond orchard and pulls around back, shielding the truck behind the long, narrow rows of meticulously maintained trees. The boughs shimmer under the high moon, their canopy blocking all but the slimmest threads of silver. "Want out?" Esau asks, swinging his door open and climbing out at my affirmative nod.

I follow around the back and we sit side by side on the tailgate, looking through the woodlet of trees toward the road. Crickets sing an eerie song that definitely could be used in a horror movie. I push the dark thoughts away. "About the play."

"About the play," Esau parrots, looking me over with his eyes hidden in shadow. "How come you changed the whole lighting scheme from what we talked about? I thought we'd agreed on it. It was done."

I exhale through my nose. "You agreed. I never did. And you didn't even look at my ideas. I just wanted to show you we had options."

"It's my play," he says with the barest hint of tension in his tone. "I'm the director." *Not you.*

"And a good director will listen to his crew when they have good ideas."

"You think I don't listen to my crew? What about Fiona's suggestion about cable placement?" Now he's definitely glaring at me a little. This is the Esau I'm used to, the one I can handle. Not the almost kind of sexy one who drives a stick shift and looks like a black-haired Aragorn with his hair down.

"Fine, you listened to that, but that was a safety issue. When it comes to anything artsy, you're like a brick wall," I say, tossing a hand up toward the trees.

Esau snorts. "I knew you wouldn't get it."

"There's nothing to get. You've got a stick up your butt about this whole thing, and you won't let anyone else contribute."

"It's my only shot!" he growls, surprising me.

A large bird cries and flies up from one of the almond trees, making me duck and throw my arms over my head.

"It's just an owl," Esau says, tracing the bird's progress across the stars. His clenched muscles relax.

"I know that," I say, uncoiling my arms.

"You're such a city girl," Esau says, his tone warming.

". . . Is that supposed to be an insult?"

He shakes his head. "You drive me absolutely insane, you know that?"

"It's one of my more endearing qualities." I sit up primly.

He laughs.

"You were saying something about the play being your one shot?"

Esau peeks at me out of the corner of his eye, his hands tightening around the edge of the tailgate. He's quiet for so long I'm not sure he's going to say anything, but then his mouth opens. "This play, *The Mousetrap*, it's my only shot at film school."

"Film school?" I shift toward him, and my knee touches his thigh. I don't move away, telling myself that I'm simply trying to annoy him.

"My parents knew my goal, so they sent me up here to live with my aunt and uncle. There's a lot more opportunity here than in the small town I'm from. My uncle is hoping I'll follow him into farm management, but…" He trails off. "I've always loved film. That's what I want to do: direct movies."

"And the play helps you how?"

"It's experience directing, isn't it? It'll help when I fill out college applications."

My head bobs in what I hope looks like agreement, even though I'm not sure I understand.

"Look." Taking out his phone, he opens his social and starts scrolling through it.

When I notice that he's continued to use some of the tips I gave him, I smile. "You're posting on regular days. And your newer photos are so much brighter."

"Thanks. Some bossy girl gave me some ideas."

"Not bossy. Entrepreneurial. She makes things happen."

My favorite owl screeches nearby, and some tiny animal squeals in terror. Inwardly, I cringe.

"She does." He runs a hand through his hair and I have to tear my eyes away. Guys with long hair are H.O.T. HOT. Who knew? Suddenly all of my mom's romance novels with that long-haired blond guy on the cover make so much more sense.

"About the lighting." I change the subject, hoping to distract my inward monologue about how not terrible Esau looks right now.

"We're back to that already?" He turns toward me, folding one foot and bumping my knee in the process. "Sorry," he says. He doesn't shift away.

Fizzing warmth skims my skin, radiating from that spot. What am I even doing? This is Esau Grumpy Pants Chavez I'm low key ogling.

"The lighting scheme you're suggesting; I don't hate it."

"Wow, what a compliment."

"Shut up and let me finish."

I make a mock frown, not in the least insulted. Esau's bark is far worse than his bite, I'm discovering. I motion for him to keep going.

"What if we combined them? Started with the soft light I planned and slowly adding harsher, more neon light as the play progresses? If we do it right, it'll highlight the tension unfolding between the characters. It'll be another layer of stress on the audience." He's ramping up to lecture me on the power of good lighting, so I interrupt, trying not to focus on the way his ear gauges gleam in the moonlight.

"Absolutely. Let's do it."

Esau's eyes widen, and he points between us. "Are you actually agreeing with me on something?"

"Let me check." I cock my head to the side and pretend to think it over. "Yes, I do believe we agree on something. One thing, but it's a start. Now, about the blocking in act two…" I trail off, grinning.

"You drive me insane." Esau is grinning too, and what I would give to keep him looking at me like that.

"You said that already."

"I did."

Somehow Esau and I have leaned closer together, our faces mere inches apart. Our knees are pressed tightly together. Hands a mere finger width from brushing. My breath hitches when Esau's attention dips to my mouth.

He sucks his bottom lip between his teeth.

I bite mine.

With a loud pop, a car rumbles up the road. Whatever spell the moonlight had woven between us like a silken spider web is broken. I peer into the dark and spot it: a dark sedan driving slowly nearer and without any headlights.

"That's odd," Esau mumbles.

My heart is pounding in my chest. It's Aunt Karen. It's gotta be. She's found out that I'm not home and has tracked me here. Crap. I am going to be in so much trouble. She probably won't let me out of the house for a month.

The car slows even more as it approaches the orchard. My blood is pumping so loud I can't hear anything else. What if it's not my guardian? What if it's him? It was so stupid to leave the house in the middle of the night. He told me he planned to come for me when the time was right, and I handed him the opportunity on a silver platter.

My shoulders sag as the car almost stops along the curb and then moves past the orchard.

Not Aunt Karen. Not a murderer come to take his final victim. Still, something about the car is bugging me.

"Did you see the giant dice that guy had hanging from his mirror?" Esau shakes his head.

"Dice?" My breath hiccups in my throat. "That car. What color would you say it was?"

"Blue or green? It was hard to tell in the dark."

A blue car with dice in the mirror. Just like the one Fiona said followed us to the beach. It can't be a coincidence. He tried to follow me out here.

Suddenly all I want to do is hide under the covers of my bed at Aunt Karen's house. Where it's safe. Where the monsters dare not come. Jumping down from the tailgate, I round the truck and pull on the door handle. "I'd like to go home now, please."

Esau follows me. "Is there something wrong?"

"No. I just want to go back."

Esau looks puzzled, but doesn't argue. We ride in silence through the deserted streets, me checking the rearview mirror every few seconds the whole way. My nerves are strung tight, my eyes narrowed as if any second a car's headlights will blind me. Esau keeps glancing my way, clearly wondering why my mood turned on a dime. His hands tighten on the steering wheel as he focuses on the road ahead. I don't take a full breath until after Esau boosts me onto the patio cover so I can crawl inside my window and lock it with a snick.

Minutes pass as I change into my pajamas and slip into bed. Only then do I allow myself to replay tonight in my head. The way Esau's gaze dipped to my mouth. My heart jogging behind my breastbone. His large hands on my waist as he boosted me easily.

Down the street, the low grumble of a car approaches. Heart skittering, I scramble out of bed and peer into the dark. Did Esau forget something? Is he coming back to finish what we started? No. It's a dark sedan. My stomach clenches. It looks like the same one that drove past the orchard.

Whoever is in that car followed me home.

Chapter 19

Day 129, Wednesday

Something scrabbles through the underbrush, making me spin. Nothing is there. I take a deep breath, trying to quiet my unease. I've been jumpy for days and I can't seem to shake the gut instinct that something is wrong. That he is closing in.

The sheriff and his guys have been looking all over town for the stolen blue car but haven't been able to find it. It's freaking me out, but I won't let it rule me. Which is why I'm standing in the middle of the eucalyptus grove behind Aunt Karen's house taking photos. The way the sun dapples the densely packed earth, the flashes of white winking in the breeze, makes my fingers itch to shoot. All around, the gray-green bark of the trees soothes my nerves. My shoulders settle away from my ears as I crouch down to snap a few photos.

Eucalyptus trees sway all around, scattered leaves spinning and twirling as they cascade to the ground. In the branches overhead, a crow caws, cutting through the rippling heat of the late afternoon. There's a bit of a respite under the boughs where I am sitting butt in the dirt, but it's still far warmer than I'm used to. Fine baby hairs stick to my neck under my ponytail.

My phone goes off in my pocket. Noah's texting, asking

when I'm coming over.

Oh crap. We're supposed to get together to work on our art project.

I'd gotten so lost in taking photos of the grove that I'd forgotten. I'll have to hustle because I'm already late. Shooting him a message to tell him I'm on my way, I go inside.

"I'm ready to go to Noah's," I call as I step into the house. The only greeting I get is the aged structure's creaking. My guardian is not in the kitchen or the living room. My feet thump up the stairs and I raise my fist to knock on the master bedroom door. Something stops me, and instead I hover near the door, listening.

Frowning, I go back downstairs. That's when I spot the sticky note on the front of the microwave. *Was needed at the store. Be back soon.*

Great. Noah lives all the way on the other end of town and I don't want to walk. It's not safe. I can't ask him to come get me, because he doesn't have car seats for Anza and Mattie in his car. Chewing on my lip, I glance out the front window. Justin's truck is parked in his cracking driveway, so it looks like our neighbor is home. Aunt Karen did say I could ask him if I needed anything. And that one time he drove me home from school wasn't terrible.

I lock the front door and pick my way across the street, not bothering to avoid stepping on the fissures in the asphalt like I did when I was a little kid. It's not like it's going to break my mother's back.

Paint peels off the wooden steps leading up to the front porch. A large plastic pot sits to one side of the wooden front door, its plant shriveled and blackened. From the thick layer of dust on the worn wood, I'm guessing that Justin expends all of his cleaning mojo at school and doesn't bother once he gets home.

When I knock, the door swings open. Huh. It must not have been latched all the way.

"Hello?" I say, peeking my head inside while carefully keeping my feet outside the threshold. No answer. Maybe he's in the back of the house and didn't hear me? I consider going out and around the building that way, but a blue flicker on the wall catches my attention. There must be a TV on, so he's got to be home, and I really need to get to Noah's.

Despite the goosebumps rising on my arms, I go in. My heart is thrumming in my throat. I've never been in what is effectively a stranger's house, and I keep expecting the boogie man to jump out and yell, "Boo."

The hallway is bare. No furniture. No family photos. It's as if no one actually lives here. As if Justin is a ghost simply passing through.

But what I find in the living room of the small house makes me wish I'd found a ghost instead.

It's not the reflection of a TV I saw from the front entryway. A long folding table spans the entire wall of the dimly lit room. Dingy curtains cover all of the windows. Unease slithers up my spine. The curtains might be there to keep the light out, but they also keep the darkness in.

The long table is lined with computer screens. Black cords snake along the floor and end in a coiled mess of surge protectors with red glaring lights. Underneath, there's a clump of computer towers and external hard drives. Each of the monitors shows a different view from a security camera. Aunt Karen's front porch. Her garage. The back door. The grove of eucalyptus trees. The entire exterior of the house and land is visible through the screens.

My breath comes in quick pants as panic starts to close its

icy fingers around my lungs. I blink rapidly, but the view from the screens doesn't change. Justin has a stalker's command center in his house. And his subjects? Aunt Karen. Me. He's got a front-row seat to everyone who comes and goes from the old house.

I was right. Justin is the one who's been watching. I have to tell her. I have to get out of here. Now.

I gasp for air, trying to run, but my feet won't budge. They've been cemented to the crusty planks that make up the floor. Digging down deep for the inner strength Aunt Karen says I've got, I turn away from the stalker's paradise.

Oh god. My stomach lurches. The other wall is worse. Justin's got a murder wall, and this one is much larger than Noah's. Shock nearly knocks me over as I register that it isn't Aunt Karen in the hundreds of crisp, color photos. In fact, there aren't any of her at all.

Images of me are plastered all over the wall. At school. The library. Noah's house. My mouth drops open in a gasp as I'm drawn to a cluster of photos near the bottom corner of the macabre collage. They're newer, pinned partially on top of others. In them Esau is sitting on his tailgate almost *smiling*. Talking to a girl. Me. I'm grinning down at my lap. Between the camera and Esau's truck is a well-manicured orchard lined with trees. Almond, I'm pretty sure.

I scan photo after photo, trying to establish a timeline. My eyes snap wide as they land on one from that day at the boardwalk. Taken while I was swimming in the ocean.

Terror clamps its hand over my mouth and nose. I try to suck in air but my mouth opens and closes ineffectively like a dying, beached fish. I can't breathe. I'm going to suffocate right here. Heaving, I take great gulps that scratch and claw down my throat. My lungs refuse to inflate.

Justin is the one helping the Mayday Killer. He's the one who has been passing me threatening notes. He was there at the beach that day. And at school. He had all the opportunity. And somehow he's completely fooled Aunt Karen.

I have to get out. I know exactly what this sicko will do if he finds me in his house. Truss me up and lead me like a lamb to the slaughter. My gaze cuts to the kitchen, to the butcher block full of shiny-handled knives. Unbidden, my hand rises to the white scar that mars my cheek. I know if I look down at my fingers they'll come away bathed in blood.

Through the archway on the left, a door opens and slams shut. Footsteps make the wooden floor vibrate beneath the soles of my shoes.

He's coming.

If I don't move now, he'll catch me.

When the time is right.

Move. Move!

Wrenching my legs into motion, I run.

Chapter 20

The sun set while I waited, shivering, for the sheriff to arrive. When he did, there were no flashing red lights. No sirens. Instead of breaking down the door of Justin's house and barging inside like they do on TV, he parked his Bronco in front of Aunt Karen's house. Stared up at it for a beat before mounting the porch and knocking on the door.

Aunt Karen admits Sheriff Lamb and closes the door securely behind him. The sheriff's hands perch on his hips as his appraising gaze lands on me. "Walk me through what you saw."

So I do. I explain that I was running late to meet a friend and Aunt Karen wasn't home, so I walked across the street to Justin's house. How the door swung open when I touched it. I describe the computer bank of surveillance footage of the house we're standing in. The wall of photos—proof that he's been stalking me all over town. I explain about the notes and the fact that he had the opportunity to pass them to me without my noticing.

A chill runs down my spine and I dig my fingers into my arms, clutching them against my chest.

"We'll keep an eye on things," is all he says.

I can't believe this.

"That's it? You're going to keep an eye on things? Justin is helping the Mayday Killer! He wasn't at school the day of the most recent murders. He was probably helping kill those people. And you aren't going to do anything?"

"Unlike what you see on TV, we can't go busting down doors whenever we feel like it. We'd have to get a warrant. And before you get any ideas, we'd have to have probable cause. No judge is going to grant us a warrant on the say-so of a teenage girl. There's no evidence of wrongdoing."

The sheriff swings his attention to Aunt Karen.

"You're sure you saw video footage of our house?" she asks, studying me as if she's waiting for me to flinch and take it all back.

I nod my head, gritting my teeth. I know what I saw.

Her expression softens. "I'll go over there."

"You can't! He's dangerous."

"I can take care of myself." With a nod to the sheriff, she marches out the door and across the street. No one answers when she knocks, but that doesn't stop her. She's inside for less than a minute.

"I didn't see anything suspicious in the house," she says as she comes back inside. "I'm sorry."

"There's no way." I move to pass her, but she catches my arm.

"I think it's best you stay here."

She wins our stare down.

I throw myself onto the couch and channel my anger and embarrassment into the carpet.

Sheriff Lamb sinks down on the ottoman near my knee and waits.

When I finally look up, his lips purse. Deep creases appear at the corners of his eyes when he puts on a placating smile. "Look. I can understand why you'd want some attention.

You're new in town, don't know anyone. Maybe you thought you'd cause a stir at school by fabricating a story about the janitor being in cahoots with the Mayday Killer—"

"I didn't *fabricate* anything. I saw it. Right over there." I jab a finger toward the house across the street.

Aunt Karen moves closer, puts an arm on my shoulder. Gives a gentle squeeze.

She had come running when I burst in the front door screaming. The carton of milk she'd brought home from the store hit the floor and burst, leaving an oozing white mess all over the linoleum. She'd stood rigid as I told her what I'd found across the street. The surveillance cameras that he'd aimed toward this place without her knowing. And then, as if I was a skittish wild animal, she'd put her arms around me. Patted my back in a gesture that was a little stiff, but not unwelcome.

It was the first time she'd ever hugged me.

Now, she stands near the window watching the empty house across the way.

"Maybe you should go upstairs," Aunt Karen says in a low voice.

"I didn't make this up. You have to believe me. I—"

"Megan." The steely look in her eyes stops me cold. With a jerky nod, I go up to my room and shut the door so they think I've closed myself inside. Then I creep toward the stairs, holding my breath.

"What are you going to do?" Sheriff Lamb asks.

"I don't know."

"He have access to the security system?"

A pause. "Yes."

I think I'm going to be sick. The woman I'm supposed to trust to care for me doesn't believe me. She doesn't even entertain the idea that her boyfriend could be a sicko. Instead, she's on the denial train all the way to the station.

Eyes pricking with unshed tears, I scurry into my room and lock the door. Make sure the window blinds are closed tight. Try to distract myself from the shame burning through me by doing some homework. My mind refuses to focus on anything but the wall of stalker photos. And the sheriff's disbelief in my story. My aunt's. It wasn't a story Before, and it's not now. I grit my teeth. The AC is blasting and for once my room is chilly. Or maybe the chill is coming from a different source. Maybe it's seeping out of my bones, which are frozen solid with fear.

I end up sitting with my back pressed against the headboard, staring at my closed door. Waiting for Aunt Karen to come in, to tell me that she's sorry. I was right. That she'll protect me from the very real monsters hiding under the bed.

Murmurs float up the stairs, but I can't make out what Aunt Karen and the sheriff are saying. Downstairs, a door opens and closes. A minute passes in silence. When I scrape together the courage to look out my window, it's in time to see the sheriff climbing into his car. He looks up at our house once more before setting his cowboy hat on the passenger seat and driving away.

Aunt Karen's distinctive knock comes on my door and I jolt upright.

"Come in." My questions start as soon as the door opens. "Are they going to look for him? Do you know where he might have gone?"

The older woman's lips thin in an expression I don't find comforting. She sits on the edge of my bed and pats the mattress beside her.

I thought this is what I wanted, but I don't like this. Not at all. Still, I scoot closer. My entire body feels weighed down with dread. My eyes find the chipped green polish on my toenails and stay there. "They're not looking for him," I mumble.

Aunt Karen folds her hands in front of her. "There wasn't anything incriminating there when I went inside. There's no proof that he's dangerous."

My eyes snap to hers. "How could that be? I was there. I saw it!"

She shakes her head, blinking her eyes closed before focusing on me. A pained expression crosses her face. "I didn't see any surveillance on the computer. And there was no wall of photos."

My hands tighten on the edges of the mattress. "That… how… It was all there. I swear. I saw it. You have to believe me, Aunt Karen."

My guardian studies my face for a moment, as if weighing what to say. Finally, she opens her mouth. "I don't believe Justin is dangerous."

I close my eyes, unwilling to show her my tears. "And the sheriff agrees."

"He doesn't know what to think."

"Maybe he has a tool shed or something? Maybe he hid everything in there?"

"Megan. The sheriff got there less than ten minutes after you called. Even if Justin had been home, he wouldn't have had time to get rid of anything. Much less hide it in a tool shed."

I shake my head. It's clear from Aunt Karen's tone that she's skeptical. It's implied. *What I'm saying is impossible.* Why would she believe me when I tell her that the guy she's been seeing is a murderer's apprentice, and he's after me? Of course she'd want to poke holes in my story.

But it's not a story. I *saw* it.

"The sheriff is going to have one of his deputies patrol our neighborhood tonight to keep an eye out for Justin. If they find him, they'll talk to him."

"A lot of good that'll do."

Aunt Karen's sigh is long and labored. She stands, pushing down her slacks as she straightens. "I told you I'd keep you safe, and I will. Try not to dwell on it, okay?"

Easy for her to say, I think once she's gone. Her disbelief hurts more than I can comprehend. Like the sheriff said, Aunt Karen must think I made it all up for attention. As if I'd want *more* attention. I've already had enough of that.

Day 8

The crowd of reporters hovers near the iron gate that bars entry into the cemetery. The security guard was decent enough to keep them out during the funeral. But even from that far away, their focus is like a laser pointed at my back. Burning my skin. Cutting through to where my heart feels completely numb, or perhaps frozen solid.

Gray clouds sit low, smothering the sky. At my feet, stiff green grass tries to swallow my only pair of high heels. Mom had put off buying them for me for so long, saying I'd have plenty of time to have them when I was a grownup. As if being seventeen isn't close enough. When she'd finally caved, she'd made a day of it. We'd gone shopping for new shoes and then out to my favorite ramen place for lunch. We'll never go shopping together like that again.

At my feet, the ground drops off into two long, six-feet-deep holes. The caskets have already been shut tight and lowered into the earth. I will never see my parents' faces again, except in photos and old videos.

I'm surrounded by friends and family in a sea of quiet, sniffling black. Aunts and uncles and cousins have come to show their love and support on this day. But even though I'm surrounded by people I've known all my life, I feel completely alone. None of them look directly at me, only out of the corner of their eyes. My pain is too raw, too ugly.

I don't blame any of them as they hover around me, afraid to speak. To extend the kindness of a hug or a tender touch. Their silent eyes graze the back of my neck, making me wish I could run. Hide. Never show my damaged face again.

The minister begins to speak, but all I can hear is the screaming in my head. A high, shrill keening that rends my soul. Echoes of that day. The day my parents were divided from me by death.

I pinch my eyes shut to ward off the gruesome images that threaten to invade. Wish someone would take my hand, squeeze my fingers to distract me from the hollow gulf that has opened in my chest, threatening to swallow me whole.

The scream replays in my mind.

I'll probably never stop hearing it.

That scream.

I'll never stop hearing it

because

it's

me.

Chapter 21

Day 130, Thursday

Tap. Tap. Tap.

My eyes pop open. There it is again—a high, tinkling rap. Not something I've heard in the old house before. Maybe it's water moving through the pipes, or a drip from the faucet in the hall bathroom. It stops, and I roll over to my other side, pulling up the sheet I kicked off in the middle of the night. My legs are cold.

The barest light is pouring over the horizon, lightening my room through the slats in the blinds.

Tap. Tap.

I sit up abruptly. That wasn't dripping water.

Tap.

"Megan?"

The name is barely a hint on the air, but I recognize that voice. I press my ear against the wall but hear nothing. I straighten the camisole I slept in and slide nimbly off my bed. My ears strain in the silence. The hallway is empty, all other doors still closed against the night.

The low voice comes again.

Spinning around, I tiptoe across my room and peek through the blinds. See a pair of black plastic frames over wide brown eyes.

I let out a surprised yelp and snap the blinds shut. I grab a t-shirt out of my dresser and yank it over my head before adding a pair of shorts. My cheeks burn in mortification at the thought of Noah seeing me in my cami and pale pink thong.

He's still crouching on top of the patio cover when I open the blinds and slide the window open.

"What are you doing out here?" I whisper.

Noah glances past me into the house. "Can I?"

"No! No," I say, quieter. Crawling out beside him, I sit carefully on the rough wooden shingles, hugging my knees to hide the fact that it's still a little cool out this early in the morning.

Some kind of bird is trilling in one of the eucalyptus trees, so I cock my head to listen. I don't think I've ever heard that particular whistle before. It sounds lonely, but beautiful.

"I went through all the photos for our collage, and I think we're pretty much set. We just need a few more black ones and we'll be done."

"Huh? Oh, that's great." I yawn, wishing I had a soda in my hand. I could use the shot of caffeine.

Noah gives me a sheepish smile. His black hair is fluffy from sleep and his anime shirt is wrinkled as if he slept in it.

"You gonna tell me why you're on my roof at four in the morning?"

The boy stretches out his legs, flexing his toes in the black athletic sandals. "Felt like a walk," he says finally. "I let my feet lead the way, and they brought me here. You okay?"

I clutch my elbows tighter as a shiver courses through me. Glance at Noah before my eyes snag on the house across the street now that it's abandoned. A deep sigh escapes. I hadn't realized how tight my chest was as it loosens. "I'm okay, I guess."

"I bet it was freaky, finding… all of that stuff in that guy's house."

There's no way I know to explain to Noah how scary it is knowing that my guardian's boyfriend is working with the murderer who destroyed my life. That he's the one who's been following me. Plotting to steal me away and finish me off. He was so close when he saw me with Esau. I bury my face in my knees. Why didn't he act then? What is he waiting for?

A black and white car pulls around the corner. The patrol they promised. Crap!

Shoving at Noah gets my message across. He scrambles in the window before helping me inside. We crouch below the sill so the deputy patrolling the block can't see us. I have no doubt that if we're spotted on the patio roof, word will get back to Aunt Karen.

Once the car passes, we both breathe a sigh of relief.

Noah sinks to the floor with his legs butterflied and his back against the wall. The look he gives me makes me go still. "You asked why I came over here. I heard about what happened, and I wanted to… I had to make sure you were okay. I need you to be okay. I couldn't sleep, thinking about how scared you might be. I… Can I, Megan?" Gently he reaches over and covers my hand with his own. His fingers are warm and rough from working odd jobs at the dairy.

I slip away and tuck both of my hands under my thighs. "Thank you. That's sweet, but I can't." There's a new awkwardness between us that I wish I could take away, but I won't. Not the way he wants.

Noah runs a hand over the shag carpet, disappointment a pall over his expression. "I'm glad you're okay." He mumbles something as he stands up that might be, "See you at school," before climbing out the window and shimmying over the edge. His eyes catch mine once more before he disappears below the roofline.

My heart is twisting in my chest as I climb back onto my bed, even though it's pointless. I won't sleep anymore tonight, not after Noah's near confession. I lean back against the headboard and pull up a streaming app.

My mind wanders, wishing I'd had the foresight to grab my recorder.

Marisa stands still on a milk crate so Viv can adjust the hem of her costume. "Can you take it up a half inch? It still feels a little long."

"It's not, trust me." Viv finishes pinning it and stands up, brushing off her knees below her long cutoffs.

They start bickering back and forth, which makes me smile. Marisa's always trying to micromanage her appearance in the play, saying her mom expects her to be perfect. Sometimes I get the feeling that deep down, she's only doing the drama club thing because her mom wants her to. My instincts are telling me that Marisa isn't nearly as vain as she comes off.

Viv, who is probably the second most chill person I know next to Fiona, lets Marisa's nagging roll right off her back. I've only ever seen Viv wound up when it comes to fried junk food. Other than that, she's unflappable. The other day we picked up Erin on the way to the diner, and not even being stared at by a hundred girls in Catholic school uniforms could faze her.

Fiona appears at my elbow. "We're all set upstairs."

"Great!" I say, too cheerfully. Esau's letting me play with some of the lighting cues today, and I'm determined to prove to him that my lighting scheme is the way to go with this play. Once he sees it all coming together—the lights, costuming, and the blocking he's been drilling into the actor's heads for weeks—I'm positive he'll come to see things my way.

"Somebody's giddy," Fiona says, nudging me with her elbow. She grins. "Something you want to tell us? Maybe why Esau is suddenly letting you change some of the lights?"

Marisa and Viv turn curious eyes toward me. Marisa points at Esau, who's pacing around the stage making sure the set is configured to his exact specifications, and winks.

"Nope." I can't stop my smile.

"Uh huh. Sure." Fiona waves a finger. "You look about how Dariel and I did when we discovered the sound booth is basically abandoned after our club meetings end. Don't think you're fooling anyone." She puckers her lips in a kissy face that makes all four of us laugh.

"You two were the worst," Viv tosses out, and Fiona gives her a playful shove.

"Let's get started, everyone," Esau yells, making Marisa jump and scurry to her mark for the first scene. "I want to get through all of act one today."

I move toward the booth with Fiona.

"Megan, wanna sit?" Esau pats the chair beside him.

I swear everyone in the room goes silent as they swivel around to look at me. I fight the flush that threatens to rush up my neck and avoid their eyes.

Fiona gives me a meaningful look, a satisfied smile on her lips.

Ignoring this, I pick my way over the cables to sit down beside Esau.

There's a tiny panda figurine the size of a penny waiting on the chair. It's just about the cutest tiny panda I've ever seen, but when I look up at Esau, he's looking studiously away. His mouth is pulled up the barest amount.

Biting back a smile, I tuck the offering in my pocket for safekeeping.

Once I'm settled he angles his body toward mine.

"I figured you'd want to see how it all looks from the audience. It's a much better view than the sound booth." Esau slides his eyes to mine. For once, the familiar intensity doesn't make me bristle. Instead, it reminds me of that night in the orchard. Not for the last time, I wonder if he would have kissed me if it weren't for Justin driving by in his car, keeping tabs on me for his black-hearted mentor.

"Where'd you go just now?" Esau asks, his head inclined toward mine. Is it just me, or is his chair closer than it was a second ago?

I blink, noticing the actors are all in place, waiting for Esau to signal them to begin. Marisa is watching us out of the corner of her eye. A dull ache starts in my chest. Please let her remember all of her lines today. "Nowhere. Sorry. Let's see how this thing looks with the new lights."

"Let's get through it, then we can go back to how it's supposed to be."

"I'm pretty sure once you see it you'll admit I was right."

"Never." My stomach flip-flops at the crooked grin Esau shoots my way.

"Never say never," I retort. "Admitting when you were wrong builds character."

Esau's deep chuckle as he pushes his French braids behind his shoulders is like a delicious licorice vine. One isn't nearly enough.

At one point during the run through, Esau slings his arm over the back of my chair, and his fingers brush my bare shoulder. My skin tingles at his touch, making me sit up straight.

Marisa's attention catches on my face and she fumbles a line before continuing red-faced.

I've been dreading it, but I'm going to have to talk to her about her focus on stage. I have no idea what I'm going to say. *Esau isn't that scary. He won't hurt you. You can't let his brooding mess with your focus when you're performing. Your entire cast is counting on you, and you're letting them down.* I mentally touch each reason and cast it aside. I haven't found the right words yet, but she's my friend and she deserves my honesty. All of it I can give her.

"Okay, you might have been right about the lighting cues," Esau says in my ear after the act is over. "It looked really good."

The warmth of his breath makes me shiver. "Care to say that again?"

"Not a chance." Standing, he offers me his hand with the rubber band. "Let's talk it over with Fiona and Dariel. See how they feel about changing it up permanently."

"Wait, you're actually going to ask someone else's opinion? Are you ill?" I press the inside of my wrist to his forehead, suddenly aware of how close it brings my body to his. Quickly, I pull back, but not before Esau hits me with a devilish grin.

"If I was sick, would you take care of me?"

"Not on your life. You'd probably want to be waited on hand and foot." I mime ringing a tiny bell with one hand.

He crosses his arms, arching one of his thick eyebrows. "Too bad. You'd be a cute nurse." Leaning in, his mouth stops inches from mine. "I'd like to see you again sometime. You in?"

I nod quickly, too ruffled to speak.

Of course Fiona is right behind him and hears the whole thing. I have never seen such a clear "Told you so" look in my life. She's never going to let me hear the end of it. And I haven't even told her about sneaking out to see him the other night. Or our almost kiss.

There's a deputy's vehicle sitting under one of the lights in the parking lot when we tromp outside after rehearsal. It's empty.

I scan around but don't see them. Aunt Karen's car is parked at the curb, and I climb inside. We exchange mechanical pleasantries as she pulls out of the lot. I'm disappointed when our conversation dies. There's no news of Justin. My guardian would have told me if there was, because she knows how scared I am.

My focus is on the black and white parked on the street. I thought the increased law enforcement presence would make me feel better, more protected, but it doesn't. Instead, seeing the deputies and their cars twice today is only freaking me out. Every time I see them I'm reminded of the fact that unlike all of my classmates, I'm not just another teenager trying to get through high school. I have to look over my shoulder when I walk. The Mayday Killer is still out there somewhere, fixated on me. Waiting to strike.

Chapter 22

Day 133, Sunday

Murky olive-brown water flows along the cement irrigation ditch, occasionally interrupted by large pipes that breach the walls and siphon water off to flood a field here or there. A welcome break in the heat wave has the people working in the fields moving just a little faster. A woman in a wide-brimmed hat waves at Noah and me from the middle of a pumpkin field.

Noah gives a friendly wave back. Mine is less steady because I'm too busy trying not to trip over the uneven, dry-cracked ground under our feet.

"Where are you taking me?" I ask. "If you're looking for a place to murder me, I'll point out that there are several witnesses right now."

A surprised laugh breaks from Noah as he turns to grin at me. "If I was trying to murder you, I wouldn't do it here, silly. I'd do it at the dairy. The cows would keep quiet. They like me."

I give a quiet, tentative laugh. "I'll have to get them on my side, then."

"Good luck with that. It would be easier getting me on your side."

There's something warm in his tone that draws my gaze to

his. "Yeah? How do I do that?"

Noah smiles at his dingy shoes. "You're off to a good start."

A pleased flush threatens to stain my already warm skin, but I fight it. I can't go there. Not with Noah. It wouldn't be fair.

Better to focus on the well he mentioned. When I look ahead, there's a low stone ring covered by a weathered sheet of plywood. It doesn't look at all like I'd pictured. "That's a well?"

"Sure is. I dropped a brand new pocket knife down there one time."

"You did?"

"Yep, and I was too embarrassed to ask my dad to replace it. Never got a new one. Want to see?" Noah shakes his head in amusement before sliding the plywood off the top of the cistern and propping it against the well's cinder block masonry. A metal grate covers the opening, and there's water inside, about twenty feet down. Noah's and my silhouettes paint the still water in the late afternoon light.

"Come on, let's keep going."

After a few more minutes Noah stops, gesturing at a spot where the irrigation ditch widens before narrowing toward an underground pipe. The water is lower here, and bugs make faint ripples over the surface of the water.

"No way, it's still here!" In an effortless leap, Noah flies across the ditch and lands in a poof of dust on the other side. Bending down, he picks up a rusty bucket with orange twine dangling from the bent handle.

"A bucket?" I ask.

"We used to use this to catch crawdads. My older brother and me," he clarifies when he sees the question on my face.

"Crawdads?"

"Yeah. Look. See?" He points toward the shallow water, and I follow his direction. Sure enough, when I look closer, I can see what look like tiny lobsters along the bottom of the ditch. They're difficult to see because of how their shells resemble the gray-brown concrete around them.

"So that's what the net is for," I say, holding up the pool skimmer Noah asked me to carry. His hands are full with the small cooler and a still-watertight bucket.

Noah grins. "Anza and Mattie have never had crawdads, and I figured it was time to rectify that situation. Plus, you like shellfish, don't you?"

I bite my lip, not sure how to respond. I'm supposed to be a vegetarian, so I was hoping he'd missed that time I mentioned how I wished it was soft-shell crab the day the cafeteria was serving tuna sandwiches.

"Um, I'm not really eating meat right now." I shrug lamely.

"More for me. Ready to learn how to catch them?"

"We're not using the bucket and string method?" Kate, Nate, and the rest of us used the bucket method to try to catch minnows at camp that summer. We never caught a single one, but when we came back to our cabins barefoot and soaking wet, I'd never felt more alive. Now those kids' parents are dead.

I climb out of the sadness threatening to drag me down, because if I let it, he wins. Pasting on an expression of interest, I focus on the boy squatting in the dirt beside me.

Noah laughs, his smile widening. "We'd be here all day. Now that you mention it…" He trails off, his eyes catching mine.

I clear my throat. "Better not. Aunt Karen wants me home by sunset."

"Right. Okay." He runs a hand through his hair, and I try

to ignore the disappointment that flashes over his expression. "Here's a foolproof way to catch crawdads. Just don't tell my mom I'm using her drumsticks, okay?"

A few minutes later, after he's shown me how to catch the crustaceans using the pool net, a raw chicken leg, and some string, he brings up a topic I'm sure everyone at school wonders about but hasn't dared to ask.

"Why did you move in with your aunt anyway? Where are your parents?" He wets his lips before looking up from the bucket of crawdads to meet my eyes.

A pit forms in my stomach. I don't want to talk about this. Don't want to have to lie to him.

"It's okay. We don't have to talk about it. Forget I asked."

I shake my head. Maybe talking, confiding in someone will help. Aunt Karen offered to send me to a therapist, but I refused. It had seemed stupid at the time, because talking about my parents wouldn't bring them back. But maybe that wasn't the point.

"They were killed," I whisper, my fingers tightening on the string as Noah ties another chicken leg to its far end. "It was… sudden."

"Oh geez. I'm so sorry, Megan. I shouldn't have asked. I just wondered—"

"No, it's okay. I don't mind." Somehow, it's the truth. Confiding in Noah about my parents being gone has lightened the constant weight on my chest the tiniest amount. He's the first person I've said these words to since it happened. Not even Aunt Karen has asked me about it, not really, since she already knew what had happened when I came to live here. I take in a breath. I can't tell Noah everything, but I can give him this. Especially after he told me about his older brother.

"Was it the car accident?" He points vaguely at the scar on

my cheek before yanking his hand back through his hair.

My throat tightens. Unable to speak the words, I nod.

We fall quiet. I'm not sure where to go from here, so I watch the chicken leg as it bobs in the water. Slowly, crawdads approach it, taking timid nibbles before latching on.

"I was nine when my brother died," Noah whispers.

I look at him, surprise bright in my eyes.

"We'd run out of popsicles, and I wanted one. Mom and Dad couldn't take me; they were still at work, but Simeon, he agreed to go down to the gas station and pick one up for me. He didn't come back."

I sit in stunned silence, trying to put together words and force them past my lips.

"What… what…?"

He trails a finger through the dirt at our feet. "Someone robbed the gas station. They killed the cashier, and Simeon. All for some measly cash. If I hadn't begged for a popsicle..."

Horror fills me at this. My heart breaks for Noah as I realize that he blames himself for his brother's death. "That wasn't your fault. You can't blame yourself for that. You were just a kid with a popsicle craving. You weren't the one with the, the gun." I swallow. His brother's death wasn't his fault. Not like me.

Because my parents' death? That's 100 percent my fault.

"It was a knife." The last word is hesitant, as if it's still difficult for him to say all these years later. Maybe it never gets easier at all.

I focus on the crawdads in the water, hoping to distract myself. Keep the threatening tears at bay. I do not want to cry out on a levy next to a bucket full of miniature lobsters. Once there are half a dozen clinging to the bait with their tiny pinchers, I glance at Noah. "Ready?"

He nods, holding the pool net low over the water.

I withdraw the chicken leg with a quick jerk, and he scoops up the crawdads before they realize they've been pulled out of the water. Dumping them in the bucket, he counts with one finger. Then he sets the net down and meets my eyes.

Somehow, despite the heartache Noah has carried since his brother's death, he hasn't let it stifle him. Noah is passionate about his family, school, his favorite anime. Noah is still among the living. He smiles easily, for goodness' sake. Not like he has to dredge it up from the bowels of his sadness.

"That's how I got into true crime. I thought I could solve it." He goes quiet. He never managed it. They never found his brother's killer. Just like they can't find the man who slaughtered my parents.

Even so, Noah hasn't let his tragedy stop him from growing, from reaching.

I can't let it stop me either.

"Hey Noah?" I ask, knowing that once I utter these words, I can't go back. I'm going to find proof that Justin is helping the Mayday Killer. No matter what Aunt Karen thinks. This is so much bigger than her now.

"Yeah?"

"Let's solve it together."

Chapter 23

Day 136, Wednesday

After my parents were murdered, I never thought I'd be in the right headspace to try growing orchids again. I stalled, all growth stunted by the grisly images that filter through my mind every other second of every day. But as day after day passes, I think about the blood, the screaming, less. Not never, just less. The worst part is no longer the mental picture of my parents' bodies sprawled on the floor in pools of their own blood, but the guilt. The knowledge that I could have stopped it.

Or that my body should have been crumpled and broken on the ground beside them.

That buzzing in my fingers has returned. The desire to touch something green and watch it grow under my tender, careful care. I'm blaming it on Noah's optimism and strolling between field after field of growing pumpkins on Sunday. Amid all those signs of life, how can I not want to be a part of it?

Aunt Karen said there were grow lights in the garage.

My head cocks to the side as I unlock the door leading into the unfinished room, wondering what other junk the previous occupants abandoned.

Shelving lines three of the walls, boxes in tall, rickety stacks. Their labels are almost indecipherable. It doesn't matter, though. On the bottom shelf in the corner are the grow lights. They're huge, long and industrial. Whoever was using these was serious about their weed. I sniff, trying to detect the smell of pot, but all I get is must. Damp cardboard. It's been so long all traces are gone.

I draw up short. After a time, are all traces of my parents going to disappear from my life? Already my memories of them are growing softer, their edges blurry. I press my eyes closed, trying to picture them. I let out a relieved breath when they materialize in my mind, reading companionably on the couch after I'd headed to my room for the night.

Running my fingers along one of the long industrial lights, I shake my head. These fixtures are way too big to use in my bedroom. Maybe Aunt Karen will let me grow a couple of plants in the east-facing window in the kitchen instead. Small ones with bright blooms.

In the house a door shuts, making me jolt against the nearest shelving unit. On the bottom shelf, a large manila envelope slides out of a half-closed box and onto the concrete floor at my feet. Bending down, I pick it up. Peek inside.

My eyes expand as my heart thuds against my ribs. What the hell? Trembling fingers make the image shake even as I try to absorb what I find. It's a photograph of me talking to Esau, sitting on his truck's tailgate. The same photo that was on Justin's murder board in his house.

Tremors cut through me as I dump out the items in the envelope. A gasp tears from my mouth when I see the contents—photos, articles, maps. All of the bits and pieces from Justin's stalker board are here, stuffed into a box in Aunt Karen's garage.

I can't believe what I'm seeing. With shaking hands, I take out my phone and snap photos for evidence. That way I'll have it on me if I need it.

When I'm done, I shove them all back into the envelope. How did this junk get in here? How did Justin sneak it past the sheriff's department and into this house?

My eyes land on the windows along the outer wall of the space. They're not too small for someone to climb through. Not barred. I creep closer to get a better look and see one of the windows is unlocked. A broken spider web hangs in one corner as if recently disturbed.

Justin has been in this room, hiding the evidence of his creepy obsession with me. He hid his scrapbook supplies in the last place any of us would look. Worse, the only barrier between him and the rest of the old house was the locked garage door.

I'm turning to flee when someone runs past the window, making me twist around to face it. I catch a glimpse of a black shirt and dark jeans before whoever it is vanishes beyond the window.

Heart and feet pounding, I fling open the door into the house and make for the front window. Scan the yard. The street. The abandoned house across the road.

There's no one there.

A vehicle turns the corner out of sight before I can get a good look at it. Was that him, back to get his things? Or worse?

I clutch at my chest, trying to get my breathing under control enough to call Aunt Karen and tell her what I found. That the evidence the authorities need to level charges at Justin is sitting in the middle of the spotless garage floor. This time I'll make them listen.

I sit on the living room sofa, staring in shock as a deputy takes custody of the envelope of horrors. My skin crawls as if covered in an army of tiny ants. What if Justin came by to visit Aunt Karen and snooped around the house? Looked in my room? Went through my stuff?

Bile rises in my throat. No, he can't have. I would have noticed if someone had riffled through the few things I own. Wouldn't I?

Once the deputy with the envelope is outside, the other approaches Aunt Karen. She rushed home in a panic when I called her at the grocery store to tell her what I'd found. She'd apologized but when I pressed, she wouldn't say what for.

It wasn't encouraging.

"Ma'am," the deputy says, glancing at me.

"Yes?" Aunt Karen asks.

"We'll catalogue everything we found, but it looks like everything is at least a few days old. Doesn't look like he's added much to his collection." She goes on, talking about increasing patrols and something about Aunt Karen's home security system, but it all turns like buzzing between my ears. The woman charged with my care is shielding someone dangerous. If push comes to shove, I can't trust her.

My stomach jerks and I make for the bathroom. Dry heaves wrack my frame.

Once I'm done, I stumble out of the bathroom toward the stairs.

Aunt Karen stands, her face lined with concern. "Megan? Are you okay?"

"Am I okay?" All of the panic and fear and anger flashes to the surface until I can't see straight.

"Don't take that tone with me." Her hands land on her hips. The perfect picture of authority. As if.

"What tone am I supposed to take? You're dating the guy who is helping a serial killer keep tabs on me. You didn't even tell me about him in the first place."

"Who I see in my personal time is none of your business."

"It is if he's a murderer's assistant."

Aunt Karen's eyes narrow as she points a finger at the empty house across the street. "Justin isn't helping anyone commit murder."

"Then why all of the photos? He's following me everywhere, day and night. Night!"

Her eyes squeeze shut, and she covers her face with one hand. "He's an amateur photographer. Happy now?"

"No!" My heart and head are pounding. "Amateur photographer? Give me a break. He's nothing more than a sleazebag, but for some reason you refuse to hear or believe me."

Aunt Karen rears back as if she's going to start shouting, hands anchoring at her hips, but barely reigns herself in. "Maybe we should table this. Discuss it when we've had the chance to cool off."

It's a dismissal if I've ever heard one. Shaking my head, I drag myself up to the second floor. Standing in the doorway to my room, I work up the courage to step inside. I look at everything as if I'll be able to see proof of Justin's presence if he did come in here. Everything looks the same. I think.

Hang on. Did I leave my headphones sprawled across the desk when I left this morning? I didn't think so, but…

The old house groans. I shut my door against it. Outside the window, a large branch from the oak tree comes right up to the roof. It's the same tree Noah used to climb onto the patio roof the other night. I freeze. If Noah could climb the tree to reach the second-floor windows, someone else could.

Panic makes my fingers tremble as I push at the stubborn old window lock and pull the shades down to ward off any evil.

To prevent anyone from seeing inside. Toeing off my shoes, I climb under the covers and throw them over my head, tucking the quilt around me like a cocoon. When I was a child, I believed that if I was completely hidden from view, I was safe. The monsters that materialized in the darkness couldn't get me. If only that were true.

My fingers run along my cheek as the tears start to come.

I'm not safe, even here.

It's happening again. Just like last time.

No, not like last time. This time is different: my parents aren't here to assuage my fears when I tell them I think I'm being followed. They aren't able to distract me when I tell them I've seen the same older, bearded man every time I've left the house. This time there is no one to tell me it's all in my imagination, even though it wasn't.

This time, I know there's someone following me. Watching me. Biding his time.

The question is, how much more will he take?

I have so

little

left

to

give.

Day 1

It's all in my head.

The rusted brown car with the rock-and-roll sticker in the back window had been parked in the street outside the school for the past few days. But it didn't mean anything.

Taryn rolls her eyes when I mention it. "Probably someone's parents picking them up," she says,

"But that doesn't explain seeing it everywhere."

"It's probably not even the same car. You must be imagining it."

Biting my lip, I watch my classic black Converse eat up the pavement. Flip my backpack around to my front to ease the soreness running along my spine. Mom said that even though our city was mashed together with a bunch of others, it's still small. It's not unheard of to run into the same person in different places.

But when I saw that car outside the school? It was hard to take Mom's assurance seriously.

"You look like such a dork when you do that. " Taryn flips her blond curls back over her shoulders, hiking her own bag up with both hands. "Did you have to stay late to talk to your teacher? Couldn't you have done it tomorrow during lunch?"

"The camera launches tonight. I had to know if she thought it was worth the hype first. I don't want to spend all of my babysitting money on a camera that I won't use."

"Why's it better than the one you use, again?"

I've answered this question a hundred times. I've been gushing about this new camera for months since it was announced. And by taking all of the babysitting gigs I could get, I have just enough money saved up to buy one.

We round the corner to our street. Sweat drips down my back. Despite the cloud cover, it's humid today, making our walk home seem longer than it is. Everyone else peeled off a couple of streets ago to their own homes, leaving Taryn and me alone for the final few minutes.

Our street is quiet. Probably because all of the adults have day jobs to stay on top of the bills and all of the latchkey kids plunk down in front of their screens as soon as they get home. I do it too.

"Hey, look." Snagging my arm with one hand, Taryn points with her other.

I stiffen. Fear bunches on my shoulder like a bird of prey about to dig in its claws.

The rusted brown car with the rock-and-roll sticker is parked under an overhanging tree right across the street from my house.

"It's real," Taryn whispers, making my heart pick up the pace.

She thought I was imagining it this whole time?

"Weird." Dropping my arm, she walks ahead.

I can't move. It's as if my brain is no longer able to send signals to my legs. They won't obey my commands.

"Come on," Taryn says, taking my hand and dragging me forward. "I bet your mom *made cookies. You know how she is on cloudy days."*

"How about your dad*? Last time he ate them all before I got even one."*

"And that's my fault how?"

Her teasing eases me into a slow walk, but I'm thankful when we cross the street away from the strange car.

Taryn stops too quickly on the sidewalk and I run into her, almost toppling us both over.

"What're you doing?" I grumble.

"Look." Her tan face has blanched white.

Following her gaze, my eyes lock on my front door. It's standing open.

"Wait!" Taryn yells as I float closer to the open portal. "Shouldn't we call the police? Have them check it out first?"

I'm no-longer listening. The car was an omen. I know it now. It wasn't in my head. It was a sign that something was coming. Dread unfurls in my gut. Something bad.

"I'm coming too," Taryn whispers, somewhere behind me.

I pause on the front step. Somehow I know instinctually that once I set foot inside, my life will be irreparably changed.

An alarming stench hits me as I step inside, making me gasp.

Taryn wrinkles her nose. "Oh, that's bad," she murmurs, wandering toward the bedrooms.

My eyes land on one of Mom's house shoes. It's sitting abandoned in the middle of the living room. It's not like her to leave it there. Mom's latest crochet project is lying upended on the couch. The yarn ball has rolled across the floor to rest at the foot of the television stand. A cup of coffee lies spilled on the rug.

"We should go back outside. Call 911." Taryn pulls at my arm.

I ignore her. Inching further into the house, I move toward the kitchen, where the smell of freshly baked snickerdoodles mixes with something sharper and rust-tinged. A smell I don't recognize.

There's a low, moaning gurgle. I clutch at my chest like I've been struck.

"T-Taryn…"

There's a puddle of crimson ebbing across the hardwood floor. A red handprint is smeared along the beige wall.

It points toward the kitchen.

Chapter 24

Day 137, Thursday

The whir of Viv's sewing machine is a settling drone in my ears as I sit on a black box, going through Act 3 with Marisa. Above our heads, Fiona and Dariel have the stage lights cued to my lighting design. It looks fantastic. Even Esau grudgingly admitted it during rehearsal last week.

I grin as I watch Marisa prepare to go through the scene again.

She's pacing back and forth in the middle of the stage, treading over the place where Esau placed her blocking tape, shaking out her hands and stretching her jaw muscles. For some reason she keeps flubbing the same line. She even asked Esau if she could change it, but our particular director declined. "It's written that way for a reason," he'd said.

I don't disagree, but I feel bad for Marisa. Her castmates are starting to tire of her mistakes. Even I have to admit, deep down where I hope she can't see, that she should have all of her lines memorized by now. But for some reason she seems rattled during rehearsals. Valley High's leading lady is falling apart before our eyes.

We begin, and she misses the line yet again.

In a low tone I hope is covered by the holler of one of the stage crew up to the booth, I feed it to her.

"I know!" Marisa snaps. "I'm sorry. You're just trying to help."

"You're supposed to have everything memorized now, Marisa."

I whirl at Esau's voice. He's standing right behind me, arms crossed, dark eyes on my friend. How long has he been standing there?

"I know," Marisa says again, cowed. Her long hair falls forward over her shoulders, partially shielding the embarrassment scrawled across her face. "I'm almost there."

"Megan has everyone's lines memorized, and she's not even in the play." Esau's large, brown hand creates a gentle cup over my shoulder. I'm surprised and pleased by the touch, but in this moment it feels like a betrayal of Marisa to side with him. I shrug the hand away, twisting in my seat to look up into his face.

"Why don't I take her for a walk around campus? We'll wind down a little. Go over lines. We won't be gone long."

"That sounds amazing." Marisa clasps her hands to her chest. "Can we go?" She bats her eyes at Esau.

I hide a smile behind my hand at her exaggerated pleading.

Esau grunts and walks away, shaking his head.

"I'll take that as a yes," I say at the same time Marisa says, "Yes! Let's go."

She grabs my hand and pulls me out of the theater building. Outside, the air is beginning to cool. The valley's summer heat is giving way to the crisp of autumn. The days of skinny jeans and cute jackets are coming and I am so ready.

Away from the high pressure of the theater, Marisa relaxes. We cross the dry grass to sit under a sapling that tries valiantly to provide enough shade for the two of us. At my prompting, Marisa begins her lines from the top, and I play the other roles in the scene. We go through the entire thing a few times until she gets it, smiling once we've finished.

"Finally," she says, raising her hands in victory. "I didn't think I'd ever get through this."

"You nailed it just now."

Marisa picks up a fallen leaf between two fingers and twirls it. "You don't have to say that. I know I'm holding everyone back."

"Nobody thinks that," I say too quickly. The grass pokes at my bare calves, making them start to itch. I shift to sit with my knees up and arms slung around my shins.

"You're sweet. Maybe you should take my role, since it all comes so easily to you." Her tone belies her words, as if she doesn't really want me to replace her. She wants a little carefully placed flattery.

The door to the theater swings open and Esau peers out. When he sees us, he meets my eyes. I wave him off and he goes back inside.

Marisa stares after him.

"Hey, don't worry about him. You did beautifully just now. Besides, it doesn't all come easy for me either. I've just done the play before."

"Still." She tosses the leaf, and it floats away on a breeze.

My hackles rise at the hint of frustration in her voice. "If this is about Esau, I—"

"Don't. This isn't about him."

"It's just that, I thought you might like him and I didn't expect—"

"I told you it's not about Esau. I don't like him like that." Marisa jumps up and brushes the bits of leaves and grass from the skirt of her costume.

"You don't? But Marisa, I've seen the way you look at

him." I shove off the ground too.

She shakes her head. "You don't know what you're talking about."

We do another lap around the gym, her staring at the grass and me at the empty path ahead. If she doesn't have a crush on him, then why is she so weird around him?

Finally, Marisa sighs. "I'm sorry. This isn't your fault. I get carried away sometimes. The pressure of having such a big part and all."

"Sure." I remember what that was like. Almost miss it a little. "So you aren't madly in love with our director?"

Marisa laughs outright. "Don't be ridiculous. It's just that, he picked me for this role, and I don't want to disappoint him. You know?"

"Ah. Well, you're doing great. By the time opening night comes, you'll have it down perfectly. The audience will thrill at your brilliance."

"Liar." We both laugh at my hyperbole.

"You think I'd lie about something as serious as the theater?" I throw my forearm up to my forehead, exaggerating the gesture Viv makes when she's pretending to be a diva fashion designer behind her sewing machine.

Marisa sighs as her giggles subside. "It feels so good to be out of that black box. I almost wish… never mind."

"What? You can tell me."

"It's nothing. Really."

My lips purse. I've only known Marisa for a few weeks, so I shouldn't be surprised that she's not ready to spill her guts to me, but it still sends a pang of dismay through my core. "We should probably get back before Esau sends out the dogs."

Marisa shoots a sly smile my way. "He'd send them out for me definitely, but something tells me he'd let you off easier.

What's going on there?"

I swallow, not sure what to say.

"I don't know."

"Oh so something *is* going on between you two. Fiona was so right! Tell me. Have you guys kissed yet?" She waggles her eyebrows.

"Uh… Well…"

"How was it?"

"I think we should go back to running lines."

Marisa curtseys. "Whatever you say."

We're almost back to the theater when I hear it: the rumble of a trash can being emptied. It could be Justin. As far as I know he still works at the school since Sheriff Lamb couldn't find any hint of wrongdoing, but I have to be sure. Maybe sometime I can sneak over to his house to snoop around while he's not home.

Marisa calls after me as I edge around the big square building until I spot it: the janitor's cart parked on the walkway outside of one of the classrooms. I draw in a breath. Tiptoe closer. The room door is propped open by a beat-up wood block. A sharp scent hits my nose, making my throat close. A tall, overweight man bends over behind the teacher's desk and stands with a small wastebasket in hand. His round face and scraggly beard make my heart stop.

"N-no," I stammer. "You can't be—" Blinking rapidly, I will my eyes to see someone different. He can't be here. He *can't* be. A wicked cackle cuts through the air, making me stumble back against the door. My eyes clamp shut and my hands cover my ears.

It's not real. He's not here on campus.

My heart is pulverizing my ribcage, making it hard to breathe.

"Help you with something?" the janitor asks.

When I peel my eyes open, an older Latino man with tan skin and no beard is watching me, holding the newly emptied garbage can in one hand.

Shaking my head, I run headlong into Marisa.

"Whoa. Are you okay?" she asks, her hands steadying me. "You look like you've seen a ghost."

"More like a demon." I wish I could take the words back as soon as they're out.

Marisa's eyebrows rise as she looks over my shoulder. "Janitor Abe? He's been here for ages. Let's get back inside before Esau really does sic someone on us. Fiona, probably. And she's scary when she gets serious."

"No kidding." I look back over my shoulder once, but the janitor has moved off down the hallway. Out of the corner of my eye, I see a car in the parking lot. The blue one. The fluffy dice are visible even from here. I'm so tired of running away.

"Hang on a sec." I'm marching toward the parking lot before Marisa can get a word in edgewise.

It's time to do something. Even check out a car whose owner I'm pretty sure is tied to a serial killer.

The parking lot is practically empty aside from the theater kids' cars. There's no one around. The blue car is unoccupied. With a frustrated yank, I check each of the doors. The driver door is unlocked.

"What are you doing?" Marisa asks, standing a few feet away, arms snug across her stomach.

"Let me know if anyone comes, okay?"

"Okay…" Marisa glances uneasily over her shoulder.

The stench of sweat and greasy fast food mingling assaults my nose as I slide into the car. Grimacing, I look in the door compartment and the center console. There's not much there but a few stray coins and a gas receipt. The floor on the passenger side is equally unhelpful. I hesitate when I get to the glove compartment. It's silly. Nothing's going to jump out at me.

I lick my lips. I make the magic happen. And it's about time for some.

Pushing the latch, I open the compartment.

It's completely, totally, frustratingly empty. No car registration or insurance papers to tell me who owns this heap.

Wait.

A corner of paper sticks out from under the floor mat below the glove box. Leaning down, I retrieve it. My heart thumps when I recognize what I'm looking at. A photo. A tree with leaves dappled by sunlight. A figure haloed by the sun leaning into the frame.

How did he get this?

Chapter 25

Day 140, Sunday

Noah groans in frustration. "There has to be something here that we're missing." He shuffles through the stack of papers he's printed about the Mayday Killer, reading bits here and there. One slides off the edge of the table and floats to the grubby library carpet. Using the toe of my shoe, I slide it toward myself and pick it up.

At the information desk, the librarian glances our way. She seems really nice, but I'm guessing that, in the tradition of all librarians, she'll shush Noah if he gets any louder.

"Did you find any connection between the victims?" he asks, looking at me over the frames of his glasses, which have fallen down his nose.

A single, solitary name printed on a piece of paper.

My lips purse. I've been prohibited from telling anyone that I already know what links each of the Mayday Killer's victims, even though the police haven't released that information. It was one of the conditions Aunt Karen had for letting me move in with her. I can't tell Noah about the survivor whose name I removed from the list he found on one of the true crime forums. I don't have the heart to tell him about my sneaking suspicion that there's nothing we can do that the police haven't thought of already. And they haven't caught the killer yet, despite the clear and bloody path he's cut through the state. If the professionals are having trouble nailing him down, how will two teenagers manage it?

My stomach rolls as I go over the talk Aunt Karen had with me this morning. When I came downstairs for breakfast, she was sitting at the dining table with her hands wrapped around her coffee thermos and her handgun resting on the table. "From here on out, you're not to go anywhere without telling me exactly where you'll be. No sneaking out under any circumstances. Understand?"

My blood had run cold at the severity of her tone. "Did something happen?"

"I'd tell you not to check the news, but isn't telling a teenager not to do something the equivalent of daring them to do it?"

"Not always," I murmured as I navigated to the news app on my phone. Dreading what I would find. There it was. The morning's top headline: *Mayday Killer Strikes Again; Two More Dead.*

My stomach had clenched as I read the article. It was short, without much information. A line at the bottom promised updates as soon as the police released more information. My eyes had lingered on the name of the city where the crime had occurred. It looked familiar somehow. Like I'd been there before.

I popped out of my chair, hoping the movement would stir a buried memory.

"The Mirror Museum. Have you ever been there?" My guardian had asked before bringing her coffee mug to her lips.

The memory had hit me so hard my knees had buckled, and I'd had to clutch at the table's edge to keep from stumbling. My parents had taken me to the Mirror Museum a couple of summers ago. There were rooms filled with mirrors in all shapes and sizes. One room had the glass panes suspended from clear wires that made them appear to be floating in empty air. Another was filled with cracked and broken mirrors that distorted your reflection in strange ways. My favorite had been the small, octagonal mirror room that, when I stepped inside, made hundreds of copies of me appear, grinning from ear to ear and making silly faces. In that moment, I had felt infinite. Powerful. Not insignificant and diminished like I usually did.

My question wasn't much more than a whispered plea. "The Chans?" The family who ran the museum.

Aunt Karen's eyes didn't leave mine as she nods.

This time I did stumble, falling back into the chair I'd just vacated.

My guardian had reached over and put a tentative hand on my shoulder. "If there's anything you can remember that might be useful, just let me know."

I'd nodded, unable to speak.

Another family had been shattered, and I couldn't help feeling that it was my fault, although I couldn't work out how. Why?

I swallow, bringing my focus back to the sheets of papers spread out over the library table. There has to be something here I can use. Something I can give to the police they've not already thought of and discarded as a dead end.

"I'm hungry. Want something from the vending machines?" Noah pushes to a stand and settles his gaze on me.

My stomach feels like an empty pit because I haven't eaten anything since Aunt Karen's news delivered over breakfast. I'm too worried the knot of nerves at the base of my spine will push any food right back up. By now I'm starving. "Yeah, okay."

Noah smiles and heads toward the front of the library where there's a water fountain and a vending machine.

When he's gone, I look down at the paper in my hands. It's a transcript of the messages the Mayday Killer has left behind at each of his crime scenes. His calling card. His crimes may be unique in their motivation, but his messages aren't. They're all bastardizations of famous poems. I read them slowly, trying to place each one. I guess I should have paid more attention in English class.

Wait.

All of these quotes are familiar.

Opening my social media app, I scroll through until I find one of the girls I follow—CuteAshleeXOXO. All of her posts are blurry nature images with famous quotes superimposed over top. I like them, usually. They're… uplifting. But right now I can't help but notice that the quotes are word for word the same as the ones the Mayday Killer has used. I start typing them into the search engine to find the originals. The social media posts contain some of the same misspellings as the killer's leavings.

My hand starts shaking as I scroll through the girl's older posts. I nearly drop my phone when I see what she posted the day Before. "Never to suffer would never to have been blessed."

My stomach contracts, sending me reeling out of my chair toward the bathroom, free hand clapped over my mouth to keep my empty stomach from puking bile all over the library floor.

I run headlong into Noah, who drops the snacks he was carrying in surprise. He tries to steady me with light hands on my shoulders. "You okay?"

Frantic, I push him away and sprint to the bathroom, letting the door slam shut behind me. I make it as far as the sink before acid climbs my throat and comes spewing out between my lips. My entire body writhes and heaves until my stomach is completely and totally empty.

Back in May. The crime scene where the Mayday Killer was interrupted before he could finish scrawling his macabre message on a wall with his victims' blood. The words he did manage to get down before he fled from the house, taking his bloody knife with him? *Never to suffer would never to…*

On a shocked gasp, I scroll back through my social. Pausing on the photos I posed of myself with Nate and Kate that summer at camp. To the photos of me with my family at the Mirror Museum.

The killer's getting ideas for victims from my posts on social media.

My entire body heaves again and again until I'm wrung out and dry as a desert.

There's a knock on the bathroom door, and then Noah's voice. "Megan? You okay?"

Wiping my mouth with a dry paper towel, I take in a few mouthfuls of air. "I'm okay," I croak.

"That wasn't reassuring. Can you come out? Do you need me to call someone? Your aunt?"

"Gimme a minute," I say, trying to speak confidently. It doesn't really work, but Noah says he'll be right outside whenever I'm ready. He doesn't mention the snacks he snagged for us, which is good because if I think about food too hard right now, I'm liable to start heaving again.

Straightening, I take a couple of careful breaths. My stomach stills. Okay. Here I go. Lifting my phone up to my eyes, I scroll to the bottom of CuteAshleeXOSO's feed. The very first quote was posted the day before the Mayday Killer's first victims were found. The quotes match. Word for word.

Either Ashlee inspired a serial killer's wannabe artistic bent, or…

I knew he was following me, even when everyone thought I was delusional. What if, to infiltrate my life even further, he created a profile on social media and posed as a cute teenage girl named Ashlee?

Taking a screenshot of one of Ashlee's few selfies, I do a reverse image search. My entire body flashes hot when the results come up. Her photos—they're stolen from a stock site. If I look closely I can see the watermarks even through the blurring filter whoever posted these used to mask them.

Another heave wells up from the base of my stomach, and I clamp my mouth shut. I've been chatting with Ashlee online for months. And the entire time, it hasn't been a teenage girl. It's someone pretending to be one.

Opening my private messages, I send her one before I can think better of it. *Who are you really? I know your name isn't Ashlee.*

Then I go to my own feed and find the first photo I posted After. Ashlee's comment was the very first.

My chest constricts when I see there's a location under my post: Valley High School. My legs nearly give out, but I catch myself on the slick edge of the sink. Gulp in air before my vision tunnels. I hit so many wrong buttons in my panic to delete it that it takes me a couple minutes, but I get it done.

Even so, I know it's too late.

Because the Mayday Killer has been moving north for the past two months. Ever since I accidentally posted a photo with my location tagged.

I meet my own gaze in the mirror. My eyes are red from

heaving, my cheeks are blotchy, my hair a mess around my shoulders. I didn't know it at the time, but the minute I posted that stupid photo, I re-lit the giant, flashing neon target sign that Aunt Karen had tried to extinguish.

It's my doing that he knows where I am.

Chapter 26

Day 142, Tuesday

Esau is standing at the base of the front porch when I crouch to jump off the roof. His hair is up in a dark bun at the back of his head, and he's bundled in a thick shearling coat. He looks so country I almost laugh. He steps right up to the roofline. "Here, give me your hands."

His fingers are warm and firm around mine as he helps me jump down. "Don't want you to land on your ass this time."

I start to shush him, but he slides an arm around my waist and pulls me against him. All of the air leaves my lungs as his eyes find mine in the glow of the moon. When I start to smile, he lowers his mouth to mine in a quick brush. Then he pulls back, just a touch. Our breaths mingle in a haze between us. His hand flinches against my waist, but before he can unhand me, I tuck my fingers into the warmth under the collar of his jacket and kiss him again. One of us groans, I'm not sure which, but it spurs Esau on. In two steps he backs me up against one of the wooden support beams under the patio cover. Esau's free hand lands on the painted wood over my head as he leans into me, sheltering me from sight with his broad body.

His nose nuzzles my throat as he places a feather-light kiss there.

We're both breathing heavy.

"This isn't… When I texted you..." I start, but it's hard to focus on words with Esau's thumb drawing circles on my side. Maybe it's exactly what I intended. To find a way to forget the repugnance of today, even for a few hours.

"Course not," he whispers, his hair tickling my nose as he caresses the shell of my ear. The pad of his thumb is coarse over my bottom lip, and then he's leaning in again. My eyes flutter shut. I don't want to merely see this moment; I want to focus on how it feels like warm elixir pouring through me.

"Not that I want to stop," I manage to say when he lifts his head long enough to take a breath. Esau could definitely help me forget.

He sighs against my mouth.

A sound from inside the old house makes us freeze.

"Go," I whisper-yell, pushing at Esau's chest. We run down the lawn and duck behind Aunt Karen's car. We sit hunched in the silence. Any second that front door is going to open and my guardian is going to be yelling at me for sneaking out again. The only reason she found out the first time was because of that box of photos from the basement. I shiver at the thought of Justin following Esau and I to the orchard. Fear raises goosebumps along my skin as I look up and down the street. No sign of who could be lurking in the shadows.

This is stupid. I'm making dangerous choices. I should go marching back into that house and lock the door behind me. But I don't.

"I think the coast is clear," Esau whispers. "Let's go." He opens the truck door for me and closes it once I'm inside. He steers out of the neighborhood easily, and once again we're coasting through town as if we're the only two people awake in all the world. It's one thing I love about this place. Unlike at home, when there are always people out no matter how late, here everything slows down after dark. Stores close. People return to their homes. One by one the lights go out. I never thought I'd prefer the quiet of night to the bustle of day, but I do.

I never considered a lot of things Before.

"That was so close," I say, relieved as the tension rolls off my shoulders. "I just knew Aunt Karen was going to throw the door open and start yelling."

"Me too." He glances at me, the corner of his mouth upturned.

"So…"

"So?"

"That kiss back there."

Esau adjusts the gear shifter as he turns out of town toward the country. "Wanted to make sure it happened this time. Didn't know you'd be so into it though." His cocky smirk sends a warm current through my veins.

"Just to be clear, that was not why I texted you."

He snorts. "Didn't think it was."

"Okay, good." Now that that's settled.

"Got to say, kissing you is way more fun than arguing, though I don't mind that either. You're so… aggravating."

"You're no piece of cake either."

"My abuela says I'm sweet as candy." Esau's confident grin makes me smirk.

"Has your abuela met you?"

Esau chuckles. "I haven't seen her in years. Maybe if she saw me now…"

"She'd still think you were sweet. Grandparents are supposed to be willfully ignorant of their grandkids' faults."

He chuckles as he drives past the iron gate that leads to the farm where he works and turns down a dirt path at the edge of the property. I bounce around on the seat as he drives beyond the house and buildings toward one of the fields. Esau parks between two patches of pumpkins and hops out, coming around to open my door.

"Where are these manners in drama club?"

"I think you like baiting me," he says, eyebrow arched.

"Yep." I slide out of the cab, pulling my jacket tighter around my neck. It's chilly out. Somewhere nearby, an owl cries.

Esau leads me around to the tailgate. There are two rolled up sleeping bags and two pillows up against the cab.

"Uh…"

"Two people. Two separate sleeping bags. Two separate pillows. Get your mind out of the gutter, Megan."

My lips part at the way he says it. It burns all the way down my throat. "So it's a totally innocent overnight camping trip."

"I have heard of such a thing."

"With teenagers? Aren't we all supposed to be raging sacks of hormones with no self-control?"

"I can control myself. You, though. I have my doubts. Is my virtue safe tonight?" He leans an elbow against the tailgate, eyeing me under lowered lashes.

"Shut. Up."

"There's supposed to be a meteor shower tonight. I was gonna come out here alone, but when I got your text…" He hoists himself up into the truck bed before giving me a hand in.

We situate ourselves in our sleeping bags, and I have to admit that despite the dropping temperature, I'm pretty cozy. There's a foam pad between my bag and the metal truck bed, and the pillow smells like laundry detergent. Without all of the light pollution, the sky is awash with stars. I can even see the Milky Way. Unlike the old house, I don't feel forced to tiptoe and whisper. There are no eggshells littering the truck bed. I sigh as the weight on me lifts. I could fall asleep out here.

Esau lies beside me with his hands behind his head. He's taken out his bun, leaving his hair to spill over the pillow. He must sense me looking at him, because he shifts just enough to meet my eyes. "What?"

I can't believe I'm out in a field in the middle of the night with you.

You make me forget.

You're beautiful.

Unlike the terrible things I've seen.

Want to argue some more?

Make out some more?

I finally settle on, "You look comfortable."

"I am. You?"

"Uh huh." We fall into a hush, me half hoping he'll breach the gap he left between his sleeping bag and mine, but knowing that, like outside the old house, he'll wait for me to up the ante on this evening. If I hadn't interfered, he would have backed off after that first, gentle kiss. If I wanted to, I could roll over right now and forget everything that's stressing me out in Esau's capable mouth. I'm about to do just that when he whispers, "Look."

His arm is outstretched, pointing toward a streak of light in the sky.

My breath hitches as flashes of glowing light paint white across the navy canvas before fading among the stars. We fall silent as we watch the sparkling galactic show. It probably only lasts for a few minutes, but it feels like hours when I'm so focused on the beauty unfolding before us I'm able to overlook the constant urge to freak out.

Yesterday, there was a possible sighting of the Mayday Killer less than a fifty miles from Hacienda. He could be here already, hiding. Waiting for his moment. Counting down the time until he can finish the job he started all those months ago. Aunt Karen was so wound up she was pacing around the living room, whispering into her phone. She threatened to pull me out of school and keep me locked in the house at all times. I had to beg her not to, especially after she found out about CuteAshleeXOXO and that location-tagged post on social media. Aunt Karen had yelled so loud I thought the ceiling was going to collapse. Afterward, she'd grounded me from everything but school.

With all of the patrols the sheriff's deputies are doing, I should be safe. Especially with Aunt Karen being constantly on high alert. I appreciate how strong my guardian's protective drive is, but I can't function in that house. Under that level of stress. Under the lingering questions about Justin's loyalty. I can't breathe. It's the reason I texted Esau tonight, hoping he'd be up for another drive.

A breeze ripples over me, making me shiver and sink deeper into the sleeping bag.

"You cold?" Esau asks, his attention on my face. When I nod, he opens his arm.

I scoot my sleeping bag next to his and snuggle down beside him. Wrapping one arm around me, he lays back and stares up at the sky.

I play up how cold I am just a little, throwing in an extra shiver. Letting out an amused huff, Esau nudges me onto my side and scoots closer behind me, shielding my entire back from the wintery air. "Better?" he whispers in my ear.

I'm glad he can't see me because I'm grinning. "Better."

"Good." He tucks his chin over my shoulder and goes quiet.

Here and there I see a shooting star, but the meteor shower seems to have stopped.

Esau's breathing evens out, his chest rising and falling in an easy rhythm against my back. He's asleep.

"Thanks for tonight," I whisper, feeling free enough to talk since the boy who's nuzzling my neck in his sleep won't hear it. "I had to get out of that house. Ever since… I've been so scared. Every day it's like waiting for the other shoe to drop. For someone to jump out of nowhere and scare the daylights out of me. It's hard. Living like that."

"Mmm." It's almost a sigh. He must be stirring. He's probably exhausted from school, theater, and his job at the farm. I get the feeling that the late night hours are the only free time Esau has. I'm surprised when he speaks.

"I've been wondering why you moved here to live with your aunt. If it has to do with the scar. You don't have to tell me, if you don't want to." His nose skims along my cheek before his head sinks back against his pillow.

My lungs squeeze in my chest. I want to tell Esau the truth about Before. Why I'm here. But I can't. "I don't… want to talk about it. Why I moved here. But I got the scar in a surfing accident."

Esau's arm tenses around me. "Ouch."

"My best friend wanted to learn, and on my first wave, I fell off. Hit my face on a rock. There was… blood everywhere." My throat goes dry at the memories that threaten to surface. I wedge my eyes shut and bury my face in the pillow.

"Hey, wanna see something?"

I look at him over my shoulder warily. "Depends."

"Not like that," he huffs. "Look." Sitting up, he lifts his sweatshirt just enough that I can see a jagged scar on his side.

I wince.

"Got it when I jumped off a moving tractor and got run over by one of the back wheels. Sharp rock cut right through my shirt."

"It looks like it hurt."

"Like hell. Serves me right for acting stupid around heavy machinery."

"Won't make that mistake again," I tease.

"Nope."

We lay back down in our bags and stare up at the starry night. I take comfort in the fact that Esau, like me, has scars. Physical reminders of what we've experienced. His isn't on his face, but it still helps a little. Somehow knowing that he's got scars too helps me feel not so alone.

Later, when Esau drives me home just as pale gray light is bleeding into Earth's indigo canopy, I delete the texts between him and me. When Aunt Karen checks my phone this weekend, a new rule she's instituted since she found out about the catfishing, there won't be anything to see.

Chapter 27

Day 147, Sunday

I run as fast as I can. Like the devil himself is chasing me. Maybe he is.

My feet crash through the underbrush. Twigs and leaves crush under my shoes like brittle bones. A branch whips across my face, lighting it on fire. My eyes water. I have to reach the house. If I ask her, Aunt Karen will fetch my books and backpack from where I abandoned them at the treeline.

My fingers tighten around my phone, and the message I finally got back from CuteAshleeXOXO. My first instinct on seeing the photo was to toss it into the irrigation ditch. Not that it would keep the Mayday Killer from finding me and finishing what he started almost six months ago. Not since he knows exactly where I am due to my own stupid actions.

Harsh, slanted words cut across the bottom of the photo.

Don't play coy. You know who I am. Do you know this place?

I have to show Aunt Karen the photo. She'll recognize where it is. She has to. And she won't be able to explain this away like she did with Justin.

"Help," I scream as I break free of the treeline. Branches cling to my sweatshirt like tiny hands holding me back. Even the trees are enemies. Swiping at the branches and leaves with frantic hands, I stumble toward the back door. If I can just get inside…

I burst into the kitchen, yelling at the top of my lungs. "You have to see this. He sent me another message. He's coming for me. Hello?" My fingers tremble as I take another look at the screen. It's a zoomed in photo of a front door with chipped blue paint. Old terra-cotta pots dripping with succulents flank the portal. I stare at it, willing my brain to come up with the rest of the image. I've seen that place. Been there before, but I can't picture it. Where is this?

The ceiling above creaks. "Aunt Karen? You up there?"

No answer.

My heart pulsates in my chest. What if he's already here in the house? What if he's up there waiting right now? Hidden in some darkened corner for me to come close enough to be snatched. I close my eyes against the fearful thoughts spiraling through me. Unbidden, a glinting knife stained crimson with blood appears. My entire body constricts at the memory.

It's not real. He isn't here. Yet.

"Are you home?" I call again once I find the courage to utter the words.

The house falls quiet.

It's strange. She was here in the kitchen attempting to make sloppy joes when I went out back to do my homework in the eucalyptus grove. The pot is still bubbling away on the stove. The meal's sweet, tangy scent fills the room. A short stack of plates sits on the counter next to it. A pair of wine glasses sit in the sink waiting to be washed.

Shoving my phone into the front pouch of my hoodie, I shuffle through the house, checking in each room.

No sign of her.

A flash of light breaks through the living room window at

the front of the house. It's narrow and cool-toned, like a flashlight. As if someone is sneaking along the front of the building. My eyes fly to the front door, and I halt. The knob and deadbolt are both unlocked.

Come on, I tell myself. Run over there and lock it before he can get inside. You can do this. You have to do this.

Still, I stand there unable to lift even a toe. Petrified by fear.

The flashlight moves outside, electrifying me into movement.

My shoes pound over the wooden floor as I sprint across the living room and throw the deadbolt. Twist the lock on the knob.

Breathing heavily, I let my forehead drop against the door.

I'm safe.

A low murmuring catches my ear. Someone is whispering outside. I can't make out what they're saying, but they're angry. Sick curiosity compels me to ease up just enough to look through the peep hole toward the driveway.

A beat-up old truck is parked there, running with its headlights off. Aunt Karen is leaning against the driver side door with her head nearly in the window. Her face is twisted into a snarl. Her phone flashlight in her hand casts swaths of light against the truck's side as she makes an angry gesture.

Dizziness makes me sway. My roots, which so recently have begun to cling to the safety of Aunt Karen's solidness, pull completely away from their foundation.

The man in the driver seat pulls her face downward and silences her with a kiss. She fights it for a second before giving in.

My brain doesn't compute what my eyes are seeing. My guardian is kissing Justin back.

When they part, he hands her a large, stuffed manila envelope. Just like the one I found in the garage. But why would Justin be giving her that?

If Justin is helping the Mayday Killer keep an eye on me, why would he show Aunt Karen more evidence of his nefarious hobby?

My joints lock up as an evil epiphany lights up my brain: she's in league with them. Somehow, she has to be. It's the only explanation that makes sense given her nonchalance when confronted with the evidence that Justin is not one of the good guys. Despite the fact that she's been tasked with protecting me.

The realization hits me like a ton of bricks. That day, the day I found the murder board. Aunt Karen must have lied about finding it to keep herself and Justin out of hot water with Sheriff Lamb. She covered for them. I'm certain of it.

Chapter 28

Hours Later

The old house falls quiet on a sigh as, down the hall, Aunt Karen closes the door to her bedroom. The low glow of the light from the hallway disappears, leaving the slim track under my door dark.

My guardian knocked before she retired for the night, feigning concern. *Are you all right, considering everything?* She'd asked through my closed door. Considering that the Mayday Killer is slithering ever closer even now, waiting for his chance to end my life in a cruel finale to the game he began in the spring? Considering that my protector is somehow involved with his little helper? That I can't trust her at all. Not after tonight.

I'm fine, thanks, I'd said, sure that she would hear the tremor in my voice and push the door open to look me over. But either she'd missed my fear or ignored it. I don't know which is worse. Do I want my guardian to be oblivious to the terror ripping through my body, or to be indifferent? It's an impossible choice.

I hold my breath the entire time I'm on the stairs, afraid with every step that the ancient planks will groan their protest and wake Aunt Karen. If she catches me trying to sneak out, I have no doubt she'll go through with her threat to slap an ankle monitor on me.

When I reach the first floor, I sag against the wall with relief. The hardest part is over. But still I linger there, indecision making it impossible to move. If Justin is watching the house, no longer safe in his nest across the street, would he be watching the front door or the back door? Which should I take?

Minutes tick by as I stand frozen against the wall, my eyes moving between the street lights glowing beyond the living room window and the pitch dark square of glass in the kitchen door. Digging up my courage and pulling it up into the gloom, I move to the back door. Slipping my feet into my worn Converse, I turn the knob so painstakingly slowly it takes me an aeon to get it open. Mercifully, it closes on a silent axis.

A twig snaps in the eucalyptus grove, making my heart skip a beat. There's a low shuffling sound in the dark.

I'm off like a shot, barreling around the house toward the street. I run like a spooked horse, my arms flailing at my sides. Down the street. Out of the neighborhood. Toward the small main drag of town.

I don't dare look behind.

Noah's house sits nestled between the trees, my only safe haven in the dark. The building lies asleep and unlit since it's so late. Gravel crunches under my feet as I finally slow my pace. My lungs heave in my chest, feeling like they're about to pop.

The low growl of a car approaching makes me squeak and jump behind one of the trees even though it's not nearly wide enough to hide me from view.

This was incredibly stupid. Justin followed me here.

He's going to nab me and bring me to the Mayday Killer. Right now.

Just like the brainless victims in a horror movie, I left the relative safety of the old house and delivered myself straight to him.

Fear fogs my brain as the car approaches, its headlights bright.

I blink as they wash over me, clamping my eyes shut as I wait for the inevitable. What will he do with me once he gets me in his grip?

A shudder runs through me as the car, a white delivery van with the company's logo emblazoned on the side, passes my hiding place without slowing.

My breaths come in shallow pants as I round the house to stand under Noah's window. Inside, it's dark and quiet. He's likely asleep. I feel bad waking him up, but I need to see a friendly face. The ghost of a smile parts my lips at the thought of a groggy Noah adjusting his glasses over his nose.

I tap on the glass twice and wait. Twice more. Brace myself against the house with one hand.

The curtain whooshes to one side and a blinking Noah appears, shirtless. He's wiry and toned like a dancer. I pull my attention back to his face, my cheeks reddening.

"Megan?" Noah mouths. He wipes at his eyes sleepily, swiping his glasses off his desk and putting them on. Only then does he seem to realize that he isn't wearing a shirt, because he slowly pulls the curtain in front of his chest.

I point to the front door, and he nods before disappearing.

Rounding to the porch, I sink down on the top step. Despite the clamminess of my skin, goosebumps break out along my arms at the damp, night air. I wish I'd thought to bring a jacket.

"Here," Noah says at my back, dropping a fuzzy cojiba blanket onto my shoulders. "You've gotta be cold out here."

"I'm freezing," I admit, pulling the blanket tighter around my shoulders.

Noah sinks down on the step beside me, pulling a blanket patterned with wild horses around himself. Taking in a long breath, he stares out at the yard. "What are you doing here? Not that I'm not happy to see you. I know you're not this anxious about our art project." His sleep-tousled curls fall over his forehead as he turns his eyes on me.

I try to smile but find I can't. "I… didn't want to be home."

His brows furrow. "Why not?"

I hesitate, torn between wanting to tell him everything and wanting to keep him out of it. Noah doesn't deserve to have all of this dumped in his lap. I don't know what kind of trouble he'd be in if anyone found out I'd told him the truth. "I just couldn't sleep."

"And you came all the way out here?" Even in the dark I can see the sheen of longing in his eyes. It twists in my chest like a knife.

"It's not like that, okay? It's just… Can I tell you something? You promise not to tell anyone?"

Noah's jaw twitches as he considers this for a long moment. Finally, he inclines his head.

"I just saw Aunt Karen kissing Justin."

Noah's expression widens in surprise. "You saw your aunt kissing the guy who was stalking you? Just now?"

"A couple of hours ago. Yeah."

"Even after everything?"

I bob my head.

"I know I promised not to tell, but Megan, you have to tell the sheriff." He readies himself to stand.

"He won't listen to me. And even if he does, he won't do

anything about it."

"You don't know that. You have to try."

When I shake my head wildly, he stands. "Then I will."

"You promised," I cry, standing too. His blanket billows around him like a superhero's cape.

Carefully, Noah steps closer, curling one hand around the edge of my blanket. "You have to tell someone. If your aunt is still with Justin, after knowing what he is, you're not safe. I don't want anything to happen to you."

My grip loosens on the blanket and one corner falls off my shoulder. Noah's fingers graze my skin as he lifts it back into place.

"You're a good friend," I whisper.

"Yeah," Noah whispers, looking out into the yard again. "Let me get some shoes on and I'll walk you to the station." He flicks on the porch light, digging around in the pile by the door.

My mouth hangs open as I stare at the door behind him. Horror pools in my gut, its level rising until I feel like I'm drowning in it, unable to breathe or speak. My ears pop as if they're underwater, failing to adjust to the pressure pulsing through my head.

Terra-cotta pots filled with succulents line the porch, flanking an old door with chipping blue paint.

Chapter 29

Even Later

Sheriff Lamb hates me. That much is obvious.

From the moment I told the deputy on duty about the photo I'd received. My suspicion that it meant the Mayday Killer was in Hacienda. He'd insisted on calling the sheriff, and that's when I'd known I was screwed.

Noah waited with me in the chairs by the door while the deputy dialed the sheriff's number, woke him up, and asked him to come down to the station. I stared at the floor, my fingers gripping the armrests so tight my palms hurt.

After what seemed like an hour, Sheriff Lamb walked into the building. He looked washed out and tired. His graying hair haphazardly combed to one side. His tan uniform shirt half-buttoned over a white undershirt and hanging untucked over his broken-in jeans.

Without a word, he'd pointed to his office.

I'd stood shakily, making to follow, but when Noah stood too, I'd gestured with one hand for him to stay. He didn't need to witness the humiliation of having the sheriff accuse me of trumping up lies for attention a second time.

Sheriff Lamb's weathered hands are splayed on top of the large wooden desk that sits like a canyon between us. The tab of one thumb taps the scratched and gouged surface in a rhythm as he stares at me.

"Let's go through this one more time," He says. "You received a photo that appears to be of the front door of the Lopez residence—"

"It *is* their residence."

"Don't interrupt me. You received this photo from an account on your social media that appears to be run by a teenage girl named Ashlee, who you think is actually the Mayday Killer toying with you." Cynicism drips from every word.

"I know it's the… him. All of the quotes he's posted match the ones found at the crime scenes. And there's no one else who would play a joke on me like this. I don't have a lot of friends, much less people who want to scare me."

The sheriff runs a hand along his scruffy chin, tapping his thumb a couple more times on his desk. "And you didn't go to your aunt with this why?"

"She's still in contact with Justin, the guy who was stalking me. I think he's helping the Mayday Killer." Behind the sheriff's desk are accolades and awards he's accumulated on the job. Surely a man so decorated in law enforcement will care. Will do something.

"I'll remind you we haven't seen any proof that he's dangerous."

"What about the envelope of photos I found in the basement? You must have seen the photos. Tonight, I saw him give her another one just like it."

Sheriff Lamb sits back, folding his hands in his lap. "I saw the photos. It's not a crime to take photos, Megan. Has he threatened you in any way?"

". . . No."

The sheriff spreads his hands, palms up as if to say, *I rest my case.*

Outrage and humiliation intertwine, sending hot flashes through my core. "Sorry we woke you up," I grind out, pushing up from the chair.

"Sit down."

Inexplicably, my legs obey him. I glare at the facade of his desk while he picks up the phone. "I'll call your aunt and have her pick you up."

"Please don't. I can walk."

"Nonsense," he says, tired. "Can't have you walking home alone in the middle of the night when there's a serial killer on the loose." His flat delivery makes me bristle, but I keep silent. This could not have gone any worse.

The only adult I kind of trust might be helping cover for a murderer's lackey.

The sheriff doesn't believe me.

And the man who started all of this with a killing spree is in Hacienda.

A place Aunt Karen assured me he'd never come.

It's all because of me.

"He's going to find and kill me," I say as soon as I'm alone with my guardian in her car. I'm trying to be flippant to keep her from seeing the depth of my dread, but it doesn't work, even for me. I wrap my arms around my middle, squeezing tight.

Noah tried to get Aunt Karen to let him come with us, but she'd refused, instead saying that he should wait for one of his parents to come pick him up as well. With an apologetic smile, he'd slipped out before the deputy had the chance to call his house, saying something about not wanting to wake them up.

"Don't cling to that self-fulfilling prophecy," Aunt Karen says, pulling out of the lot and on to the dark road. "I thought we were clear on the 'no sneaking out' rule. Are you really going to make me put an ankle monitor on you? I could get one, and Sheriff Lamb would go along with it. He's no fan of yours."

Everything in me I've been bottling up bursts out in a rush I know I'm going to regret.

"You'd love that, wouldn't you? Then you could let your boyfriend know where I am every second of the day. He could deliver me to the Mayday Killer soooo easily then."

Aunt Karen slams on the breaks when a yellow light abruptly turns red even though there aren't any other cars around. When she whirls on me, her eyes are blazing with anger. "Is that really what you think? That I'm stupid enough to date a guy who's a stalker? Come on, Megan. I think in the last few weeks you've gotten to know me better than that."

"Don't try to lie. I saw him giving you that envelope tonight. What was in it? More photos of me? Since his hobby is photography? What am I to him? Wildlife?"

She goes silent.

Arguments and thoughts spin in my head, but I don't voice any of them. I don't want to provoke the woman who has sole responsibility for me any further. The truth is, I don't know what she'll do if I keep pushing her. I don't know what she's truly capable of doing. A shudder moves through me, making me hug myself tighter.

I have never felt so completely, utterly alone.

My so-called guardian pulls into the driveway and shuts off the car, but instead of getting out, she stares into the rearview mirror.

I twist in my seat to see what she's looking at. There's

nothing back there but Justin's house, illuminated by a too-orange street light. Is she thinking of delivering me to him after all?

"I asked him to keep an eye on you when I couldn't," Aunt Karen says finally.

"Wait, what?" I whip around to look at her.

Aunt Karen's hands loosen from the steering wheel and fall into her lap. "Justin. You're right. He's been following you, observing you. But it wasn't because he's helping the Mayday Killer. He's been helping me."

"Helping. . . you."

There's a weak smile on her face when she looks at me. "I was nervous about being a teenager mom, so I asked him to back me up. I never thought you'd figure it out, or that it would feed into your fear like it did."

"So, Justin was working with you. He's not a homicidal maniac's BFF." Something clicks in my head. My roaring instincts go quiet. Somehow, I know she's telling the truth.

"That's what I'm saying, yes."

"You could have just told me."

Aunt Karen reaches over to take my hand, tentatively, then more firmly. "I thought it'd be easier if you didn't know. I thought it'd be easier for you to find some sense of normalcy. Clearly I was wrong."

"Clearly."

"Let's go inside. I could use some coffee. Want some?"

We're halfway up the walkway to the front door when I grab her arm.

"If Justin wasn't the one passing me those threatening notes, who was?"

Aunt Karen purses her lips. "I don't know yet, but we're going to find out."

Chapter 30

Day 149, Tuesday

Being back on stage is glorious. Neon pink light shines down from above, bathing me in a glowing halo of happiness. It's the first bit of peace I've felt all week. For just a moment, surrounded by the friends I've made in the drama club, I can relax. The rush of performing bubbles through my body as I recite the lines, putting all of the tension in my shoulders into the character I'm embodying.

I don't even look at my backpack in the corner where I left it to see if anyone's messed with it yet. If anyone does try to put another note inside, it'll trigger the tiny camera Aunt Karen tucked inside.

Marisa didn't show up for rehearsal today, and after we waited for her for twenty minutes, Esau told me to step in. I protested.

A little.

But the truth is that hiding behind the scenes has been killing me. The first time I did this play, I absolutely loved it. The uncertainty. The suspicion. The thrill was like the one I get when I go swimming in the ocean. Euphoric.

So as concerned as I am that Marisa has flaked, which is unlike her, I can't pass up an opportunity this good.

The other actors and I flow as if we've been rehearsing together for weeks instead of minutes. We hit line after line, cue after cue, seamlessly. In a beat of quiet, I chance a look around the theater. All of our clubmates are watching us, mesmerized by the performance. Knock 'em down, roll 'em around. Come on actors, work! I want to shout, but stifle the impulse.

This is only temporary. Marisa will be back and I'll have to retreat from the limelight and fade back into the shadows.

"That was really good," Esau says once we've finished the run-through of our scene. "Take a second, everyone. I need a word with our understudy."

I flush when the intensity of his gaze lands on me. Putting a hand on my elbow, he draws me down the hall toward our advisor's abandoned office.

"What are you…?" I ask when Esau nudges me into the empty room and closes the door behind us. He turns toward me, his expression unreadable.

"Did I do something wrong? Wait, are you about to critique my performance? Because I thought it went well, and I'm only the understudy anyway. Marisa will be back and—"

"That was perfection," he says, walking purposefully toward me.

"Then why are you looking at me like I'm in trouble?" I say, relief fluttering in my stomach. Gliding backward until the backs of my thighs touch our advisor's unoccupied desk, I lean back on my palms. A pile of papers slides across the floor at my feet.

Esau boxes me in between his arms. "Take over Marisa's part. She's good, but you're breathtaking. With you in the lead, this play will be… Have you considered being an actress? Together we could be a fantastic team."

I go still. “I can’t.”

“Why not?”

“Marisa. She’s worked her butt off for this part, and I can’t do that to her.” As much as I’d love to reclaim the title of actress. But with everything that’s going on, I can’t expose myself like that. I shiver.

“You cold?” Esau’s fingers skate up my arms and land on either side of my neck.

I shake my head. “We should get back.”

“Just one more thing first.” Exhaling, he moves to kiss me.

Miss Crabtree pushes the door open, halting in the doorway when she spots us.

“Am I interrupting something?” she asks, coming closer. Her long, velvety dress knocks over another pile of papers. “You haven’t been poking around on my e-reader, have you?” She scoops up the item and tucks it into her side.

“No, ma’am,” Esau says. “Just giving our understudy some acting tips.”

“Good then. Carry on, but maybe not in my office next time, hmm?” She sits in her desk chair and picks up one of the papers to read. I can tell through the page that it’s upside down. Her phone rings and she waits for us to leave before answering it.

When we’re alone in the hall, Esau snorts. “That was close.”

“No kidding.” I move toward the theater, but he takes my hand.

“Wait.” He presses his lips to mine. I’m surprised by the heat behind it as I kiss him back. This isn’t a quick, consuming kiss like the one the other night on my front porch. No, this one is more assured, as if it’s a dance we’ve done together before. I'm falling into it, his warm scent teasing my nose, when I snap back. I can't do this. Use him like this. He's a real person, not a memory-erasing spell.

That was perfection.

If he only knew how far from it I truly am.

Pulling back, I take a few steps away.

"Hey," Esau protests, leaning forward on the balls of his feet. "What was that for?"

"Why did you bring me back here?"

Something flashes in his eyes. "You were captivating out there. I had to do something about it. Didn't think you'd mind."

"I didn't, but it can't happen again."

One of his hands gestures over me. "Clearly you hated it. You're all pink."

"I'm serious. You might want to fix your hair." I point to where his bun is hanging lopsided to one side.

"Right." Esau's biceps flex as he reaches up and re-does his dark locks, wrapping them expertly into a messy bun at his crown.

The murmur of voices coming from the theater gets louder. "What's going on out there?" I wonder out loud to distract myself from the boy in front of me.

Gesturing with a hand, Esau lets me lead him out. I'm careful not to touch him as I pass. He turns his face away, toward the middle of the larger room.

Everyone is standing in a clump, huddling around Marisa.

"What's goin' on?" Esau asks, cutting through the crowd to where the girl is standing at the center, cheeks flushed and panting as if she's just sprinted across campus.

"Sorry," she breathes. "Have to catch my breath."

"Spit it out, girl," Fiona says, putting a hand on the girl's shoulder.

"I went to the coffee shop in the grocery store after school. Needed some caffeine. And there was something going on in the manager's office. There were serious-looking guys there wearing suits and asking Javier all these questions. I was curious, you know, so I inched closer by pretending to look at the racks of DVDs along the front wall. Turns out, the suits were asking about some security footage."

"What for?" Viv asks, eyes alight. Her measuring tape dangles from one hand.

Marisa looks around at all of us. "Someone called in a tip. They think they saw the Mayday Killer in there this morning. In our grocery store. Here in town."

I stagger back as my knees give out. He really is here in Hacienda. Less than a mile from Aunt Karen's house and the school. My heart ratchets as if it's going to hack its way out of my chest. I clutch at it with one hand, struggling to breathe.

Esau catches me under the arm. "Are you okay?" he asks.

All I can manage is to shake my head as I struggle to get my feet under control.

"Don't worry," Marisa says. "No one was hurt. Your aunt is fine. Apparently he bought a couple things and left. No one recognized him until one of the employees saw a sketch on the news on their lunch break. Guys, I think those dudes in the suits were from the FBI." She looks from me to the crowd around her as all of my clubmates start to chatter among themselves.

"Hear that?" Fiona says to me. "Your aunt is fine."

"I'm kind of freaking out," Viv says. "My mom stays home alone during the day."

Marisa shakes her head. "I'm sure she's fine. Your mom's single. So far he's only attacked married couples, right?"

I nearly jump out of my skin when the theater door opens and Mr. Baugh comes in, his face drawn. Miss Crabtree emerges from her office. "All right everyone. We're ending rehearsal early today. The sheriff's office has requested that all of you go straight home immediately."

"Do we have school tomorrow?" someone asks.

"We plan to, yes. For now, everyone just go home. Megan?"

My nose wrinkles at being singled out. What could she possibly have to tell me? I inch over to her, taking my time to avoid stepping on the cables and cords snaking across the theater floor.

"Yes, Miss Crabtree?"

"I got a call from your aunt. She's been delayed at the store, so she's asked me to make sure you have a ride home."

Mr. Baugh puts a hand on my shoulder. "I'll make sure she gets home safe." He winks at our advisor. Flushing, she smiles back.

"Okay.... Let me get my stuff."

"I'll drive you," Esau says, stepping closer to the three of us. "I can take her."

Miss Crabtree starts to shake her head. "Miss Biel was insistent that an adult accompany Megan home."

"I'm eighteen," Esau says, squaring his shoulders. His warm fingers enclose mine.

Mr. Baugh looks between Esau's clenched jaw and the advisor's worried expression. "How about if I follow them? Will that work?"

Miss Crabtree's lips pucker, but then she nods.

My legs still feel like putty as I climb into Esau's truck, dropping my bag at my feet. I stare out the windshield as he closes my door and comes around to the driver side. "Are you okay?" he whispers once the cab is closed. "You're pretty worried about your aunt, huh?"

Not sure how to answer, I don't say anything for a long minute. "Aunt Karen. Yes. She's all I have left. I don't want to talk about it."

Esau's eyes try to meet mine, but I look down at my lap. I'm tired of lying to him, so I don't elaborate.

Unbidden, my hand rises to run my fingertips over the scar on my cheek.

"Look," he says, hands gripping the steering wheel. "I wasn't going to ask what happened before you came to live here. Why you had to move in with your aunt, but Fiona told me—She said you told her your scar was from a car accident. But you told me you were surfing." He lets the question linger as his eyes flick to my scar.

"I'm sorry I lied." I don't elaborate.

"Why did you?"

I shrug, trying to hold myself together, but it feels like I'm fragmenting, like an iceberg drifting out to sea.

"I know what it's like to miss your parents," he says quietly, gazing out the window. "I haven't seen mine—"

"It's not the same," I blurt. Anger boils up in me, mixing with the terror, the helplessness I've felt since that day. "My parents are *dead*."

"Sorry. I'm just. . . wondering why you didn't tell me. I thought we were becoming something. I thought we understood each other."

I scoff. He can never understand me, because all I've done is lie to him. From day one. Esau has seen only bits and pieces of what remains of me. Somehow, by trying to hide myself, I've become a shade of something that draws Esau. But it has to stop. The shadow who has lurked in the corners of my vision for the past six months is looming large, crowding out everything else I thought I had to look forward to. It's all a blurry mess.

"Let me in, please."

Hot tears well in my eyes and I swipe at them with my free hand. "Just… take me home, okay?"

With a tense frown, Esau turns the key and pulls out of the parking lot. Mr. Baugh follows us in his car.

Silence hangs between Esau and me the entire drive.

My eyes dart back and forth over the roads. Looking for *him*. Every second I expect him to jump out in front of the truck, knife in hand. I start at the glimpse of a man with his back turned, but when we pass, it isn't the one I'm looking for but praying I never again set eyes on.

My mind is spinning. Esau knows I lied about how I got my scar. He knows my parents are dead. How long until he puts all of that together with the fact that I almost fainted when Marisa said the serial killer who haunts me waking or sleeping was spotted in town?

Aunt Karen will be furious if I blow my own cover.

Esau pulls up in front of the old house. Cutting the engine, he turns to me. "Talk to me. Whatever it is, let me help fix it."

"You can't. I have to go." I hop out of his car and jog up the walk without looking back. It'll be better for Esau if he believes I'm nothing more than a liar. I can't pretend anymore that what I feel for him is purely physical, so it has to end. It would never have lasted anyway, I argue. A relationship based on lies is doomed to fail.

I'm so absorbed in the darkness of my thoughts that I don't notice the bouquet of fall flowers on the front porch until I almost knock it over. Gasping in surprise, I scoop it up before the vase can crash on its side. Water dribbles down my fingers as I take in the bouquet. The flowers are beautiful.

What if *he* sent them?

I almost drop them in revulsion.

"I'll wait until you're inside." Mr. Baugh is standing in the middle of the dead, yellowed grass, watching me warily.

"Someone sent you flowers?" Esau calls, standing against the door of his truck.

I shake my head. No one would send me flowers. They're probably for Aunt Karen. Maybe now that I know about Justin, he won't have to be so secretive about dating my guardian.

There's a white card tucked into the bouquet. I fish it out and open it with one hand, desperately hoping to see Justin's name. Instead, there's a note scrawled hastily in cursive.

Audrey,

I hope you know it's all for you.

Yours,

I stand frozen, the edges of the card cutting into my palm as I clench it between my fingers.

Esau's boots clomp on the wood as he mounts the stairs.

I should move, run inside before he gets a look at the card. My legs don't bend under my control. Any magic I had is used up and gone.

"Looks like they delivered it to the wrong house," Esau says over my shoulder. "Do you know an Audrey?"

"No," I lie.

Chapter 31

Day 152, Friday

School on Wednesday was torture.

I couldn't focus on anything but the killer's calculated trip to the store. The flowers. They were bright red flares fired into the sky. Warnings that the game wasn't over.

The entire town seemed to be suspended in a state of wary trepidation. Would the killer strike anyone they knew? Maybe someone who had lived in the sleepy valley their entire life? Several of the students who had stay-at-home parents walked around with their phones clutched in their hands as if waiting for them to ring with the dreaded news.

I wanted to scream, but the knowledge that all of this was my fault kept me quiet. I floated through the halls like a ghost.

Thursday was only marginally better. It seemed that because the Mayday Killer had been spotted in town, every teacher had given up on their lesson plans and spent the day tuned in to various news channels. The students bobbed from class to class, catching the new repetitive reports. No more sightings of the fugitive since Tuesday. The newscaster on the late night news said that the authorities didn't know where the killer was hiding or if he was merely passing through town and would continue the trek north he'd begun in September.

Talk show anchors in sharp suits and bright red dresses speculated as to his motives. How he chose his victims. Why he used a knife rather than a gun.

I spent the entire day trying to drown out their voices with the music streaming through my earbuds. I kept thinking one of the teachers would confiscate them, but if they noticed they didn't care.

I already knew the truth.

None of the town's people were in any real danger. Not if the killer sticks to his established modus operandi.

The town's people weren't the reason the deranged killer had made his way up the state with such single-minded focus, only taking breaks to slake the blood-thirst that drove him.

No, I was the reason.

It was me.

Vehicles from the sheriff's department passed the school at a near constant rate. Or at least they seemed to whenever I looked out one of the windows. I longed to be out there with them doing something. But my guardian had assured me that the best thing I could do was to stay inside. Stay safe. My time to step up would come, God willing.

Aunt Karen picked me up from school without a word. Her mouth flattened in a grim line. *You're safest at school,* she'd said when I balked at going. *You'll be surrounded by people, all of them on alert. Try not to worry.* Like that was possible.

Today, the town-wide frenzy seems to have broken. The teachers are back to their various subjects. My friends have begun to relax, drawing their shoulders down from their ears.

The killer hasn't been spotted again. He hasn't spilled even a drop of blood. And I have it on good authority that the police are on high alert in case he tries.

"He must have moved on," Fiona says at lunch. "There's

nothing interesting about this town."

"I hope so," Viv says, looking up from the notebook where her doodles expand over the page like black and white galaxies. She's been texting back and forth with her mom constantly for the past three days. She said it was because her mom worried, but I could see the line between her brows every time she checked for new messages.

"It blows my mind that there was an actual killer in our town. I go to that grocery store all the time," Marisa says, adjusting the scarf looped around her neck. "I wonder what made him go in there anyway. He's been hiding out for months. Why go someplace so public now?"

My mouth drops open.

She's right. The man has proven he's more than good at staying out of the public eye. Evading the police for days and weeks and months. Why did he allow himself to be seen on Tuesday? They played the surveillance footage on the news. The Mayday Killer had the gall to stroll up and down the aisles, even glancing at the cameras mounted on the ceiling more than once. It was as if he was daring them to identify him, since they hadn't been able to yet.

Not even when they showed me the surveillance footage from the supermarket and I confirmed it was him

Ice cuts through me like a sharp winter wind. He did it on purpose.

He wanted to be seen.

He wanted me to know he's here.

The time is right. He's coming for me.

Cold weather has blown in with conviction, thrashing the trees until their leaves concede the battle and fall. Crystal white dew clings to the roofs of all the houses when morning breaks. The library door opens and an icy gust slices through my sweater, chilling me to the bone.

I whip around, hoping to see Noah walking this way. Finally.

Instead, two old women cluck at the cold as they walk past the front desk toward the romance section. They're so bundled up against the autumn chill they're waddling like penguins.

Forcing my gaze down, I try to focus on my homework, but the words in my textbook might as well be in ancient Greek. I'm not getting anything done tonight.

The deputy in the corner who the sheriff tasked with keeping an eye on me doesn't help my focus.

My eyes drift toward the large window and the moonlight beyond. It's already dark; the days are getting shorter. And fewer in number, I think, unable to shake off the macabre idea. I run my fingers inside the rim of my bracelet, absently wishing for survival.

Police sirens ring outside the building, and when I look up a sheriff department vehicle rips up the street as it passes. I wonder where they're headed. If they spotted the serial killer who haunts my waking hours as well as my nightmares. My eyes fall on my phone, which is still open to my photos. The photo of Noah's front door, specifically.

Terror chokes me. What if they're going to Noah's house? What if something happened to him or his family? The sirens recede in that direction.

Crossing the lobby, I plant my feet in front of the deputy. "Can you tell me what's going on?"

The woman looks up with a stern face. "I'm not at liberty to say."

"Please?"

"No can do. Sorry." With a sympathetic tilt of her head,

her attention shifts back to the card game she's got open on her phone.

Putting my hand on top to block her vision, I lower my voice. "Please. I just need to know my friends are safe. The Lopezes?"

The woman's expression softens. "There's a fire at a storage unit across town. Nowhere near the Lopez house. Nothing to worry about."

It still doesn't explain why Noah is so uncharacteristically late. Scooping up my phone from the table where I've been working gives me something to cling to as I send a message asking where he is.

A frigid wind slams into me as the library door opens.

"Sorry I'm late," Noah says as he slides into the chair across from mine. "My mom took another shift, so I had to take Anza and Mattie to my abuelo and abuela's house for their party. Where are we at with our project?"

"Party?" I ask absentmindedly, sinking in my seat in relief that he's sitting across from me hale and whole.

Noah gets a stack of books out of his backpack and flips through until he finds the one he wants.

"Tomorrow's their birthday. My grandparents will keep them and bring them back to our place when we're all ready. Speaking of, how are you at hanging streamers or stuffing piñatas?" His eyes are warm behind his thick frames, but his smile starts to teeter under my horrified gaping. "You don't have to come, but Anza asked about you, so I was thinking—"

"They share a birthday. Are they twins?" I choke out the words, my mind careening around my skull like a bug trapped in a jar. I blink when Noah gives a slow nod.

"I thought you knew."

"But they're different heights. They don't look the same

age." I mumble, connecting the dots. The Mayday Killer must know that the youngest Lopez kids are twins. That's the reason he sent me that photo. Not because I'm friends with Noah, but because their family makeup fits his sick criteria. My throat feels stuffed with cotton and I can't seem to wet it even though I swallow over and over.

I work my tongue, trying desperately to quell the panic clawing up my throat. I can't breathe. Can't look at my friend.

His parents are in danger. He could be an orphan tomorrow. Because of me.

Noah leans across the table, nudging my hand. "Megan? You're freaking me out a little. What's wrong?"

The textbook pages cut into my fingers, but I can't seem to loosen my grip on them. The lemony sharp pain is the only thing grounding me right here, right now. My eyes flit absently around the library, to the window. I'm trying to figure out how much to tell Noah. If there's anything I can say to help him without ruining everything. His deep brown eyes are on me, filled with concern.

I have to tell him. There's no other choice.

"Are there any other sets of twins in town?" I manage.

"Not that I know of. Why?" Noah's head angles to one side.

"You said your mom was working. Is your dad home?"

"Yeah. Again, why?"

I lick my lips. Once I say this I can never take it back. Noah will never look at me the same. All of the warmth and openness I see in his eyes will be replaced with pity. Revulsion. Still, it's no reason to keep him in the dark. Even if he never speaks to me again, I have to tell him.

"The cops don't call the Mayday Killer by that name. They use another one, but they kept it out of the press. The Gemini

Killer."

"Because he only kills Geminis?" Noah looks incredulous.

My entire body trembles as I shake my head. "Because he only kills the parents of twins. They buried that fact to keep people from panicking, but it's true. He always goes after families of twins."

Noah's brown skin pales. "How— Megan. How do you know that?"

"He killed my parents,"—I gulp—"and my sister."

Noah's eyes skim over my scar. His gaze darts from me to the deputy sitting in the corner of the room with her nose buried in a thick history book. Abruptly, he stands up. His backpack falls off the table with a thunk. "He came here for you. You're the reason he's here."

My head hangs heavy with guilt. My eyes drop to the floor. "I'm his unfinished business. And once he's done with me, he'll target your parents. I know it. I didn't tell you, but he sent me a photo of your house. I thought it was just to taunt me, but I think it was his way of telling me his plans."

He knifes a hand through his hair. A hiss escapes from his lips.

I keep my eyes down, unwilling to look into his eyes and see the disgust I'm sure is there.

"Hey. Hey, look at me."

When I refuse, he walks around the table. Kneels at my side. With gentle fingers, he lifts my chin until our eyes meet.

My breath hitches.

The things I see in his eyes are not what I expected. No hatred or revulsion or anger.

"It seems like you're blaming yourself for this, and it's not your fault. None of it."

Noah's eyes are filled with conviction, compassion, and

more I can't afford to name.

"You don't get it. I'm sorry I didn't tell you, but Aunt Karen made me swear not to. To protect my identity. I moved here to lie low until they catch him. Because I saw him. He's here to silence me. I brought him here."

Noah shakes his head gently. My knee is warm under his gentle hand. He looks in the deputy's direction. "You're not responsible for that psycho's actions. We have to tell someone though."

"The sheriff already knows. He knows all of it."

Chapter 32

Day 156, Tuesday

The pumpkin field is quiet except for the rumble of the tractor's engine between my legs. I let its loud hum overtake the swarm of thoughts that threaten to overwhelm me.

It's been four stifling days since Noah found out the truth about the Gemini Killer. Four days of him eyeing me warily in hallways and classrooms. Four days of waiting for the gossip and rumors to start, for the furtive, curious glances to begin again.

But for whatever reason, the contents of my late night conversation with the sheriff haven't spread. Nor have the revelations I shared with Noah. He might be wary of me, but he hasn't told anyone.

At home, Aunt Karen keeps tabs on me, constantly checking to make sure I'm wearing my bracelet. I'd had enough of the scrutiny, so I'd texted Esau. I'd hoped he'd be up for hanging out, even though we haven't really talked since he found out I'd been lying to him about how I got my scar.

My bracelet sits on my wrist. Despite everything, I put it back on. *Your parents would have wanted you to wear it.*

"There are so many," I say, looking at each row of leafy green vines as we pass to see all of the different varieties of gourds. Esau's arms sling casually on either side of me as he steers the big three-wheel tractor between two fields of pumpkins. Some are smooth, vivid orange while others are white and wart-speckled. There's something unsettling about the way the vines sprawl over the ground, as if they'd grab my ankle and drag me under if given the chance.

The frigid weather of a few days ago has given way to an Indian summer. Despite being mid-October, it's a hot day. I opted for a cute dress, even though it wasn't from Aunt Karen's closet of approved wardrobe choices. I had hoped that the frivolity of it would take my mind off the shadows closing in. A breeze flutters the ruffles along my shoulders. It's not really working.

"Twelve varieties," Esau says. "Mr. Dell'Osso loves pumpkins. Grows more kinds than any other farmer in the area. You should see the place once Halloween hits. It's a zoo."

"Sounds fun," I say, forcing my interest. I used to love Halloween. Morbid costumes. Horror movies. Going to haunted houses with friends. But now it all seems far too real. My fists clench on my knees. I'm not going to let *him* ruin it like he has everything else.

The tractor hits a rut in the dirt and I bounce back against Esau's chest with a surprised squeal.

One of his arms bands around my waist. "Stay close," he whispers in my ear. "Wouldn't want you to end up like me, or that guy in that old Reese Witherspoon movie."

My eyes widen in dismay. "There's no plow on the back of this thing!"

He chuckles, doesn't remove his arm from my waist. Instead, he steers one-handed. Whistling. Esau is whistling. It's such an astonishing, happy sound that I can't stop the genuine grin that splits my features.

For once I'm not tiptoeing around wondering when everyone will connect the dots and accuse me of luring a serial killer to Hacienda. When they'll ask me what happened that day. To recount what I saw when I stepped into that kitchen, painted red with blood.

I force the memories away, focusing on the cheery orange of the growing pumpkins, the sun shining in a cloudless blue autumn sky. Esau's warmth at my back. His arm resting on the tops of my thighs.

"Do you miss your parents?" I ask before I've even fully decided to.

Over my shoulder, he nods. "My mom calls me pretty often, so we talk. My dad sends me texts with random emojis. Not sure what he's trying to say, but yeah. My tia and tio are great, but..."

"It's not the same." I understand. Aunt Karen tries. She does. But she doesn't know from years of experience making my lunches that I don't eat mayo. That I love having piles of blankets on the end of my bed for when I get cold. That I would occasionally climb into my dad's lap to cuddle for just a minute, even though I'm far too old for stuff like that.

"I'm sorry about your parents." His words are kind and matter-of-fact. Not whispered like grief is something to be hidden and ashamed of.

"Thanks. What's the thing you miss most, about home?" I ask, not sure if the boy steering the machine under us can hear me over its grumbling.

"The ease of it," Esau says immediately. "Being with people who know me without constantly expecting something. I can just be myself, you know?"

I nod. I get it. More importantly, Esau gets it. The constant nagging at the back of my mind that everything I do is a performance. Not for my benefit, but for the benefit of the people around me. Aunt Karen. My classmates and teachers. The sheriff and his deputies.

"I feel a little of that. When I'm with you," he whispers in my ear.

My cheeks warm. "Me too." It's the reason I came out here. Because as much as I told myself I was using Esau as a distraction, it becomes less and less true with each minute we spend together. I've learned so much about him these past few weeks. And I'm starting to give him glimpses of the real me in return. The version I hide underneath. He never rejects the flashes of truth I show him.

We ride in comfortable silence, the sun and the warm breeze our only company. Water burbles in the irrigation ditch as we drive alongside it. Something slips beneath the surface of the water. Probably one of those crawdad things.

I am 100 percent glad I played hookie today. V. I. C. T. O. R. Y.

"Want to see the corn maze?" he asks over the coughing of the engine.

"Is that allowed?" I ask, turning to look up at him.

In lieu of answering, he winks.

"What's it shaped like?"

"Let's see if you can figure it out. Just give me a minute." Cutting off the tractor's engine, Esau jumps down from the high seat and turns off an irrigation valve. The rich dirt beneath the sprawling vines is a rich cocoa brown.

When he swings himself up behind me, I nestle against him again. Being here, with Esau, I actually feel something. It's been so long since I felt that way that it takes me a second to recognize it. Safety. I feel safe with Esau.

The corn looms up before us, rows and rows and rows of

it so dense and wide and tall that it takes my breath away. The stalks wave in the gentle air as Esau helps me down, his hands tightening on my sides. His attention dips to my mouth.

"You can't catch me!" I squeal, bolting toward the shelter of the maze. My laughter trails behind as Esau gives chase.

I run under the wooden arch into the maze, making turns at random. Left. Left. Right. Dead end.

I crouch in the corner and wait, listening.

"I helped cut this maze," Esau calls from nearby, a cocky slant in his tone. "You can only hide from me for so long."

"We'll see." I'm off, running down another path.

Footsteps thud behind me as I push my legs to their limit. Suddenly I stop in a little alcove where there's a bale of hay set up as a bench. Easing down on it, I wait for Esau. My heart is drumming a gleeful rhythm in my chest. Whatever this game is, I'm pretty sure I'm winning.

Esau calls a taunt from somewhere to my right just as something snags the back of my dress. I stifle a gasp as I whirl around.

Nothing there but giant stalks of corn.

Weird.

Shaking it off, I wait for Esau to come around that corner, his eyes lighting up when he spots me.

A minute stretches out. I can hear Esau moving in a distant part of the maze. Somehow, he hasn't found me yet.

Nearby, something snaps.

I whip my attention in that direction, but there's nothing there. Slowly, I turn to face the path. Listening.

I can't hear Esau anymore. He must be at the other end of the cornfield.

How big is this maze anyway?

The aisle feels narrower than it did before, as if the corn is looming in toward where I'm sitting. There's a rustling in the next row.

"Took you long enough," I say, but Esau doesn't appear.

"Esau?" I call. "Hello?"

No response.

Nervous energy tingles up my back, making me pull my shoulder blades in. Being alone in this place is starting to get a little creepy. Like that Stephen King movie about people who were lost in an endless corn field for so long that they started to lose their minds.

Around me, the corn creates a tall, green wall that blocks everything from view. Above, the blue sky is empty. No clouds, no airplanes, no birds.

Maybe I should keep moving.

I make lots of noise as I advance through the maze, trying to find the way out.

I yell for Esau again, louder this time. He doesn't answer.

A crow flies out of nowhere, cawing in my face, flapping its wings as it ascends.

I scream in surprise, and then I'm running blind. My feet beat a path over the dusty ground as I try vainly to find the exit. A stalk whips across my face as I take a sharp corner. My cheek stings, but I don't stop. I have to get out of here.

I round another corner and run smack into Esau.

"Whoa, whoa. What's wrong?" he asks, his hands gently rounding my shoulders.

I shake my head. Take in a shaky breath.

I can't tell him. He'll think I'm a scaredy cat. A paranoid kitten.

"Got scared by a crow," I say with false bravado. Force out a laugh that's faker than a blizzard in July.

But when I look up, Esau isn't focused on me. His

attention is on something over my shoulder, his mouth is parted in shock.

When I spin around, I see it. A black pillar of smoke coming from the edge of the cornfield. Birds flee with loud squawks from the growing spark of flame. Slowly, corn stalks begin to burn. Then more quickly.

"Shit!" Esau runs down the narrow path between the maze and the next field of corn. "Flip the valve!" he yells over his shoulder.

I'm frozen in incomprehension for a second before I spring into action. Running to the spot where the irrigation valve meets the larger line from the ditch, I open it wide. Rushing water spurts into the pipe leading toward the field, dowsing the ground in water. But I don't know if it will be enough to stop the burning tide moving across one corner of the maze.

The fire department arrived quickly. It was dumb luck that they were doing a drill in an abandoned barn nearby and saw the smoke.

Esau and I stand off to one side, watching as they put out the fire with expert teamwork. I'm shaking with adrenaline, watching with rapt attention.

Once it's done, the firefighter in charge comes over to us. "You two okay?"

We nod.

"How's the maze?" Esau asks, looking past the man toward the blackened corner of the field.

"Far as we can tell, it didn't get far enough to burn into any of the cut paths. Lucky we were close by. If we'd gotten here any later, the entire field would have gone up. Quick thinking, turning the irrigation back on. Looks like you'll be able to open as planned on Friday, and I'm glad. My kids look forward to opening night every year."

Esau gives him a customer service smile. "Us too. How'd the, uh, fire start?"

The firefighter shrugs. "Don't know yet."

With a pat on Esau's shoulder and a nod to me, the man moves toward where the rest of his crew are working around the fire engine.

An EMT approaches us. "Are either of you hurt? Need looking over?" She leaves when we insist we're fine.

"Come on then. I'll take you home." Esau slings an arm around me and steers me toward where his pickup is parked in the dirt. "You look like you could use something cold to drink."

I stick close to him even though he's filthy from using an irrigation hose to hold back the flames until help arrived. As we pick our way to where the truck is parked, I take one more glance over my shoulder at the maze. From out here it looks like an ordinary, harmless field of growing plants. But when I was in its heart, alone? It didn't feel benign. It felt like I wasn't alone. Like someone was watching me. Waiting for the opportune moment to slash my throat.

And then the fire started.

Chapter 33

Esau glances over to make sure I'm buckled in before he starts the truck. Gravel crunches under the tires as he pulls on to the street.

I sigh, relaxing into the bench seat. Today, being near Esau as he moved through the fields, quiet purposefulness emitting from his every muscle and bone, it was exactly what I needed. Never mind that Aunt Karen will be livid about me sneaking out again. Plus, the fact that I could have been burned to a crisp.

A truck I recognize turns into the road ahead of us. Justin's. I thought I'd slipped past him, but he must have followed me to the empty lot where I met Esau, and then on to the farm. Did he see how the fire began? If he saw Esau and I leaving, did he decide to get a head start? It doesn't make sense. My finger lingers over my phone, just in case I need to call Aunt Karen.

Instead of turning down the road that leads to home, Justin's truck leads farther away from town. My chest squeezes when the truck pulls off the road into a stand of trees near the Lopez's driveway. Fear flaps its scraping wings along my insides. Did something happen to Noah and his family?

My heart stills under my sternum. "Pull over," I hiss, tugging at Esau's elbow. The truck's wheel jerks under his hands.

"Careful," he commands even as his hands move to heed mine.

My focus is locked on his dark, hooded figure as it moves quietly through the trees toward Noah's house. If I didn't know what Justin's truck looked like, I wouldn't know it was him. He takes careful steps, swinging low-hanging branches out of the way with ease. It's clear that he's had practice moving around without being detected.

My stomach drops. If he left me to come here, there can only be one reason. He must have gotten a call from Aunt Karen telling him to come over here. What if it's already too late to stop whatever bloody tragedy is playing out inside Noah's house?

Esau parks his truck far enough away that Justin doesn't notice. Instead, the man is careful as his figure fades into the dusk between the eucalyptus trees.

"This is getting strange," Esau says, swinging his gaze toward me. "Who is that?"

"Shh." Pushing open the door, I slide down, praying my cute but impractical shoes are quiet over the gravel.

The hooded figure has disappeared. I can't see him at all. Hopefully that means he can't see us either.

Esau's door opens and he steps out, shutting the door too loudly.

I wince, but start walking toward Noah's house, rolling onto the balls of my feet in silence. The weight of Esau's gaze, and his lingering questions, presses against the back of my neck like a large hand. I'll owe him an explanation after this. My lips thin. How much will I have to tell him? How much do I want him to know?

Blood roars in my ears as I tiptoe through the trees, half

expecting Justin to jump out at me from behind every trunk.

He doesn't.

He doesn't.

He doesn't.

Dread creeps in. I have the sickening thought that I wish he was coming here to retrieve me, because it would mean the people inside the house a few yards away would be safer. Maybe I should have called the sheriff after all, risked the tang of his disdain.

At the treeline, I stop, hiding behind a wide, old eucalyptus. Its bark is craggy and rough under my palms. Esau hovers behind me, but his heat can't penetrate the cold coursing through my body. I scan the yard, but there's no sign of the tell-tale blue car.

Esau's hand lands on the back of my neck in a gentle, protective caress. "There something you need to tell me, Megan?" he whispers.

I give the slightest shake of my head even as the air whooshes out of my chest.

Justin is slinking around the side of the dingy house, peeking into each window before moving on to the next. He stops, his back pressed against the building's worn wooden siding. What horrors does he see when he looks in those windows? His lips are moving as if he's talking to someone. With one hand, he returns his gun to the holster at his side.

A blaring crow makes me nearly jump out of my skin as it takes to the skies somewhere above. I'm beginning to hate those big black menaces. In the distance, a dog barks.

The Lopez's attack rooster comes winging around the side of the house with a screech like a battle cry and starts jabbing its needle-sharp beak into Justin's shins. The man growls in surprise and kicks at the bird.

A light flicks on inside the house, and someone shouts.

My eyes widen as Justin throws himself at the treeline, heading straight for us.

"We have to get out of here."

I whirl, but Esau's arms tighten around me, tugging me behind a girthy eucalyptus. "I'm calling the sheriff. Just let me…"

"Don't call him! There's no need for—"

Justin crashes through the trees mere feet away from where we're hidden. His lack of stealth would be funny if I wasn't so afraid of what he saw inside Noah's house.

Instead, I'm breathless with fear as he draws level with us. Any second he's going to glance this way. His eyes will lock on mine.

It happens just as he streaks past, leaves crunching and twigs snapping as the rooster chases him all the way to the road. He doesn't turn back. The scent of burning rubber permeates the air as the truck peels out.

I sag against the patchy bark of the tree, frustration and relief battling within me. He's gone. I have no idea what Justin was doing here, but I do know that if there was something bad happening inside Noah's house, the man wouldn't have run off.

"Let's go," I whisper, turning toward Esau.

Esau shakes his head. "They're putting me through to the sheriff. They should know your favorite janitor was scoping out a student's house." His entire body is rigid, his phone to his ear. Through it I can hear the receptionist at the sheriff's office talking. Esau's eyes are locked on the Lopez house.

Noah is standing on the front porch, squinting out into the trees. "Stay inside," he yells to someone inside. "Stay with Anza and Mattie."

Someone answers low enough that I can't make it out.

I pinch my eyes closed, wishing I had the power to vanish into the gathering dusk. My hands claw at the bark, wishing I could slough it off the sturdy trunk and cloak myself in it. I should not have followed Justin here.

Esau clears his throat and moves away from me, closer to where Noah is rustling through the undergrowth.

"Hello?" Noah says, his voice closer this time. "Esau? What are you doing here?"

"Saw a truck parked in the trees and thought I'd check on you."

"Thanks," Noah says, his voice high and nervous. "I think we're okay, but Anza is pretty spooked. She saw a man peering in her window."

Esau nods. "It was the new janitor at school. Justin."

"Oh." Noah looks over his shoulder at the house, his body visibly uncoiling.

"You don't sound surprised."

"Naw. I, um, forgot he was going to come by. He's interested in some of our baby chicks. Too bad Napoleon scared him off," Noah says with the fakest laugh I've ever heard. He's such a terrible liar, it's kind of endearing.

A pulse throbs in my neck. Justin must have come out here to see if I was with Noah, since I wasn't where I was supposed to be. So I guess he didn't know I was at the cornfield with Esau.

Noah is standing an arm's length away from where I'm hidden, and I pray he doesn't see me.

"Sheriff's on his way," Esau grunts. "You can explain it to him."

Thanking him, Noah's footsteps get farther away, back toward the house.

Esau takes my hand and leads me back to the truck. I keep

peeking over my shoulder to make sure Noah doesn't see me.

"Care to tell me what that was about?" he asks once we're back on the road heading toward town.

"My guess is Justin went over there to see if I was with Noah, since I snuck out. Aunt Karen has him check up on me sometimes." I won't meet his eye, and from the way Esau's jaw flexes, he knows I'm not telling him the whole story.

The rest of the drive is tense and silent.

It's not until I get up to my bedroom that I discover how close I was to death in that cornfield. There's a wide knife slash through my dress, and a shallow line of red cuts across my back.

Chapter 34

Day 159, Friday

Aunt Karen went on a tear when she found out about Esau and the cornfield. She reinforced that taking off my bracelet was not an option. Then she started laying out an ironclad argument about how slipping past Justin was incomprehensibly perilous.

Then early this morning we got the call that the fire at the cornfield was arson. Someone tried to burn it to the ground knowing two people were inside. The knowledge has sent me spiraling even further into a pit of regret. All of this is my fault. My parents' death. The deaths of the Andersons. The Chans. Every single person who has died at the hands of that psycho since May. If only I had pushed harder, made my parents listen to me about the man who showed up everywhere I went. If only I had made them listen, maybe all of this could have been stopped.

But they didn't hear the desperation in my voice.

And I didn't push.

Instead I let it go, and my parents were butchered.

And the Mayday Killer is still free. Lurking in the dark crevices of my mind and waiting for his next chance to cut and rend with his bloody blade.

Now, I can add siccing a tail on the Lopez family to my list of transgressions. Justin didn't mean them any harm, but it didn't prevent Anza and Mattie from being scared enough to keep their parents up all that night, crying from the nightmares.

I did not envy Aunt Karen for having to come up with an explanation to give Mr. and Mrs. Lopez about why Justin was sneaking around their property.

Aunt Karen informed me that the sheriff's deputies are keeping a close watch on the Lopez house for signs of the Mayday Killer, and that they're doing everything they can to warn twin families in nearby towns. But it's the same as before: how do they warn the public without causing panic? If every twin family in the state knows what's going on, how long before the public makes a spectacle out of it? How long before they whisper his name, sizing up their neighbors and friends as future murder victims. How long before the true crime fanatics descend on our town, digging for clues the sheriff and his cronies may have missed?

My stomach clenches tight and doesn't loosen.

I can't let that happen.

In May, when I thought I was being followed, I let my need for my parents' approval, my need to please them win out over my instincts that were screaming something bad was happening. No longer. I can stop this, now. The time to be a shy orchid bud tucked behind a leaf is over. Instead, it's time to be a vivid purple bloom. Demanding attention.

Taking the cuff off my wrist, I leave it on the desk. I pull on my favorite hoodie and zip it to my chin. Its over-large bulk is like a security blanket, even though it's lost any hint of my dad's scent. The greasy musk he'd track into the house after spending hours in the garage working on his latest car project. It's the first time I've worn it out, because I know if Aunt Karen saw it she'd make me change clothes.

I allow myself one heartbeat to wallow in the absence of it, of him, and then I'm opening my door and peering down the hallway.

The master bedroom door is closed, just like it's been since I moved here in August.

Downstairs, the house is quiet. I don't know where Aunt Karen is, but she can't be far. The fire in the corn field almost put her over the edge. She checks on me every half hour, it feels like. Not to mention the constant inquiries about my phone. The uneasy rhythm we've fallen into is coiling tighter and tighter. Living in this house is to be on high alert every minute. It makes it difficult to breathe.

I manage to hit every creaking board on the staircase on the way down, but still there's no sign of my guardian.

My heart is chugging around my chest like a toy train flying off its tiny rails as I reach the front door. I slide open the deadbolt achingly slowly. Turn the knob at such a glacial pace that it may never actually open. Then I'm outside.

A noise in the house makes me bolt down the sidewalk and away from the building that I've never warmed to and will probably never feel like home.

I run through town as if being chased by Aunt Karen herself. I refuse to stop, knowing that if I pause even a second to re-think this I may not go through with it.

My lungs are burning and I can't catch my breath. I run headlong into somebody, and Chinese takeout rains over the sidewalk.

"Urgh," the man says, scrambling to catch the rest of the Styrofoam containers before every bit of his dinner is on the concrete.

"Oh no. I'm so sorry, Mr. Baugh. I have some money. I can buy you more dinner. Here, take this." Digging into the pouch of my hoodie, I dig out my phone and slip out the twenty Aunt Karen handed over because she ordered me to always carry cash. But even as I'm holding it out to him, it occurs to me that twenty dollars won't be nearly enough to replace all of the food he's dropped.

"It's fine, Megan. Really. I can't take your money," he says even as his fingers close around the green in my hand.

"It's the least I can do," I say as I duck past him.

"You seem like you're in a hurry. Going somewhere?"

"Thought I'd check out the corn maze," I say between choppy breaths. Now that I've stopped running, I don't know if I'll be able to begin again. My hands press into my knees as I take great gulps of air and force them into my lungs.

"Do you need a ride? It's on my way."

"No thanks! I don't want you to be late for whatever party you're taking all that food to."

"Party? Oh, right." Mr. Baugh's eyebrows draw together as he glances down at the large quantity of food splattered over his shoes. "I don't mind being a little late."

"That's okay. See you Monday!" I shove my body into a jog. I can't let my teacher distract me from the task I've set myself.

The maze is packed with couples kissing in out-of-the way corners. Screams of delight and panic fill the air. The heady scent of apple cider and fried cinnamon-sugar donuts makes my mouth water as I meander through the towering stalks of corn.

Footsteps approach, and I whirl, expecting to find a face nearly smothered by a grizzled beard and thick, unkempt eyebrows.

A pack of laughing guys hoots and hollers at the way I

nearly jump out of my skin, but then they're rushing past me further into the depths of the maze.

I posted on my photography profile over an hour ago that I would be here, but the Mayday Killer hasn't shown his face.

A knife-wielding scarecrow makes me scream when I run right into it, even though it's the third time. Its twisted burlap sack face and fake blood freak me out even though I know it's all for show. Whoever put this creepy spectre together had too much fun with the corn syrup blood that looks all too real.

Twisting away, I spot Fiona, Marisa, Viv, Erin, Dariel, and Esau through the crowd.

I freeze, not sure how to react. Esau's been acting coolly toward me since the other day at Noah's. Since there is no reasonable explanation to give him for what happened. I take a slow step back, hoping to melt into the corn like a cartoon character in a hedge.

Esau meets my eyes for the barest of seconds before he looks away, arms crossed tightly over his chest. Even he is dwarfed by the towering stalks of green corn.

"Hey Megan!" Fiona says when she spots me, waving me over.

My feet war with my brain as they propel me to the edge of their circle.

"Girl, we thought about calling you but weren't sure your aunt would let you come out with everything that's going on."

"She doesn't know I'm here. Been here for hours, actually," I say, biting my lip.

"Oh, rebel. I like your style. Want to join us?"

"We're hopelessly lost," Viv says with a grin.

"Somehow I think you don't mind," I say, letting the corner of my mouth curve upward despite how heavy the muscles in my face feel. "Where's Noah?"

"Babysitting," Fiona shrugs. "His mom got called in to work."

I wish he was here.

"You any good at these things?" Dariel asks, slinging an arm over my shoulders. "Help us, Obi Wan. You're our only hope."

I'm about to shake my head when Esau speaks. "I'm hungry. Let's go get something to eat."

"The exit's that way. I'm pretty sure." I point.

"It's the other way," Esau murmurs, leading the group.

Fiona raises her eyebrows at me but doesn't ask.

Everyone follows Esau through the twists and turns and out of the maze, a chorus of voices talking about how delicious a slice of pumpkin pie sounds piled high with fresh whipped cream.

I don't fight it as Dariel steers Fiona and me with a hand on each of our shoulders. "Funnel cake," he drones, imitating a mindless zombie on the hunt for its next sugar hit.

I almost laugh as my entire body begins to unwind. I'm unspeakably relieved to be leaving the maze. I regretted it one second after I posted that image of me standing at the maze's entrance. How stupid was it to post on the Internet telling a murderous lunatic who's obsessed with me exactly where I'll be tonight? I must have a death wish.

Every second of being in that endless sea of giant corn was torture. Every footstep and every snap of a branch made my nerves spiral higher and tighter. Sure that the next figure who stepped around the corner would be him. A murderous gleam in his eyes and a bloody blade clutched in one hand.

My friends pile into the back of the line at the snack shack. I wrap my arms around myself to hold in the warmth that builds in my chest. Even though I've told these wonderful people lies, lies, and more lies over the past few months, they've somehow become my friends. I've teased Fiona for her snacking habit. Asked Viv for recommendations of places to clothes shop. Run so many lines with Marisa that she's finally perfected them. And Esau, despite his hard-ass director's ways, is a friend too. Underneath that grumpy exterior is a softish center. Okay, so he'll never be an effusive person, but that's fine.

The warmth starts to seep away when I realize that eventually all of them will know what I've done. Once they do, they may change their minds about wanting me around.

"Be right back," I say, ducking out of line.

I can feel Esau's eyes tracking me as I run past the snack shake toward the line of bright green porta-potties.

"Megan!"

I spin around to see Mr. Baugh jogging this way. "I'm so glad I found you. You have to come with me. There's been an incident at the Lopez's house, and your aunt wants you home right away."

Dread slices through my gut like a black hole. The Mayday Killer got to them. Maybe he didn't see my post and instead decided to add more bodies to his grizzly count. I clutch my face. More bodies lying at my feet.

My fault.

My fault.

My fault.

"Are… are they okay?" I manage to push the words out as Mr. Baugh herds me toward the parking lot.

He cuts a look toward me, something worrying in the lines of his face. He got to them. They're not okay.

My knees start to buckle, but Mr. Baugh holds me up. "Come on, we're almost there." He coaxes me across the lot to his car and helps me climb inside.

"Thanks," I mumble as he drives me through town.

He nods, eyes focused on the road.

My mind is flailing for purchase, but I can't hold on to any single thought. My chest is so tight it feels like I'm being crushed by a car rather than riding inside of one. Town whooshes by in an unfocused blur. The packed diner a din of noise. The grocery store where Aunt Karen would be working if something bad hadn't occurred. The sheriff's station where only half of their patrol cars are parked, unattended, in the lot.

"Mr. Baugh? Can you tell me what happened?"

"I'm not sure. Your aunt didn't give me the details. Just asked me to go to the corn maze for you while she and Justin were tied up at the house."

I glance at my teacher, whose knuckles are white on the steering wheel as if he's clinging to this tiny act of normalcy even as it propels us closer to whatever devastation has been wrought on Noah and his family. Noah's warm smile films my memories. Anza's inquisitive eyes and hot-seat-like manner of questioning me. The shy way Mattie tucked his hand into mine the last time I was there.

Fiona said Noah was home babysitting, which means his parents aren't home. It's odd for the Gemini Killer to change his MO this late in the game, but who am I to try to reason out the actions of a deranged murderer?

Whatever. Please, just let them be alive.

Mr. Baugh is clearly upset by what has happened, and I wonder if he's deliberately keeping the worst of it from me.

I open my mouth to tell him that he doesn't have to protect me from the evil in the world. I've already seen it firsthand. But the tight pallor of his face stops me. If he's upset, I don't want to pile on. The horror of my complicity can wait for another day.

Chapter 35

An Hour Later

I'm pacing, still waiting for Aunt Karen to get home with news. She and Justin aren't answering their phones. Neither is Noah. The wait is driving me wild with fright.

A clipped knock on the door downstairs brings my head up.

Finally! I slap my textbook closed and push off the worn carpet. It's dark out, and enough shadows have gathered in my room that it's hard to see anyway. I ought to have turned on a light ages ago, but I was too distracted to crawl the five feet to the desk to flip on the lamp. Anything to take my mind off what's happening across town.

When I open the door, Noah is there, his eyes red-rimmed and his curly hair disheveled as if he's clutched at it with sweaty hands.

"What—?"

The air whooshes out of my lungs when he lurches forward and wraps his arms around me. I'm stock still, caught off guard by his unembarrassed embrace, until I realize the shudders of his body against mine are sobs. Instinctually, my arms wrap around his back.

"It's okay," I murmur, patting his shoulder blade. "It's

going to be okay." I don't know why I say the words; they're a blatant lie. Sometimes horrible things happen that change a person's reality forever. Something wrenches apart the threads that weave your life together. You can try to glue everything back together, but it will never be the same. An ugly, jagged scar will always be there, staring you right in the face.

You can choose to make the best of it and move forward with the hope that life will get better. It has to. Or the brokenness can drag you under, if you let it. Twist you into a bitter, angry husk.

With a sharp intake of breath, I realize that I'm so very close to letting everything that's happened to me ruin what remains of my life Before. I've let the bad memories poison all of it, my memories, my words, my heart.

Noah's whispered confession jolts me out of my self-loathing.

"I was supposed to be watching them, but someone posted on the true crime forum about the Mayday Killer. A new guess as to who he might be. I got distracted by the theories and conjectures, and then Anza screamed. It was so loud. I—I thought I was going to lose them too."

At his choked revelation, my entire body seizes. No, please, not Anza and Mattie. I haven't spent a ton of time with them, but those two sweet kids have weaseled their way into my heart. Anza with her gap-toothed chatter and Mattie with his shy, empathetic nature. Please, let them be okay.

Noah drags me tighter against him, burying his face in my neck. Desperate for comfort.

"Noah, you're scaring me. What happened? Are they all right?" I hold on to him tightly until his grip eases.

He takes in an unsteady breath before letting go of my waist, slowly, as if he'd rather stay here in my arms. With a swipe of his hand across his eyes, he finally looks me in the face. "Anza convinced Mattie to climb the kitchen counter to try to get the cookie tin off the fridge. He fell and broke his foot in three places. I can't get his wailing out of my head." He winces, his face beginning to crumple again.

I sag in relief. They're both alive.

"It's not your fault." My fingers wind around his and squeeze. "Kids get hurt sometimes. His foot, it'll heal, right?"

Noah gives a slow nod. "He looks ridiculous in the boot they've got him in. It's so heavy he's listing to one side." A weary laugh escapes his lips.

I giggle too, overcome with relief, and that single, cheerful sound breaks the dam of tension between us. We're both laughing at the mental image of Mattie in an oversized boot. Noah is doubled over with his hands on his knees and I'm pressing my hands into my warm cheeks.

When we're both down from our giddy high, Noah meets my gaze. "Thanks," he whispers, "for letting me, you know."

My eyes fall to the wet spot on the front of my sweater dress. "I think it goes well with my tights, don't you think?"

Noah's mouth turns up appreciatively. When his eyes meet mine, there's something there I haven't seen in a few weeks. Interest, I think. "Definitely. Look, um, I know when I asked before, you weren't—I mean, since you and Esau aren't official. I was wondering if you'd consider—"

My lips part in surprise. I thought I'd been pretty careful around Esau at school, but I don't know why I'm surprised that Noah has noticed. He's observant and smart.

I don't like hurting him.

My phone vibrating in my dress pocket cuts him off. I resist the urge to reach for it.

"Is that him?" Noah asks, his voice carefully modulated.

"I can get it later."

"No, it's fine. It might be important."

"It's not," I say too quickly. But I take out my phone and check the message anyway.

Pushing his hair back off his forehead, Noah takes a step back. "I should get home. Check on Mattie."

"Wait." I hold the sleeve of his flannel shirt with a claw-like grip, but I can't tear my eyes away from the message shining from my phone.

Are you still here? What did Mr. Baugh want?

Hello?

If you don't answer, I'm assuming you've been kidnapped. ;)

Megan? Is everything okay?

They're from Esau, starting over an hour ago. I stare at the messages, not sure how I missed them.

We both jump when a hard knock comes against the front door.

"Megan? You home?" Esau.

My eyes go large in surprise.

Noah's eyes dart between me and the door. "Is it okay that he's here? I can stay, if you need."

"It's fine." I open the door to Esau, who looks like a Greek god with his black hair streaming out behind him and his face fixed in an avenging snarl.

He takes in Noah and I standing in the foyer and zips it all back inside his protective shell until he's his usual, well-controlled self. "I guess I was worried for nothing."

"You were worried about me?" My heart melts into a puddle of goo and my words come out in a coo.

Esau huffs. "No."

My lips curve upward. "Liar."

"I'll just see myself out," Noah mutters, his cheeks tinged

red. "Thanks again," he tosses back, and then he's gone.

Esau swallows, his Adam's apple bobbing. He closes the front door without taking his eyes off me. Shrugs out of his shearling coat and drops it on the floor. With a deep inhale, he advances with intent in his eyes.

A welcome shiver rolls up my spine at that look. My toes curl in my cutesy slippers. Esau may be an expert at hiding his emotions at school, but right now I can almost read his mind.

Our mouths crash together in a kiss full of heat and want. He backs us up to the wall and leans against it, banding me to his torso with muscled arms braced across my back. Breaking off to take a sniff of my neck, he murmurs. "When you left the maze with Mr. Baugh, I thought something had happened. And then you didn't answer your phone…"

He moves to kiss me again, and I barely get a word out before my brain is a fog of fizzing sparks and the velvety caress of Esau's fingers down my arms.

"Maze?"

"Corn maze," he breathes against my mouth.

"Wait." My hands press against his chest, but it's not necessary. Esau has pulled away to get a better look at my expression. "You saw me leaving the maze with Mr. Baugh earlier?"

I'm panting, anxiety spiraling upward through me and slicing through the endorphin-fueled haze. Aunt Karen never could figure out who was behind the Mayday's Killer's notes I found in my backpack. But Mr. Baugh has been around the entire time, hovering. I thought he was being a teacher, worried about how the new kid would do at Valley High. But what if that wasn't it at all?

Esau nods.

"A little over an hour ago?"

"Yes."

I swallow as I glance up the stairs, hoping Aunt Karen will materialize on the landing. It's a futile wish. I already know she isn't here. I square my shoulders and look to Esau, who is studying me with hungry eyes. A dull pain cuts through my chest.

"Whatever you're thinking is going to have to wait. I think I left something in Mr. Baugh's car. Can you drive me over there?" He doesn't see the fingers I have crossed behind my back.

He shrugs.

"Be right back," I toss over my shoulder as I run up the stairs. With hurried, unfocused movements, I toss on my jacket, shoving my bracelet into the front pocket. I stomp down the stairs in time with the throbbing pulses of my heart.

"You ready? It's getting windy." Esau asks as he stands in the doorway. Already wearing his coat. He drags a hair tie off his wrist and pulls his hair back into a bun on the crown of his head.

Over the blood rushing in my ears, the wind whips around the sides of the old house, howling as if begging to be welcomed inside. But I know better than to welcome monsters in.

The door flies against the wall with a smack when Esau opens it. Opposite, a frame falls to the ground and shatters.

"I'll get it later," I say when Esau moves, his boots crunching on the shards of glass littering the floor.

I pull him outside. Drag him after me as I run to his truck and jump inside.

My hands grow clammy in my jacket as he drives through town, which has already begun falling asleep even though it's only just after 6 PM. Many of the stores are dark. There are only a few stragglers on the sidewalk.

"Everyone's still out at the maze." Esau glances at me before focusing on the road. "What's so important that you have to go get it now?"

I squirm in my seat, not sure how to answer. So I don't. My eyes are fastened to the red light ahead.

"Can you drive a little faster?"

Esau's black eyebrow cocks upward, but he presses the gas harder with his boot and the truck guns forward.

My feet tap on the floorboards in a nervous rhythm as we ride out into the country. Rows and rows of almond trees flank the street. During the day, I find their spindly branches kind of pretty. Right now they look as if they're about to grab me and drag me down like the ghostly trees in Snow White. But unlike the warbling princess, I'm not running away from my worst nightmare, but toward it.

I only hope I get there in time.

Chapter 36

Esau pulls on to a dirt road surrounded by gangly, overgrown trees on all sides. Up ahead there's a pale green ranch house tucked under the naked boughs. A rusted metal playset sits on a dead, yellowed lawn. Mr. Baugh's yard is so overgrown we could hide in the tangle of brambles and tall grasses and never be found. The screaming wind will cover any noises we make. I'm counting it as a sign that this isn't going to be a total disaster. Not that it would stop me. I have to do this.

With one hand slung over the wheel, Esau turns to me. "What did you forget?"

"My phone."

"You grabbed it off the counter before we left. Try again." Esau's expression is firm, brooking no argument.

My terror burbles up and bursts. "We don't have *time* for this." Panic has a stranglehold on my throat.

"Fine! Fine. But it doesn't look like he's home," Esau grumbles, leaning past me to study the house's darkened windows.

"You're forgetting something."

Esau's deep eyes slide to mine.

"I make the magic happen." I hate how unsteady I sound, but I keep eye contact with him and hope that he reads it as conviction. If Mr. Baugh isn't home, I don't know what I'll do.

But I press forward.

Opening the door and sliding out of the truck, I zip my jacket up to my chin. The wind's fingers snag in my hair, throwing it in my face and whipping it against my cheeks. When I manage to get it under control, Esau is holding an extra hair tie in front of my face. Snatching it off his pointed finger, I toss my hair up into a messy bun like his. It probably looks like hell, but at least I can see now.

My jaw drops to the ground when Esau pulls the bench seat forward and retrieves a hefty shotgun from a pair of hooks mounted to the truck's rear interior wall. He checks and loads it with deft hands.

I swallow a nervous squeak.

"Is that necessary?"

He eyes me, resting the shotgun against one shoulder. "You tell me."

". . . Let's go." With a rushed breath, I move toward the yard and plow into the needling grasses.

The parallels of this experience and that day at the corn maze don't escape me as I'm slinking around the side of Mr. Baugh's house in a hunch, lifting just enough to peek in each window before I move on. Esau was right; the house looks completely empty. The TV sits dormant in the front room. Piles of Chinese takeout cartons litter the kitchen counter. When I dare to try the handle on the back door, it's locked.

Almost imperceptibly, my pulse begins to slow. I've read this situation all wrong. Mr. Baugh isn't the bad guy here. I'm tilting at windmills.

Then my eyes slide over the unkempt backyard to land on a barn so flimsy I'm dumbfounded the winds battering it haven't caused it to collapse.

Esau stops me with a hand to my elbow when I start to

move toward the leaning structure. "Whatever you forgot can wait. Let's go."

He's giving me a chance to come clean about the reason I've dragged him to Mr. Baugh's house and am sneaking around the place like a burglar with a hot tip about an easy take. But none of this is easy. If I come clean with Esau now, he'll never understand. The drive inside him that pushes him to direct and control everything in theater has to be warring with whatever he might feel for me. I've given him less than nothing to go on, and yet he drove me over here on a flimsy excuse.

I can't tell him everything, but I still have to try.

"Someone's been putting notes in my backpack when I'm at school. Threatening ones."

Esau's eyebrows go up and his grip tightens on the rifle. "Someone has been threatening you?"

I nod. "And it occurred to me that it could be Mr. Baugh. At first I thought it was Justin, but it turns out Aunt Karen asked him to keep an eye on me while she's at work."

"What? Why didn't she—"

"I can't explain right now. Please trust me."

I reach for his hand even as questions scrawl across his beautiful face.

"Lower your rifle."

The sudden, rough words make me put my hands up and twirl around.

But it's not the police doing the commanding. It's Mr. Baugh. And he has a gun pointed at my chest.

"Mr. Baugh?" The words crack at the same instant the puzzle pieces begin to snap together to show the completed image.

Esau lowers his weapon slowly, never taking his eyes off the barrel of the other man's firearm. "No need for that," he says once the shotgun is leveled at the ground. "Megan just left something in your car."

"Did she? Drop it." He gestures with his free hand. Reluctantly, Esau complies.

"Why?" I ask my favorite teacher.

"I'm doing this for the same reason you are, *Megan*."

Finally, Esau's eyes jump from the man to where I'm frozen with my hands still up in the air like a freaking statue. I command them to lower, and my fingers twitch as they come down. My hands curl into fists at my sides. My eyes dart over the yard. Looking for a sign. Anything. There's nothing.

"Go on." The gleam in Mr. Baugh's eyes turns greedy as he gestures for us to precede him to the barn. Inside, he marches us to a concrete structure. A tack or storage room, maybe.

I look around the cave-like space, once more sweeping for any shred of evidence that she's been here, and come up empty. There's no sign of her. I clench my teeth at my own stupidity. I practically frog-marched Esau right into what is clearly a trap.

Tossing a key on a ring to Esau, Mr. Baugh orders, "Unlock it."

Esau does, lobbing the keychain into our teacher's outstretched hand.

"Now go inside, nice and slow."

I start to protest; my instincts screaming at me to flee. If Esau and I go into the small, cave-like room Mr. Baugh is forcing us toward, we will never make it out alive. My hand clamps around my naked wrist, cursing myself. No one will be able to find us out here. No one will hear if I scream. Steeling myself, I ready the muscles in my calves to run. Cut a glance toward Esau, who looks primed to punch Mr. Baugh in the face with his tightened fists. His eyes meet mine. He's ready.

The feel of cold metal on the back of my neck silences me before I can push the words over my tongue.

Esau's mouth curls into a snarl, and his angry eyes smolder a glare at the man just behind my left shoulder. "Don't touch her."

"Inside. Now."

"Run!" someone cries from within the dimly lit concrete room.

It's the proof I've been looking for. With my heart thundering in my ears, I lunge inside.

There's a scuffle at my back. A grunt. A curse. The squelching of metal hitting flesh. Esau stumbles into me, holding a hand up to his bleeding nose. His lip is split and crimson dribbles down his chin.

At our back, the door slams closed. There's a scraping as the lock is thrown in place. We're trapped.

Esau's eyes land on me. "You okay?"

I stare at him blankly as my tongue struggles and fails to catch up with my fishtailing mind.

Rustling against the far wall draws his gaze, and he freezes. The color drains out of his beautiful face. His carefully constructed facade of calm control shatters into pieces.

Knowing what I'll find, I look.

In the corner, tied to a chair, her cheeks stained with grime and tears, she sits.

The person responsible for all of the unfortunate events that have slowly embalmed us in misery, despite the fact that I'm kicking and screaming at the closed coffin lid, begging for air.

My mirror image, minus the scar that mars my cheek.

My twin sister.

Audrey.

Chapter 37

Audrey

Bafflement contorts Esau's face. Hurt flickers behind his eyes as they bob back and forth between Taryn and me. I'm sure the makeup I used to draw on a fake scar is smeared by this point, adding to the mental wallop Esau is experiencing right now. His hands flex at his sides as realization works its way through his features.

My eyes fall to my wrist where my tracking bracelet is supposed to be. My plan to lure the killer out of hiding backfired, and now three people will pay for it instead of just me.

I turn my attention to my twin. "Where is Aunt Karen? Is she coming?"

"I don't know," Taryn says, shuffling her feet.

"Are you wearing your bracelet?" I ask, my last tinge of hope staining the words.

"I stuffed it in my pocket, but…" Taryn turns out both her jacket pockets ruthlessly; they're empty.

My expression crumbles.

"So she has no idea where we are," Taryn says. "This is it. We're dead."

I shake my head. "Untie me. Please. Now that you're here,

we can find a way out. There are tools on the workbench and—We'll figure it out."

Taryn doesn't make a move. She glares in my general direction, but I don't care. She's acknowledging me. Talking to me. For the first time in months. Even with her arms crossed tightly like a shield over her chest, I'll take it. It's something. Hopefully, a new beginning.

When a beat passes and Taryn still doesn't move, Esau lumbers over. Kneeling behind the rickety wooden chair I'm sitting in, he begins working at the knotted, rough cord.

"There are two of you," he growls as he works. "Which one of you was Megan?"

The tender skin at my wrists pinches as he pulls at the rope, and I wince.

Esau huffs, which I take as an apology.

"We both were. We're identical twins," I say, straining against my urge to yank at the ropes, knowing it would not help Esau untie my bound hands any faster. After a minute, the ropes fall away and he moves to the side to work on the rope twined around my left leg. I bend to untie the one on the other side.

Nostrils flaring, he glares at me out of the corner of his eye as he works.

"I'm sorry."

Esau yanks his gaze away.

A shuddering sigh escapes my lips as the last of the bindings falls away and I'm able to stand. I stumble toward my sister on wobbly legs. Pins and needles shoot through my calves as feeling returns to my muscles. "You have no idea how glad I am to see you," I whimper, moving to put my arms around her.

She stands limp in my embrace, and it hurts as if she'd

stabbed me straight through the heart. This distance she's put between us since our parents were killed. We were always so close, thick as thieves our mom would say, and the distance Taryn has insisted upon the past five and a half months has been nearly unbearable.

It's impossible to say how long I was strapped to that chair, and being left alone in a dank, dimly lit cage nearly pushed me to panic. But that's not me anymore. I may have made the mistakes that led us here, but over the past few months I've gotten stronger. Bolder. Before Taryn and Esau showed up, I had begun to believe that I was skirting the cliff overhanging death. But having them here has snapped me out of it.

With a little shake, my sister pushes me away.

"Taryn, please. I'm so sorry…" I trail off, guilt choking off my throat. I should have said that a long time ago.

Something in my twin finally snaps.

"You're sorry?" She spits, her visage a contorted mask of anger. All of it comes spewing out of her at last. All the words I knew she'd been bottling all the time she refused to speak to me. Any relief I might have felt that she was finally talking withers beneath the heat of the unadulterated fury in her eyes. "You're sorry? Well *I'm sorry*, but that isn't good enough. Your *sorry* can't fix the fact that our parents are *dead.* They were murdered in our kitchen because you just had to show your stupid teacher that camera you'd been eyeing. You don't even use the stupid thing. My face is ruined because of you. I can't even look in the mirror without going back to that day. Our lives are ruined. Because of you. And now the Mayday Killer's lackey has trapped us in a concrete room, again your fault, and he's going to kill us."

She might as well have shot a cannonball through my

chest for the amount of pain firing through me.

"Taryn, please. You're all I have left." We're going to get out of this. I'm going to get you out of this.

"How, prey tell?" Taryn bites off, making me realize I'd spoken that last bit aloud.

"With these." I scan the workbench, unfamiliar with most of the tools abandoned there. They're old, rusty and dirty. Falling apart with disuse, but there has to be something we can use to get the aged door open.

Esau stays where he is, watching.

Ridged metal bites into my palms, but I don't stop. I can't. This chisel, or whatever it is, has to work. It's the fourth or fifth tool I've grabbed to try to pry the door open, but it's not budging. Taryn is pacing around the small room, anger coming off her in waves. I want to say something, anything, but I'm not willing to get yelled at any more.

Esau leans against the workbench, arms crossed, saying nothing. I have no idea what is going on in that calculating head of his. I've never been able to read him.

I wonder if they've kissed yet. Glancing at my sister over my shoulder, I consider it. She was always more confident with guys than me. More sure of herself. She was the blond cheerleader involved in every aspect of school, surrounded by friends and admirers. I was the quiet one who worked hard and kept my head down. Despite our differences, we were best friends. If she and her friends schemed to drive to San Diego for a can't-miss concert, I was always included. There were no barriers, no questions between us. We were *sisters*. Twins.

Until we weren't.

Pushing off the workbench, Esau comes over to the door. "Let me try."

Instinctively, I hand him the rusted tool and step aside. He bends to work.

Taryn mutters something under her breath, and Esau glances over his shoulder in her direction. That I can understand. I'm sure there's a lot that he'd like to say, to ask her. Because somehow, ever since Mr. Baugh locked them in this room with me, Esau has been carefully focused on her. Somehow, even though he's only known we're twins for mere minutes, he knows that she is his match. She's the one who snuck out to see him that night in the orchard.

"Theater was her. Photography was you." Esau's dark eyes catch mine for a breath, and then he's back to attacking the door's hinge.

"Yes. She's always been… more than me."

"Don't sell yourself short," he growls, still angry. "You picked everything up pretty quickly. You had everyone's lines memorized too, after a while."

A corner of my mouth flicks up. "Yeah."

"And she learned how to use a camera." It comes out more like a curse than a statement of fact.

My eyebrows scrunch up. I hadn't thought about that, but it's true. In order to maintain the illusion, we had to meet in the middle of ourselves. Become each other when we stepped outside the old house. At the end of each day, whichever one of us had been to school handed the recorder off to the other for listening. Taryn may not have been our face every day, but she experienced all of it, just as I did. Taryn had to work at being Megan just as much as me, if not more. While I had to step outside my comfort zone, she had to stifle herself. Make herself smaller. The realization makes me feel even worse, if that's possible.

"Why?" It's a rough whisper on Esau's tongue.

"We didn't have a choice," Taryn says. I didn't know she'd been listening to our hushed conversation.

Both Esau and I turn to look at where she stands with her hands on her hips. "Made any progress on that door yet?" Her body is rigid as if she's fighting its instinct to cross to where we are. And why should she give in to it? All of this is my fault.

Our parents' death.

The long, painful scar that's faded to a white line along her cheek.

The Mayday Killer's presence here in Hacienda.

His threats against Noah's parents.

Esau looks at Taryn, his expression cool. A handsome statue chiseled out of granite. "You're a pain in the ass."

She scowls at him. "You love it."

Yanking viciously at the rubber band on his wrist, he mumbles something.

"What was that?" Taryn's eyes are locked on him.

He clears his throat. "Not anymore."

"What do you mean?" For the first time tonight, she sounds less sure of herself.

"You were using me the whole time. It was all a power play."

"That's not true."

"It is, Taryn. I thought you and I were building something together. I thought we made a great team. The lighting. The blocking. Hell, the performances you've gotten out of all of the actors this semester. The play would have been fantastic. It would have been more than enough to give me a shot at film school. But none of it was real. The whole time, you were using me. Trying to take the play for yourself. Weren't you?"

Taryn's face flashes white and then red. "I admit it started that way. I lost everything, Esau. Everything. But if I could take one play and put my own spin on it, it would mean that I wasn't completely lost. That there is some of the old me buried inside somewhere. But as I got to know you, everything changed. You said it yourself. We make a great team."

"Made."

"What?"

"We made a great team. No more." His hand slashes the air between them.

Taryn's jaw clenches. She glares at him, breathing hard. "That's really what you want?"

Esau's harsh look silences her.

I stand between them, torn. Half of me wants to explain to Esau that we only lied because we were forced into it. The other half wants to wrap my arms around my sister and beg her forgiveness.

A low rattle comes from somewhere outside the concrete room. Something skitters over the floor. A shaft of light flashes under the seam of the door.

My heart kicks into my throat. Mr. Baugh is back, and there's no telling what he'll do now that he has both of us trapped. Esau, too. Swallowing, I put a hand on his arm. Wait until he meets my gaze. "If you get the chance, run. Tell Aunt Karen what happened to us. You'll do that, won't you?"

Esau's eyes blaze. "You think I'm a coward?"

"Yes, if you're so willing to believe that what we had didn't mean anything," Taryn bites off.

I shoot a look at my sister, annoyed at her caustic attitude, even though I know it's a front she's using to hide behind.

"It's not cowardly to go for help," I say to Esau. "Please."

We fall into a hushed silence as something scuffs right outside the locked door.

He's coming.

I've been running from the demons in my mind for six months, but it ends now. I'm not going to run from this. If Mr. Baugh thinks he's going to help the Mayday Killer do whatever he has planned for us without having a fight on his hands, he's mistaken. Hiding the rusted chisel behind my back, I square my shoulders.

"Megan?" someone whispers. "Are you in there?"

I know that voice. Relief floods through me as the chisel hits the ground with a plunk. I'm at the door before I can blink, hands pressed to the gnarled wooden planks. Rough splinters dig into my fingertips, but I don't care.

"Noah, we're in here. Help us!"

"Get away from the door, and be ready to run."

I take a big step back, confused by why he'd—

BANG

The door convulses and flies open, slamming against its frame. Fragments of wood scatter through the air. My hands fly up to cover my eyes. I peek out from between my fingertips and my mouth falls open.

Noah stands in the doorway with Esau's rifle hitched to one shoulder. His wild curls fall over his forehead and the sleeves of his flannel are shoved up over his elbows to reveal the capable arms underneath. Did he just shoot the lock off the door? I gape, staring, and can't seem to stop.

Beyond him, the barn door hangs partially open to reveal the pitch dark of the night beyond. Bats fly across the moon.

"I'm sorry, but I followed you guys. I'm here to rescue you…" Noah trails off when he sees who else is in need of rescuing.

"Thanks, Noah," Taryn says as she passes him in the doorway. "Let's get out of here."

Esau snorts as he moves to follow, prompting me with

one hand between my shoulders. Despite the anger flaring across his brow, Esau doesn't take his gaze off my sister's back.

Noah blinks, eyes skirting between my twin and me as the four of us approach the barn door on quiet feet. He hands the rifle to Esau and falls into step beside me since Esau is like a wall behind Taryn. Esau snaps the gun's loading chamber open, finds it empty, and closes it again.

Noah gulps, something akin to hurt in his eyes. "There are two of you."

I focus on the ground as we creep through the wild backyard toward the side of the house nearest the street. The house is quiet and unlit. Maybe we got lucky and Mr. Baugh had to go out, missing the blast of a rifle being fired in his backyard.

Noah's presence is like a spectre beside me. Unfocused and immaterial. For the first time, I wonder what it must feel like for Noah when he looks at me. What thoughts and emotions are coursing through him now that our duplicity is plain. For the first time, I can admit that we led them on, Taryn and I, without thinking ahead to how it would make them feel. I tried to keep things with Noah platonic, but I didn't entirely succeed. And based on the photos of Taryn and Esau that Justin got, my perfect sister failed spectacularly at keeping our director at arm's length.

I reach out and take Noah's hand, needing the warmth of human contact. When he doesn't pull away, I whisper, "If you'll let me, I'll explain everything. Later."

With a gentle flick of his wrist, Noah lets go. He adjusts his glasses and averts his gaze.

The tatters of my heart tear asunder. Whatever was beginning to sprout between Noah and me, it's blackened and dead now. Rotten from the roots.

"Well, isn't this adorable?"

Up ahead, Taryn gasps, the tall weeds and grasses pawing at her hips.

Esau curses, shoving my sister behind his back to shield her from the two shadowed figures blocking our access to the street and our only avenue of escape. One of them holds a flashlight in our eyes, nearly blinding us.

Noah shifts his weight in front of me so I can only see a sliver of the phantoms over his shoulder.

As the two figures come closer, their shapes come into focus. Two men. Both armed. When they're a few feet away from us, the one holding the flashlight lowers it.

My vision sharpens. My breath floods out of my chest, leaving me agape in shock and horror.

One of them, the one with the flashlight, is Mr. Baugh. My favorite teacher turned kidnapper. But until this moment, I didn't understand why he did this to me. Why he used the pretense of the Lopezes being hurt to lure me into his car earlier tonight at the corn maze and absconded with me to this broken-down house out in the boonies.

The other man is heavier, bearded, with a bedraggled appearance that suggests an unpleasant smell, but the juxtaposition of him with Mr. Baugh shakes something loose. If they stood side by side, they'd be nearly identical.

This man has hunted me for months, making my every waking hour a nightmare impossible to wake from. He looks at me with intensity in his gaze, and I realize that I wasn't a player in this game.

No, I'm the prize awarded to the winner.

The Mayday Killer has revealed himself at last, and we're trapped.

Day 1

"Mom? Hello?"

Taryn is rooted to the wooden planks in the foyer, the police dispatcher talking into her ear through her phone.

But I step into the kitchen. My gasp snatches her attention. My ragged sobs make my sister's eyes well and spill over.

Two bloodied human forms lie ravaged on the kitchen floor. Their blood splattered over the faces of the appliances and cabinets.

My breath hitches as I reach toward the form that was our mother. I can't bring myself to touch the still, lifeless twist of flesh that wrapped us in a warm goodbye hug only hours ago.

My knees knock together. "Taryn! Are they coming?" I stammer, but I can't think. Can't remember what I'm supposed to do in an emergency.

The squeak of a rubber sole against the wood floors makes my eyes fly to my sister's in terror. I can't move. I've turned to stone.

A man emerges from the hallway and skirts toward her. His blood-spotted face is twisted in a hungry scowl, but his movements ooze unearthly calm. Small, beady eyes move between us under thick, unkempt eyebrows. "Audrey?" he asks.

Taryn swivels toward me, mouth open in shock. "How does he—?"

Sirens wail nearby, but I can't look away from him.

With a furious cry that I will never, ever forget, the man's blade slashes through Taryn's cheek. Blood spills down her neck as she tries to stop it with white fingers. I lunge toward her, my tongue twisted hopelessly.

Her wail of pain lacerates my organs to shreds.

Footsteps thud across the wood floor. The front door slams against the wall, and he's gone.

Sirens claxon as they draw closer.

I pray they're coming for us.

Chapter 38

Taryn

"Just let us go. Let us go and we won't tell anyone we saw you. You can escape."

"And give up my mate? I don't think so."

A sickening swoop crashes through my stomach as the Mayday Killer looks past us, his eyes locking on my twin. Did he just say… *mate*? This middle-aged monster thinks my sister is his match?

A menacing grin crosses the man's face as his eyes glimmer. He's far more dangerous than I imagined.

My fists clench. He can have Audrey when hell freezes over.

A sharp steel knife flashes as it catches the moon. It's such a sudden, savage move that I don't register what's happening until the blade has slashed along Esau's arm. Esau's blood is almost black under the pale moon's light as he pulls his wounded arm into his chest with a guttural yell.

In an instant the psycho out maneuvers him, whipping me around and pulling me viciously against his chest.

My breath halts in my throat as he presses the warm, sticky blade against my throat. "Any more heroics, and this one dies."

Esau is glaring daggers at my captor, but I can't focus on

anything but the dark liquid seeping between his fingers. He's losing a lot of blood, and if he doesn't get help soon...

The whites of Noah's eyes shine in the dark as he stands in front of Audrey. He's made of more than I knew, but the resigned look Audrey gives him as she gently steps around him betrays her. I didn't truly see Noah, but she did. She does. He stuck with her all these months, even when she evaded his questions, avoided his hints about being more than friends, and outright lied to him when she absolutely had to. I've listened to all of the recordings, and whatever the thing was that they'd begun between them, it's as real as the blade against my throat.

Audrey isn't looking at me.

"Hey, it's okay," she says, centering her attention on the man who has me locked in a brutal embrace. "There's no need for that. I'm not going anywhere."

The paunchy, pungent barrier behind me shifts. "I knew you'd understand, Audrey. You know it was all for you, right? Everything I did was to prove to you how right we are for each other."

Esau's face is pale as he wavers on his feet.

Audrey ignores Esau, taking another careful step closer. Her eyes are pinned on the murderer whose knife is digging into the flesh below my trembling chin. "I saw," she whispers. "How could I not? It was all—very sweet."

Noah looks like he's going to be sick.

The man at my back stands up straighter. The acrid stench of rot washes over me when he laughs. "I knew. The moment you told me that you felt overshadowed by your sister, that you felt like your parents didn't even see you, I knew. My parents didn't see me either."

Mr. Baugh starts as if he's just remembered where he is, and looks down at the gun he has aimed at Noah's chest. He blinks and glances at me, but before I can react, he looks away. The last, desperate flicker of hope I had that he would have a change of heart withers in my chest.

"Tell her what you said to me. Tell her you meant it," the Mayday Killer urges.

The eagerness in the man's voice makes horror dawn in the pit of my stomach. There is no way Audrey could have known—much less spoken to—this man before he eviscerated our parents, could she? She wouldn't do that. Not my best friend. My twin sister. The gentle, quiet soul who grounded me when I needed a jumping off point to fly.

Look at me.

I will it with all my might, but Audrey's attention is fixed on the man holding me hostage. Her expression is a mix of so many emotions I can't hope to pick them apart. When she speaks, everything I thought was true is obliterated.

"I told you sometimes I wished I wasn't a twin. Wished I didn't have a mirror image reflecting all that I lack back at me. And you said you wished there was something you could do to help me. You figured out a way." Audrey bites her lip, eyes darting toward mine and back over my head.

This cannot be happening. I am not hearing this. Audrey, my Audrey, would never join up with this psycho. She would never heap kindling and fuel on his hatred in an attempt to build it into a fire capable of murder. But by the determined look on her face, I guess I was wrong. I don't know anything about this girl. Not anymore.

I cringe and try to pull away from the killer's punishing grip, but I can't as the blade at my throat begins to cleave my skin. Maybe it would be better if I died quickly, before the true horror of my situation comes to fruition. Still, I can't look away.

The knife bites deeper, and I close my eyes. My heart is a sledge-hammer behind my ribcage, each punishing beat forcing the blood through my body in a gush as it surges toward the small cut at my throat. The man threatens to pull it wider with a flick of his fingers.

"Are you ready?" he asks, his tone less hungry, more placating.

Audrey nods. "But don't kill Taryn. She doesn't deserve it."

The knife backs just a hair's-breadth away from my skin, and I take in a slow, careful breath.

"Let's move inside," Mr. Baugh says. "We can have the ceremony in the living room."

"I, I think I'm going to—" Esau topples into the mud and doesn't move.

"What ceremony?" Noah asks in a strangled voice.

"You'll see," my captor says, shoving me toward the house's warped back door.

"What about the boy?" Mr. Baugh asks from somewhere behind me, not even deigning to say Esau's name. Anger starts to spark low in my belly. Audrey may be lost to me forever, but I won't lose Esau too. He's the only person I have left to fight for, and I will never give up.

"He dead?" my captor asks his brother.

When he fell, Esau made no move to catch himself. His body was so still, and there was so much blood...

"Not yet."

"Leave him."

"No!" I cry. "Let me go, you freak." I kick and yank with every bit of strength I can call forth. The man at my back hisses as my heel connects with his kneecap. His fingers on my upper arm loosen a fraction, and if I can just—

My vision goes white at the hot, shearing pain at my throat. The man's breath is moist on my ear, and revulsion works its way through every cell in my body.

"Not yet, girlie. I need you and the scrawny boy as witnesses."

Inside, once Noah and I are zip tied hand and foot and shoved on to a musty plaid couch, I realize how truly screwed we are. I stupidly left my phone in Esau's truck. Audrey isn't wearing her bracelet, although if she was planning this with that murderer, she probably left it off on purpose.

Was all of this an act? The fear that crowded her expression when Mr. Baugh shoved Esau and me into that concrete cell he built in his barn. The dirty tear streaks on her cheeks. The fact tools were left on the workbench where we could reach them.

If Noah hadn't arrived and shot the lock off the door, would Audrey have magically figured out how to get the door open and feigned helping us escape? Were Mr. Baugh and his twin lying in wait for her to lead us right to them?

Now, Mr. Baugh is across the room leaning against the smoke-stained brick fireplace with his gun leveled at Noah and me. He checks his wristwatch and steals a glance toward the back bedroom where his brother disappeared a minute ago.

Audrey, too, stepped away into the bathroom, leaving Noah and me alone out here, gaping like idiots. A fist clenches around my stomach, making it gurgle in acidic protest. There has to be a *reason* she's going along with this. But what?

Could she really be as angry and hateful as she sounded outside?

I wished I wasn't a twin.

The reverberation cuts as deeply as it did the first time I heard it. I never wished Audrey wasn't my twin. But maybe that's the problem. I always thought of her as my twin, as someone whose existence was attached to mine. Not the other way around. And our parents? They fawned over me, I'll admit, but they never treated Audrey badly. Not that I noticed.

In my peripheral vision, Noah adjusts his shoulders. A pungent cloud is dislodged from the couch cushions, making me wrinkle my nose in disgust. It smells like a hundred cats lived and peed in this house.

Noah's mouth twists in a grimace as he attempts to shift his arms. He looks pained at the way they're wrenched and tied behind his back. He's been oddly silent since he arrived, not that I blame him.

"You okay?" I whisper.

He's staring at our teacher, eyes narrowed.

"Years ago, when my brother… died. The security video from the gas station was really grainy, but… Would it be crazy if I told you it looked like the Mayday Killer?" When his eyes meet mine, so full of the extreme sadness I can only imagine is the result of years of open-ended wondering, it takes my breath away.

My hands are tied, so the only thing I can do to comfort him is lean over enough to press my forehead into his shoulder.

"I'm so sorry, Noah. I wish I could get you out of this."

Noah's breath hitches, making me whip around.

The killer has emerged from one of the bedrooms wearing an old, ill-fitting tux. Its ruffled shirt looks like it was plucked right out of the 1970s. Or a *Dumb and Dumber* movie. He makes the final adjustments to his bow tie in a scratched mirror that hangs over the dust-coated fireplace.

Noah's eyes dart from him to me. "What is happening?"

My mouth goes dry when Audrey exits the bathroom wearing a yellowed, floral wedding dress and veil. The gown is loose along the neckline and at the hips; it was obviously made for a taller, curvier woman.

Slowly, she steps up beside our parents' murderer and gives him a tentative smile.

The hungry flash of his teeth makes bile rise in my throat. I fight to push it back down, but it explodes out of me in sharp, livid words that fill the room with a prickling heat.

"This was your plan all along? To murder our parents and marry this… this monster? How could you do something so evil?"

Audrey turns a hard look on me. Her silence is telling. Any doubt I had about her involvement slips away.

"Why do you think she dallied after school that day? She was giving me time to take care of your parents. Too bad I messed up with you, though." Yellowed teeth part in a wicked smile as the man's eyes rover over the white scar on my cheek.

I jerk at my arms, wishing I could cover it. He doesn't deserve to see it, especially if he's getting some sort of sick pleasure out of seeing his handiwork written across my face.

"You're lying," Noah yells. "Meg—she would never do something like that."

I envy Noah's faith in my sister.

The Mayday Killer cocks a bushy eyebrow. "Wanna tell him, pet?"

Under the lacy veil, Audrey pales.

"Meg—Audrey, please." Noah's voice cracks but he doesn't drop his gaze from hers.

"What he says is true. I told him I was planning to talk to my teacher, show him the camera. He took care of the rest."

"Call me Eugene," the killer says, making final adjustments to his suit jacket. "No need for manners now that we're getting hitched. I know it won't be official until you turn eighteen, but

I can't wait any longer to take you as mine. You ready, Mr. Officiant?" The man's greasy hair shines as looks to his brother, who nods.

My entire body starts to quake. I can't control it no matter how much I wish it would stop. My heart pounds in my chest. Chills run down my spine.

Noah leans over, resting his head on top of mine. "Just breathe," he whispers. "It'll be over soon."

Can't he tell that's the reason dread is filling my abdomen like a bunch of lead weights, dragging me down below the surface of control into a whirling ocean of fear and chaos? What will the Baugh brothers do to us once this sham of a wedding ceremony is over? What will Audrey permit them to do?

The two of us watch in horror as Mr. Baugh begins to recite the familiar words I've heard a bunch of times in movies and TV shows. He has Eugene recite his vows first. Words like *honor, respect*, and *provide* have no meaning as they bounce off my shaking body and pop like poison bubbles in the air.

Audrey gets through her vows—with emphasis on *obedience* and *subjugation*—with no more than the slightest tremor of her lips.

Behind his glasses, Noah's got his eyes clamped shut, but I can't look away from this horror show.

Mr. Baugh is wrapping up the ceremony. It's going too fast. Any second I'm expecting a wicked magician to appear and tell us that he hypnotized my sister, but it doesn't happen. My trepidation grows as each word draws my twin into an unholy alliance with a psychotic killer. Each word forces Noah and I closer to a gruesome, bloody death. Because I have no doubt that once he gets what he wants, the Mayday Killer will slit our throats and bathe his hideous suit in our blood.

"I now pronounce you man and wife. You may kiss your bride."

Noah buries his face in my neck, but I still don't look away.

Mr. Baugh has the courtesy to avert his eyes as his gross brother grips Audrey's upper arms in his grubby hands and yanks her into him. Audrey squeals in disgust when his lips meet hers.

When he finally lets her go, Audrey shrinks back against the wall.

"Ready for your wedding present?" the man asks gleefully as he withdraws a huge knife from his boot. "I'm going to take care of your lesser half for you. Just like you asked me to. I tried to get rid of her by setting fire to that corn field, but it didn't go like I planned. I won't make that mistake again." He lunges for me so quickly I don't have time to panic.

His body bucks and crumbles to the floor, almost before the gunshot has stopped echoing through my ears. Blood oozes out of a hole in his forehead as his limbs jerk. And stop.

The back door crashes open and a pack of FBI agents in bullet-proof vests come storming into the room, weapons raised. One pins Mr. Baugh to the wall while Justin leads several others down the hall to sweep the rest of the house.

Audrey is frozen, the hem of her dress beginning to soak up the crimson stain seeping from underneath the killer's lifeless body. Tears stream down her cheeks.

Noah gapes as Aunt Karen steps into the room between the busted door and frame, looking fierce in her government-issued gear and holding a gun like it's an extension of her arm. She rushes over with eyes blazing, giving Noah a once over to make sure he's okay before drawing me into her chest and beckoning to Audrey to join. When she does, the older woman pulls both of us into her chest. Holds on tight. "I'm so glad you girls are okay," she swears. "I got here as quickly as I could."

"Took you long enough," Audrey manages through a sob.

Chapter 39

Audrey

Esau is sitting in an ambulance while an EMT looks at his arm. Taryn is trying to talk to him, but from where I'm standing on the front porch it looks like he's refusing to even look at her. She puts a hand on the shoulder of his uninjured arm, but he shrugs her off and shows her his back. Her shoulders slump as she takes a few steps away, trailed by an FBI agent I don't recognize. My sister glances at me before turning away, pulling the borrowed coat she's wearing tighter around her shoulders.

Four deputy's vehicles, a fire truck, and the sheriff's Bronco are parked on the gravel drive and the overgrown front lawn. I saw one officer come out of the house a few minutes ago with evidence bags full of various stuff I didn't care to examine too closely. I never want to see the knife that severed my parents from me ever again.

Aunt Karen, or Agent Biel, I should say, is standing a few feet away having a chat with her boss on her cell phone. Her eyes catch mine in a way that I recognize. *Are you okay?*

I shrug. I have no idea if I'm okay, or if I ever will be. My eyes land on my sister again. We have so much to talk about, and suddenly I can't wait another minute. I run over to where she's sitting on the trunk of one of the deputy's cars, but stop a couple steps away.

We stare at each other, and I'm not sure we'll ever be able to bridge the gap that has yawned wide between us in the past almost six months. It's partly my fault, yes, but it's hers too. Instead of coming clean about my discovery that I'd been chatting with the Gemini Killer online for months, I kept that from her. Instead of forgiving me for being naïve, she shut me out of her heart and bolted the door.

Exhaling to alleviate the nervous energy coursing through my arms and legs, I haul myself up beside her on the cool metal. We sit side by side in silence for a beat, watching the frenzy of movement in and out of the house.

The ambulance carrying Esau pulls away, and Taryn frowns as her eyes follow its progress up the street.

"What's going on between you two?" I ask.

She shrugs. "Nothing. He wouldn't listen to me."

"Now you know how it feels." The words come out sharper than I intend, but as I open my mouth to apologize, I stop. If Taryn and I have even a shot at getting past this and being sisters again, I'm going to have to start being more honest with her about how I'm feeling. Especially when it's one of the uglier emotions. So instead of apologizing, I brace myself for a fight. Fighting will be infinitely better than pretending the other doesn't exist.

When Taryn's eyes meet mine, they're not full of anger but… remorse. I suck in a breath.

"It wasn't your fault," she whispers. "You had no idea there was a psycho killer who was obsessed with you and following you. You had no idea he was catfishing you over social media and twisting everything you said to suit what he wanted. I mean, come on, any guy would have to be truly twisted to think you'd want to marry him in that truly criminal wedding dress."

She cracks a hint of a smile, but I shake my head.

"It's not funny. If I hadn't made you hang back after school while I talked to my teacher—"

"He would have killed me and taken you, Audrey. You wouldn't have been able to stop him."

"I could have tried." My eyes start to well.

Taryn shakes her head. "I blamed you because it was easier than admitting the truth: that our parents died in a senseless and cruel attack, for no reason other than someone chose to do evil. It was easier blaming you because at least then I had someone to be mad at. I'm so sorry." The overlarge coat she's wearing falls off her shoulders as she flings her arms around my neck and clings to me. "I missed you so much. Nothing is the same without you. I just want to be sisters again, okay?"

I cry into her hair, hugging her back fiercely.

"What were you thinking, pretending you wanted to marry him? That was the grossest, freakiest thing I've ever seen!" She yells, shoving at my shoulders. "Are you insane?"

"I thought if I played along he'd let you go. I realize how stupid that sounds now that I say it out loud."

"You think?" Taryn wraps her arm around my shoulders and rests her head against mine. "No more pretending, okay? From now on we're Audrey and Taryn, no matter what."

"Deal."

Agent Biel hangs up her phone call and marches over, examining us with a wary expression. "You two girls okay?"

We both nod, still huddled together.

"That was my boss. He's sorry the Gemini Killer won't face justice in court, but he thinks we'll have enough evidence to put a case together against his brother. Do you girls think you'll be up to testifying when the time comes?"

We nod again.

"Good. Let's get you home. It's freezing out here."

Taryn and I slide down off the car, and my sister points before tucking the borrowed jacket around her thin frame. "There's someone Audrey needs to talk to first."

I follow her direction and spot Noah standing nearby, hands shoved in his pockets, studying me like I'm a puzzle he can't quite work out.

"Gimme a minute?"

Agent Biel nods, gesturing with her chin for me to go over to him.

"Hey," I say when I get close enough. It's awkward. I've spent hours and hours with Noah studying or hanging out, but now that he knows who I am, I don't know where to start.

"Hey," he answers, staring at my shoes behind his glasses. "So…"

"You lied to me."

My mouth drops open, but I quickly close it again. It's true. I did lie to Noah. I had reasons, but still. "I did, and I'm sorry."

"You're both Megan."

"I was her on Mondays, Wednesdays, Fridays, and Sundays. Taryn did Tuesdays, Thursdays, and Saturdays. She was self-conscious about her scar, so I took more days. And I used special effects makeup to create a matching scar on my cheek."

"That's why you've been so hot and cold all semester. Why some days it feels like you're barely tolerating me while other days... " Noah speaks as if he has to get the words out while he has the chance. His cheeks flush in embarrassment, and he still won't look directly at me.

"Taryn didn't just tolerate you. She thinks of you as a

friend."

Noah shakes his head. Glances between my mirror image and me as if he's still in disbelief that the girl he knows as Megan is actually two separate souls. "I didn't. You meant more to me."

I don't miss the past tense in what he says. I meant more. As if I don't mean anything to him now. My heart, which had just begun to draw its jagged pieces into something resembling one piece, splinters into impossibly tinier bits.

"Noah, please…"

The crunch of tires over gravel grabs our attention, and the four of us turn to see the sheriff's car making a three-point turn on the driveway. The engine cuts off and the man swings out the driver door, thumbs in his belt as he saunters closer.

Agent Biel stops him with a hand.

"I'll have to talk to them sometime, Ma'am," he drawls, cutting a glance through Noah and me and settling on Taryn. "Guess I can give you a little more time."

"Thank you," Agent Biel says.

"He knew too?" Noah asks, incredulous. Rakes a hand through his curls. "I'm such an idiot."

The sheriff lolls his head lazily to one side. "You think the FBI would hide their only witnesses in their case against the most violent serial killer this state has seen in a decade in my town without so much as a courtesy call? Please, boy."

Noah starts to fold in on himself.

"Noah, please let me explain." My mouth dries up when he finally meets my eyes.

"How can I believe anything that comes out of your mouth? I didn't even know your real name."

My own face begins to scrunch, but I bite my tongue to ward off the urge to cry. Forthcoming honesty, always. From now on.

"The FBI swore us to secrecy," Taryn says, but stops herself. Gestures toward me. "Go ahead."

Taryn takes my hand with a gentle squeeze, letting me know she's with me before letting go. I compose myself, stronger with my twin backing me up.

"We were supposed to be in hiding until they caught the psycho. I'm so sorry. If you give me a chance, I'll tell you everything. Whatever you want to know. Just please don't shut me out."

Noah turns on me with a fiery expression. "I told you all about my brother. About why I got into true crime. I showed you all of the research I've done on his murder. The security footage. The crime scene photos. All of it. The least you could do was be honest with me. Your twin is alive. You were in communication with the Mayday Killer. I don't—how am I supposed to take all this?"

With trembling fingers I take the smudged paper out of my pocket. I've gotten into the habit of carrying it around as a reminder of what I'm fighting for. The reason I lied to everyone around me. To save her.

Noah's eyes widen as he takes the proffered sheet and looks at the name printed there.

Audrey Thomas

He stares and stares. Runs a finger over the footer that identifies it as the final page in the list of survivor's names that he found on that true crime forum weeks ago. "This is, you took this from me?"

"Yes," I whisper. "I wanted to tell you, but—"

His shoulders slump. "Stop. Just, stop. I don't know you at all."

"Noah, please listen. You know me. This is me. Audrey."

My voice breaks on the name I haven't voiced in nearly six months.

But Noah's already stepping away, widening the space between us. Taking his glasses off, he swipes at his eyes. Replaces the frames. "I can't. I just… I need some time. Oh, your sister dropped this." He hands me a silver bracelet before he goes.

Sheriff Lamb's mouth twists in an expression that I would almost label sympathy, if I didn't know any better.

"Come on," the older man says to Noah, taking him under his wing. "I'll take you home."

With a final heartbreaking look in my direction, Noah follows the sheriff over to his Bronco. The car's engine roars to life, and then they're gone.

Chapter 40

Day 174, Saturday

Taryn

Audrey and I agreed to stay away from the drama room for a few days to give Esau time to breathe. Truthfully, she convinced me that it wasn't always the best course of action to go into a complex situation with guns blazing. It's been weird seeing her speak up about her thoughts and preferences over the past couple of weeks since the FBI's showdown with the Gemini Killer. Not bad, only different from before. I never realized how much she was stifling herself when we were two. Seeing her now as she speaks up in class and with our new friends, I can't help but smile.

Fiona, Marisa, and Viv were understandably shocked when Audrey and I showed up to school on the same day. They asked us tons of questions and we answered as many as we legally could, seeing as we're still witnesses in the state's case against our former teacher, Mr. Baugh. The rest of our teachers were pretty cool with the switcheroo since they'd been notified by the principal about what was happening.

Esau and Noah, though?

Noah is polite in class, but other than that he doesn't

speak to either me or my sister. It's hard watching Audrey's heart get crushed a little more in art every day, but she insists I should stay out of it. I'm trying to let her fight her own battles, so other than sitting at the same table as them since we're technically a threesome for our project now, I have.

Since neither Audrey nor I have been to drama club in the last fifteen days, I have no idea how Esau's doing, other than to say that when I see him in the halls, he looks tired and strained. Yesterday his bun was haphazard at best. He wasn't at school at all today. I have no idea if it's because he simply didn't want to be there, or if there was some work at the farm that needed doing.

I pull my knees up to my chest. The prematurely dark sky, courtesy of gray clouds heavy with rain, mimics my mood.

Tonight is opening night of *The Mousetrap*, and I won't be there. It's the first time I have ever missed an opening night, but Esau doesn't want me there. If he did, he would have asked. So instead of bundling up and leaving when my sister and Agent Biel, er, Karen, did, I watched them drive away from the shelter of the front window.

My fingers itch for something to do, but I'm done with my schoolwork and I am not taking Karen up on her idea to clean all of the fast food containers out of the fridge. Stinky leftover mushroom chicken? No thanks.

My phone buzzes and I glance down at it, chin resting on one knee.

It's a message from Fiona. The show starts in half an hour and Esau's a no-show.

They need me.

I'm throwing on a raincoat and Karen's black rubber boots before I have a chance to think. I'm not going to miss opening night for anything.

The heavens wait until I'm halfway between the old house and the school before opening their floodgates and dousing me with rain. Even being soaked to the bones can't dampen my smile.

The roar of the crowd is thunderous as the curtain falls. The show went off perfectly, and I have a fantastic cast and crew to thank for it. It helped that they were used to me giving suggestions (and arguing with Esau), so when I showed up fifteen minutes before curtain looking like a drowned rat, they took it in stride.

Marisa hugged me despite already being in costume. Fiona and Dariel asked me to mediate a lighting dispute (Fiona was totally right). And I stood in Esau's usual spot to one side as the show began. By the time the curtain went up, I was soaked in rain and a thin sheen of cold sweat. I had never felt more alive.

Being on stage is nothing like the rush of directing a show. It's so much better.

No wonder Esau didn't want me anywhere near this place. One taste of power and I want more. I tried texting him before it began, but he didn't answer.

Director or not, the show had to go on. Marisa and the rest of the cast absolutely killed it. As evidenced by the hoots and whistles coming from the audience.

The cast goes through their practiced show wrap-up, bowing in order, before Marisa grabs the microphone. It's my cue to leave, and I'm about to do exactly that when our leading lady says, "Not so fast, Director Thomas. Everyone, please welcome Taryn Thomas to the stage."

I shake my head vehemently, hissing, "I'm not going out there."

"Yes you are," Viv says, pushing me out of the shadows and under the bright stage lights.

The crowd starts clapping again. Audrey and Karen beam up at me from third row center.

"Give Taryn a hand," Marisa says, grinning. "Our original director couldn't be here tonight, so this lady here stepped in and made sure *The Mousetrap* went fantastically. Taryn, you're the best. You started this semester as the new kid, but now you're so much more. A fabulous director, and a great friend. Thanks, girl."

She hands me the microphone and steps back. I stand in surprise for a second, basking in the limelight for the first time in what feels like aeons. A surge of joy at the adoration of the crowd, the power I wielded tonight, flutters over my skin. Maybe it was a good thing Esau wasn't here, so I could find my own directorial bent. I know exactly what to say.

"Marisa is right. I started this semester as just the new girl. I didn't know anyone, and I didn't have a place here at Valley High. But over the past few months, I've found my niche. Here with the drama crew. I've learned so much about lighting and costuming and blocking and team management. It's been kind of a whirlwind. A wild, stressful one.

The truth is, I never could have done any of it without the help of our director, Esau Chavez. This play you saw tonight was his vision, and I was honored to step in and make it happen since he couldn't be here. Esau is a lot of things: demanding, exacting, detail oriented. He had a picture in his head for how this play would look, and it turned out amazing. Even more amazing, over the weeks, Esau took the time to listen to his cast and crew. When they had ideas, he considered their merit instead of simply shutting people down. He got more out of us than any of us expected, including me. He did it with grace, even when I argued with him about pretty much everything. We couldn't have pulled off this show without him. Let's hear it for Esau!"

The crowd bursts into another round of applause along with the cast. Handing the microphone back to Marisa, I jog toward the side. And stop.

A tingling sensation skitters along my nape, making me shade my eyes to scan the crowd. Someone is watching me. I know that's stupid to say when there are in fact several hundred people watching me, but I can feel it.

There.

Leaning against the back wall, almost completely hidden by the shadows, is Esau. Even from so far away, we lock eyes. When I point to the exit, he nods. He'll meet me outside.

Esau is already there, leaning against the wall with his arms crossed over his chest when I exit the back of the theater. His neck is craned, and he's watching the moon and stars as they peek out from behind a tear in the clouds. Black hair winds down his chest as it rises and falls in several deep breaths.

I take the spot next to him in silence. Tilting my head back, I find a couple of the constellations he pointed out to me that night in the orchard. The memory feels fuzzy, as if I'm viewing it through a pane of rippling water.

So much has happened since then, and I don't know if that boy and girl exist anymore.

The screeches and laughter of the crowd leaving the theater fill the night air. People hug on the curb. Car doors slam. The crush in the parking lot drains away.

Finally, when a hush wraps around us like a scratchy wool blanket, he tilts his head to look at me. "I want to know if any of it was real."

My sharp intake of breath jerks his attention to my mouth for the barest of seconds before his jaw ticks and he looks away again. Seeing Esau, beautifully capable, assured Esau with that uncertainty in his eyes physically hurts.

"All of it. I mean, my name wasn't, but the rest of it—that was me."

His hands slide down into his pockets as he stares out into the darkness. "Hard to believe."

"I'm sorry. Again. I don't know what else I can say."

Esau sighs and turns toward me. "I don't get you. You spend all semester arguing with me about the play. About *everything*, and the minute you get the chance to take credit… you don't. If you weren't trying to steal my role, what were you doing? It doesn't make sense." With a huff, he pushes his hair back behind his ears.

"Didn't take credit…" The truth behind what he is saying dawns on me in a blaze of lightning.

"You didn't show up tonight just to see what I would do? Did Fiona know?" But even before I finish getting the words out, I know she did. Everyone was too eager to see me when I arrived at the theater earlier tonight. They were far too earnest when they peppered me with questions during our last few precious minutes before the start of the show. They were baiting me to see if I'd buck Esau's vision and do my own thing. Testing my loyalty to their friend to see if I'd remain true or stab him in the back. Behind their complaints about Esau's griping, they care for him. They're loyal to him.

Those terrible, wonderful people.

"It was a test. You were testing me."

An owl screeches on the wind, making me start and glare out into the inky black. I don't know if I'll ever grow accustomed to that. But everything else about living in the country? I could get used to it.

Esau's laugh floats away in a puff of hot air. His eyes fall to mine. The piercing clarity of his gaze feels like it could penetrate clear down to my soul, which is ridiculous. No one can read my mind, not even this boy who I've spent the past three months sparring with by day and kissing by night.

"No one makes me as mad as you do. No one drives me as wild, wondering what you're going to do next. No one has ever pushed me to expand my vision like you do. I tried to make myself stop thinking of you, but even physical pain couldn't change how I feel." Yanking the rubber band off his wrist, he throws it in the garbage can I used to prop the door open.

"So you're here to tell me how much you hate me?" It comes out more breathy than teasing. How can it not when Esau is looking at me with such intent in his eyes?

"I have to know. How much of it was real?" The weight in his eyes slays me.

In the distance, a train whistles. Often at night, when I'm snuggled safe in my bed at home, I can hear it in the distance. It's become one of my favorite night sounds. Hearing it now gives me serenity. A tremble ruffles my fingers as I reach out and take Esau's hand. Gently, I fold his fingers down but for his pointer and middle fingers and press them into the thrumming at the side of my neck.

"Your heart is racing." He starts to withdraw his fingers, but I cover them with my own to stop him.

"You asked me if any of it was real. You can feel the proof of it under your fingers. Being with you makes my heart come alive. These past few months, arguing with you, talking to you were exactly what I needed. No, more than that. Being with you was the one good thing about moving here. After my parents were killed, I thought I'd never feel anything but anger. But you, you re-ignited my spark. You reminded me that there is so much more to being alive than hatred. There are so many good things too. Friendship, laughter, hard work… love. I've been saying that I make the magic happen, but it's you. You make the magic. You brought me back to life, Esau. I hope you know that."

Esau steps into my space. The toe of his work boot bumps up against my rain boot. Warmth folds over me as he brings his hand up to cup my jaw. The other hand hovers barely there over my scar, above it to the curve of my brow. "You're the magic," he whispers just before his mouth covers mine. Esau kisses me like I'm the sweetest oxygen he's ever tasted and now that he knows it, it'll never be enough.

I kiss him right back, letting him know with every brush of my fingers down his cheeks or through his hair that we were both right. I make the magic happen. He makes the magic happen. Together, we're a miracle.

Chapter 41

Day 178, Wednesday

Audrey

Noah answers the door a full minute after I knock. Inside, Anza whispers, "Megan's here! Do you think she'll play with me?"

"Shh. Quiet. She'll hear you. Her name's Audrey. "

"Are we playing hide and seek?" Mattie asks.

My cheeks flush.

"No! No, I just… Don't open that. I'll do it."

When the door finally swings inward, Noah frowns behind his glasses, which are crooked on his nose. The ivory waffle shirt he's wearing is open at the collar, exposing the way his throat bobs when he swallows nervously. "How much of that did you hear?"

"I didn't hear anything." My completely convincing shrug almost makes him shake his head. One hand grips the wooden frame.

"Right." Shutting the door behind him, Noah motions me toward the wicker chairs at the far end of the porch.

My shoulders slump at the realization that he doesn't want me in his house. I'd been looking forward to seeing the twins again. Their beaming smiles and bright energy were always a welcome shot of hope when I fumbled in the dark.

My hands dangle awkwardly between my thighs as I try to find a comfortable position in the hard chair. Noah sits on the edge of the seat, elbows resting on his knees. He scans the yard, looking for something.

"An animal tried to get into our chicken coop last night. Napoleon scared it away."

"Is he okay?"

"Yeah. Got a couple of shallow scrapes and a hurt wing, but he'll live."

"Wow. Knowing that bird, I wish I could see the other guy."

A loud crow caws from behind the house, and I pull my feet up off the ground. As if that would protect me if Napoleon comes running in defense of his castle.

A small laugh escapes Noah's pursed lips. He shifts, sneaking a peek at me with his peripheral vision.

I pretend not to notice, just like I do whenever I catch him covertly studying me at school. Geez, it's freezing out here. A shiver runs through me.

Noah stands abruptly and goes into the house.

My brow furrows in disappointment. I guess being near me was simply too much. He's still too mad at me to hear what I have to say. Frowning, I make my way down the porch steps, rubbing at my arms in a vain attempt to warm up. The long walk back to Karen's house will help. I hope.

"Where are you going?"

I whirl at the note of incredulity in the question.

Noah is standing on the top step, jacket on and a blanket draped over one arm.

"You left, so…"

"To get a blanket for you."

"Oh." I retake the chair, acutely aware of the strain between us. Noah's even more withdrawn than he usually is at school. Maybe it's because when we're there at least he has class work to focus on.

Careful not to touch my shoulders, he wraps the thick afghan around me. I tuck it under my chin and let the warm cover hang down over my legs.

"Better?"

"So much. Thanks."

Noah's eyes catch mine and linger there for a beat. I hold perfectly still in the hopes that he'll forget he's mad at me long enough to let me explain. Just as I open my mouth, he blurts, "You look different without the scar."

Surprised, I cover my newly-bare cheek with one icy hand. "It's weird not seeing it when I look in the mirror. This might sound… strange, but I kind of miss it. Having that scar made it easy for me to blend in with my sister, but without it. I can't hide anymore. When people look at me, they see Audrey. Not Taryn. It's not something I'm used to."

"You were hiding?"

I nod, eyes on the wooden slats under my shoes.

"You could keep wearing it, but you shouldn't hide who you are."

Biting my lip, I meet his look again. "I don't want to anymore. If I've learned anything from all of this, it's that before, it was the hiding that made me feel like my parents—like everyone—overlooked me. But it was my own fault. I let Taryn shine while I faded into the background. But over the past few months, I've figured out that it doesn't have to be one or the other. Taryn and I can both shine in the same space. Just look at what happened with her and Esau. Even with only spending half his time with her, he fell for her. And you—" I stop, my cheeks flushing red, not from the cold. "What I'm trying to say is that my sister and I are pretty different, and that's okay. We don't have to be the same. We can love what we love and still be close. She listens to me talking about orchids and I help her brainstorm ideas for drama club. It's the give and take that makes us work. I forgot that once. I won't make the same mistake again."

Noah runs a hand through his curls. "All of that's great. Really, Audrey. I'm glad you're finding yourself again. But why are you here?"

"Right." I ignore the pangs of hurt that ripple over my heart as I reach into my pocket and pull out my phone. Opening the photo app, my fingers hover over the last image. One I took this morning, in a room buzzing with activity and bad fluorescent lighting.

"You remember that green and yellow sweatband you showed me once? The one you wore on your wrist when you were younger? You said your brother was wearing the other one when he, you know."

"What about it?"

Turning my phone toward him, I wait.

Noah stares at the image of a green and yellow sweatband covered in blood for so long that my arm starts to ache, but I don't move. We're done with our art project, so once I give him this one last thing—something he deserves so much—I'll leave him alone.

Noah's Adam's apple bobs as he swallows, pulling his eyes from the screen to my face. "Where, where did you see it? I spent so many hours crawling around in the dirt behind the gas station looking for it, but I never—It wasn't there."

"Sheriff Lamb had me at the station this morning looking

through photos of some of the items they found in the Baugh house. Albert Baugh, he, he kept trinkets as mementos of each of his kills. They wanted to know if I recognized any of them. They'd already identified most of them, but the sweat band. I was pretty sure it was the twin to yours. Noah, I'm sorry." My expression collapses as the weight of all of the horrible things I saw in those photos finally hits me.

I sat in that cold metal chair in the Sheriff's office sifting through images as if they didn't affect me, with Taryn and Karen right there for support. But now? I let a few tears fall before I swipe my eyes on my sleeve.

"Lamb thinks the sweatband was from his first victim, but when they ran the blood, they didn't get any results. I think it's because your brother wasn't in their system. Does that sound right to you?"

Noah's eyes are round and glassy as he stares at the image. I'm not sure he even heard me until he jumps up. "I have to go down there. Maybe they can take a sample from me to verify. I can't believe after all these years—I have to tell my parents."

I stand up too. "I hope this news brings all of you some closure. I'm sorry you had to wait so long."

He looks at me over his shoulder, his hand wrapped around the doorknob. "Thanks, Audrey."

It's the first time he's called me by my real name, and it sends a bolt of lightning through me.

"Hey!" I call as the door is closing.

Noah pokes his head out. "Yeah?"

"I was wondering; would you be interested in going to the diner with me sometime? We could get shakes. Maybe even some of those animal fries you like. My treat."

Inside the house, Anza yells something I can't make out, and Mattie starts to cry.

Noah shoots a look over his shoulder and then drags his attention back to me. The line of his forehead tightens. "I don't think I can. Thanks, though. Audrey."

I stare at the closed door for a long moment before I start the walk home. Noah's rejection hurts, but I can understand why he did it.

My feet crunch over the pavement with each step. It's solid and reassuring under my soles. For the first time since May, I'm determined to enjoy being outdoors since there's no one lurking in the shadows waiting to kidnap me. I take a deep breath, absorbing the sounds of twilight. Birds chirping their final songs before bedding down. Crickets join the chorus. An owl hoots, pulling a smile to my lips.

Chapter 42

One Month Later

Audrey

I've stopped counting the days since our parents were taken from us. Once Taryn and I made up, once she helped me lever the massive weight of guilt off my shoulders and toss it away, it no longer felt like a penance I had to pay. I'll never forget the day they were killed. It's seared into my memory. But with each passing sunset, the tightness in my chest lessens the tiniest bit. I learn a little more about forgiving myself for something I couldn't control. I learn a little more about what it means to put down new roots, to grow, to bloom.

"You ready for this?" Karen looks back at us from the front passenger seat of the armored van the FBI used to transport us from home to a hotel near the courthouse. We'd had just enough time to change into nicer clothes and fix our hair before Justin, Karen's partner, told us it was time to go. After spending some time with him, he's not so bad.

Now, I stare out the window at the chaos on the courthouse steps. Reporters with microphones and cameras swarm on both sides of the path up to the large, ornately paneled wooden doors. Men and women with homemade signs scream and yell. One says "Burn him in hell" while another says "Free John Baugh." Law enforcement officers line the walk to make sure the swarm doesn't turn into a riot. My stomach churns.

Taryn's grip tightens on my hand. Her fingers are a welcome anchor in this media storm.

"Hey, you can do this," she says, her expression one of firm encouragement. "All you have to do is tell the truth, and then we can go home."

Home. For the longest time, it wasn't a word I associate with the creaky old house in Hacienda. Hiding place. Cage. Temporary. Those were the words I would have chosen if asked, but somewhere over the past few months, the two story with whiny stairs and ancient clapboard siding has become just that: home. It's the place where I found myself again. Where I found my sister again. Found freedom from having to look over my shoulder. I'm not in any hurry to leave.

I just have to get through today, and we can go back there. Looking forward to eating hot soup from giant bowls while watching some melodramatic reality show with Karen and Taryn is what finally allows me to nod.

"Let's do this."

Together, we climb out of the vehicle.

The noise level rises to a roar as the crowd spots us. Journalists and bloggers yell questions, shoving their microphones in our faces in search of the perfect quote or sound bite. Karen and Justin are at our side in an instant, parting the crush of eager bodies so my twin and I can make the climb up the steps of the large concrete building. The doors whoosh closed behind us, the clang bringing an abrupt end to the clatter.

The interior of the courthouse is well lit by large pendant

lights hanging from the ceiling. Up and down the long space, people in suits whisper back and forth. Lawyers and their clients confer before they're ushered into the halls of justice.

Nearby, a door opens and an officer leads forth a man in an orange jumpsuit. His wrists are handcuffed, but his legs are free.

I freeze as Mr. Baugh catches sight of us. His haunted eyes lock on me, sending a chill down my spine.

Our lawyer says that the state's case against him is ironclad, but what if it isn't? What if he gets off and decides to kill us to honor his dead twin's memory? A shudder of fear threatens to turn my veins to ice, but I fight it off. I've come this far, found my courage, and I won't be ruled by fear now that the end of this horrible journey is in sight.

Squaring my chin, I march right past him with my twin at my side.

Inside, the courtroom is not as grand as I thought it would be. It's not cavernous with ornately carved architecture like the ones on television. It's a smallish, wood-paneled room with two long wooden tables facing a raised podium where the judge will sit. Behind the tables are several rows of plain chairs for members of the press and the audience. My eyes catch on a tall, broad back with long black hair neatly combed.

Esau turns toward us with warmth in his eyes. "You look amazing," he whispers to Taryn when she hugs him.

"You too," she says, running a hand down the buttoned front of his shirt. "Is that a panda under there?"

Esau grins, pulling his collar aside far enough that I can see there's a panda on his undershirt.

Taryn giggles.

Something in my chest tightens. I'm so happy for them that they found each other in all of this. Taryn has never seemed happier than she does these days. She grins like the Cheshire cat when she comes in from a date with Esau, minutes before curfew. And Karen's taken her guardian duties extra seriously and instituted Friday night dinners so she can get to know Esau too.

I wish Noah was here.

We haven't spoken since the day I told him about the sweatband. My lawyer wouldn't tell me anything, either, because it was a separate case and I didn't need to know. I don't know if they proved the bloody band had belonged to Noah's murdered brother, or if it was just another dead end. For Noah's sake, I hope they found answers.

"Look who I found outside?" Esau steps to one side and pulls Noah forward.

My mouth drops open in shock.

"Hey," Noah says nervously, shuffling around Esau and Taryn to stand beside me. I never understood the phrase, "A sight for sore eyes" until this moment. Noah looks like an oasis in the desert in his crisp flannel, dark wash jeans, and shiny dress shoes. "They're my dad's," he says, shuffling his feet.

"They look nice."

"We'll start in five minutes. You girls ready?" our lawyer asks. At our nod, she says, "Meet me up there when you're done here." Pointing to one of the wooden tables, she moves in that direction.

Taryn and Esau are whispering and grinning at each other like there's no one else in the room. I turn to Noah and find him staring at me. My mouth runs dry. We speak at once.

"Look—"

"Audrey, I—"

Shaky laughter breaks the tense air between us.

"You go first," he says, his hands in his pockets.

Swallowing, I do. "Thanks for coming today. It means a lot that you're here. I don't know what's happening with the investigation into your brother's death, but I'm sure it can't be easy for you to be here knowing he hasn't gotten justice yet. Or that he might never. If that guy was responsible, that really sucks. But at least he can't hurt anyone else." I'm babbling but I can't curb the tide. My word vomit spills out until I clap a hand over my mouth to stop myself from digging myself farther into the pit that I've dug for myself.

Noah shifts his weight. Sighs. "It's not bad, really. Being here. I am glad that he's dead. It helps." He pauses, chewing at the corner of his lower lip. "I wanted to tell you. They tested the sweatband. It was my brother's. After that they went back to the evidence they had and re-tested some of the DNA they found on my brother's body. It was the Mayday Killer. He killed Simeon. They think it was his first."

"I'm so sorry, Noah. I don't know what to say."

With surprising certainty, he puts a hand on my shoulder. A gentle finger lifts my chin until our gazes meet.

"None of this is your fault," he says. "Especially not my brother's death."

"I know, but thanks."

The corner of his mouth tips up. Something low in my belly flutters back to life. "I was thinking, once this is over, you'll probably be pretty hungry. Famished, even. Can I interest you in a trip to the diner? I hear their peanut butter milkshakes are the best ever." At something in my eyes, Noah's smile grows.

The butterflies in my stomach are doing a line dance now, complete with switching partners and do-si-does.

"How can I pass up such a delicious-sounding milkshake? And maybe a burger?"

"I thought you were a vegetarian."

"Taryn's the vegetarian. I'm a meat-atarian. It's been so hard not eating burgers the past few months. If I never eat another bite of tofu, it'll still be too soon."

He laughs. "That would be great."

"Double date?" Taryn chimes in, beaming in her spot underneath Esau's arm.

Noah nods, and his smile makes my entire being puff up with happiness.

"We can talk about what play to do in the spring. I've got some ideas." Taryn's eyes twinkle as she looks up at Esau. He arches an eyebrow.

"Othello," he suggests.

"The Importance of Being Earnest," she counters.

"We can discuss it later," he growls into her ear, making her titter.

"It's time," our lawyer says from where she's standing behind the table, making all four of us stand straighter. "Come have a seat."

I nod, turning to go, but Noah puts a hand on my arm to stop me. "You're going to do great," he whispers in my ear. His lips brush against my cheek for the barest of moments before he withdraws, but I swear the warmth of that kiss will linger for the rest of the day.

"All rise for the honorable Judge Jay Houser." The court officer opens a door at the back of the room.

Outside the Courthouse

Reporters talk into their phones, into cameras, or type notes on devices as quickly as they can. Each one races to get their story into their station so they can be the first to break the news about the start of the most widely talked about and publicized trial the state of California has seen in years.

"Families of twins can sleep more soundly tonight knowing that the man who terrorized them this summer is gone. His brother, a teacher who aided him in luring his final victims to a country farmhouse, will likely be jailed for quite some time, if the testimony by survivors Audrey and Taryn Thomas is any indication of his extensive crimes.

Investigation into the Baugh brothers' past indicates abuse perpetrated by their parents, who pitted them against each other and punished the brothers who did not measure up by depriving them of meals, beds to sleep in, and on occasion, proper shelter.

Mr. John Baugh, the oldest brother and former high school teacher, is being brought up on charges of kidnapping. The youngest brother, Albert, otherwise known as the Gemini Killer, was killed by law enforcement in the rescue of the Thomas twins. The authorities have been unable to contact the killer's twin brother, Robert. Yesterday the sheriff issued a statement saying that no evidence of his participation in the crimes has been found, suggesting that he was not involved in the string of murders that brought fear to our state. Authorities speculate that he has gone into hiding to avoid the censure of the public wrath against his brothers. They ask that he come forward if he has any information regarding the crimes of his siblings. For channel four news, this is Chelsea Ichaso."

At the edge of the crowd, a man holding a sign with the words, "They got the wrong man," lowers it with care. Turning away from the throng, he sets the sign against the side of an adjacent building.

His heart thuds as he rounds a corner, and his hand falls to the lump in his inner jacket pocket. The hard curve of the hunting knife's hilt is reassuring. If there had been trouble, he would have handled it.

Getting into his brother's blue car—he'd ditched the dice—he drives north out of town.

Robert would always be grateful for his younger twin brother, Albert, who's obsession with that teen girl saved his neck. Albert's decision to reveal himself to her on that grocery store camera took the heat off him. It was convenient that the police killed him before Albert could tell them he wasn't responsible for the killings.

All of his life, Robert had hated having a twin. Had hated feeling like he was simply a spare.

Finally, he realized Albert had been the spare. He'd been sacrificed so that Robert could continue his work. There were many more parents of twins who deserved punishment, and he would ensure that they got it.

One by one, they would feel the severing plunge of his knife.

And someday, once Robert judged that retribution had been paid, he would return to finish what he'd started with the

Thomas twins.

About the Author

Emily lives in sunny Southern California with her husband and daughters. When she's not writing, she enjoys cuddling with her two dachshunds Nestlé and Kiefer, making homemade ice cream, watching television, and enjoying the sunshine with her daughters and their flock of backyard chickens.

To learn more about Emily, visit her website: www.emilykazmierski.com

www.ingramcontent.com/pod-product-compliance
Lightning Source LLC
Chambersburg PA
CBHW020337310726
48979CB00015B/2400/J

* 9 7 8 1 7 3 2 2 4 3 5 9 0 *